The Story of Owen

The Story of

OWEN

Dragon Slayer of Trondheim

E. K. JOHNSTON

SCHOLASTIC INC.

ISBN 978-0-545-83894-8

12 11 10 9 8 7 6 5 4 3 2 1   15 16 17 18 19 20/0

Printed in the U.S.A.   40

First Scholastic printing, March 2015

Main body text set in Janson Text LT Std 10/14
Typeface provided by Linotype AG

— ❖ — — ❖ —

TO EJ, WHO HAS ALWAYS
BEEN MY FAVOURITE JEDI;

TO THE F-LIST, THE
GREATEST SUPPORT GROUP
I HAVE (N)EVER MET;

AND TO THE G.O.D.S.,
BECAUSE I PROMISED.

Fairy tales

do not tell children the dragons exist. Children already know that dragons exist. Fairy tales tell children the dragons can be killed.

—G.K. Chesterton

THE STORY OF LOTTIE

Before the Thorskards came to Trondheim, we didn't have a permanent dragon slayer. When a dragon attacked, you had to petition town hall (assuming it wasn't on fire), and they would send to Toronto (assuming the phone lines weren't on fire), and Queen's Park would send out one of the government dragon slayers (assuming nothing in Toronto was on fire). By the time the dragon slayer arrived, anything not already lit on fire in the original attack would be, and whether the dragon was eventually slayed or not, we'd be stuck with reconstruction. Again.

Needless to say, when it was announced that Lottie Thorskard was moving to town permanently, it was like freaking Mardi Gras.

Everyone knew the story of Lottie Thorskard. She had been one of the most famous up-and-coming dragon slayers of the late eighties, and she'd celebrated the end of her mandatory tour with the Pearson Oil Watch by signing the largest contract on record with the Hamilton Consortium of Steel Mills. It was the dawn of a new era in corporate dragon slaying. For eighteen years, Lottie defended The Hammer against an onslaught of dragons, none of which ever seemed to understand that all the fire and smoke stacks in the region weren't actually an invitation to an all-you-can-eat buffet. Lottie Thorskard was a living legend.

Every morning, Lottie would go up to the top of the CN Tower and look out over the Greater Toronto Area, watching for dragons. Sometimes, they'd come in from over the lake, concealing their size and species in voluminous billows of black smoke that laid a trail of soot across the water in their wake. Other times, they'd come from the north, from the hatching grounds in Muskoka or the Kawarthas. When Lottie saw a dragon coming toward her beloved Hamilton, she would rush to her designated elevator, and once she was on the ground, she would make for battle with all haste.

Very little of that is true, obviously. There's no reason Lottie would watch Hamilton from the CN Tower. And if the Steel Mills had to hope for clear traffic on the QEW for the prompt arrival of their very highly paid dragon slayer, they'd never see another dragon slayed. But it makes a good story, those pictures of Lottie in the tower, watching over the city with a fond expression on her face, and without a story, there's not much to dragon slaying.

The truth was very nearly as fascinating, if somewhat less picturesque. Lottie spent her mornings on the Burlington Sky-way, defending the commuters who drove back and forth across the bridge every morning. She cut an impressive figure, a high, clear note against the smoggy sky as she held her sword aloft in both hands, protecting those below her on the road or in the harbor, but it was difficult for cameras to get a clear picture of her through the girders and beams. As far as most of the people in Hamilton knew, Lottie defended them from on high, and from far away.

Everyone knew the end of Lottie's story. It had been dramatic and terrifying, everything a good dragon-slaying disaster should be, and even though we in Trondheim didn't know it at the time, it would change our lives forever. Lottie was alone on top of the bridge, as always, the last bastion of defense between the morning rush hour below and a fiery end. She had, as she often did, forgone a safety harness in order to maintain maximum mobility, and everyone with an iPhone was able to record her leaping back and forth between the girders as the dragon flew down to harry the bridge from above.

It was nearly impossible to stop people from watching a dragon slaying, even though it was exceptionally dangerous and only made Lottie's job more difficult. The bridge was quickly closed after the dragon was sighted, but that didn't prevent the drivers already crossing from stopping to watch, and it certainly didn't stop the media from showing up. Accordingly, the whole event was exceptionally well televised, even by the standards of Lottie's usual following, and nearly everyone in the Greater Toronto Area and Hamilton saw it live over breakfast.

My favorite account came from a little girl named Amelia who saw the whole thing through bird-watching binoculars from her house on top of the escarpment in Burlington, miles away from the actual fight. Though she was too far away to see the individual exchange of blows, she wasn't hampered by the noise and chaos that muddied the perceptions of everyone on the bridge that morning. The journalists on the Skyway were too close to the action, too terrified for their own lives to really appreciate the final act of heroism Lottie showed, taking a risky jump to bury her sword in the dragon's chest before being swatted off the girder by its tail. Amelia saw it all. So far removed from the action, she had a nearly unobstructed view of Lottie's terrible fall, which she was able to describe in tearful detail on nearly every major news channel in the following weeks.

Lottie Thorskard slayed her last officially recorded dragon on my sixteenth birthday. I didn't see it live. I was in my parents' bedroom, opening presents, and we didn't turn on the radio until we went downstairs for the one surprise my parents couldn't giftwrap, and breakfast before school. When Lottie plummeted off that girder, an entire city screamed as one choir and then held its breath for three days while she fought her injuries at the University of McMaster Hospital. Doctors from across the country were flown in to consult. The Prime Minister himself visited her in the hospital, even though she was unconscious. All he could really do was stand awkwardly by her bedside for photos and hope that no one mentioned how he'd done his level best to block the legislation that had allowed Lottie to get married. Lottie survived, but after her bones knit she was too stiff and too slow to fight dragons professionally anymore.

For a whole week, even the playoffs were a footnote in the news. Speculation of what Lottie would do next took up almost all the air time. There were rumors that the Steel Mills weren't going to let her out of her contract—that they were going to find her another job somewhere in their organization. There were theories that she would go back to the Pearson Oil Watch and run logistics for their overseas campaigns. There was even talk of outright retirement, and retirement with honors for a stellar career cut short. There was never so much as a whisper of a town in southwestern Ontario called Trondheim.

She could have stayed in Hamilton, lived out her life as a hero there and done the motivational speaking circuit, but she didn't. Instead, she announced that her brother Aodhan would be taking over her duties until a permanent replacement could be found. Aodhan was a fair dragon slayer, in the tradition of his family. He'd done his time in the Oil Watch and served as faithfully as Lottie had, if not to such renown. He was still on the official roles, but he held no contract and seemed content to live unnoticed in his sister's shadow, raising his son to follow in her footsteps. Lottie's accident thrust him into the limelight.

It soon became apparent that Aodhan couldn't cope with the pressures of slaying dragons in an urban environment, particularly not one so hard-fought as Hamilton. He could handle the dragons well enough, but the constant audience, the way the media watched him and criticized his every move like he was a goalie for the Leafs, was something he had trouble with. Still, he might have learned to deal with it. What he really couldn't handle was protecting actual people, the stupid ones with camera phones and no survival instincts. So Lottie made another announcement: After much consideration and research into local areas that needed help, the family had decided to move to the countryside. There, she said, her brother would be able to protect barns and chickens, and perhaps as her physical therapy progressed, she might even be able to help him.

The nation reacted in shock. Never before had such a high-profile dragon slayer moved to the middle of nowhere and set up shop. Cities were always the focus of government-mandated and independently contracted protection, and with good reason. Centers of industry attracted dragons by the score. In the country, a town might get one dragon attack a week, and even then, only a single farm or one residential block of some town no one had ever heard of would be lost. But Lottie was determined, and she refused to let anyone gainsay her decision. Neither she nor Aodhan had contracts, she pointed out, which was true, as she had been released from hers and Aodhan still didn't have any official paperwork, so they were free to move wherever they liked.

As the country watched, the Thorskards put their house up for sale and began, as quietly as they could, to organize their move. The coverage lessened after a few days, as the media moved on to other topics. There were plenty of other dragons in the sky, after all, and it *was* the playoffs. By the time all the Canadian teams were eliminated, it was almost like everyone had forgotten—or at least stopped thinking about—Lottie's sacrifice. And, in the city, they mostly had.

The countryside was different, though. Small towns across the province waited on edge for the announcement of which of them would be profiting from this unexpected piece of luck, as morbid as it was. No one cared that Lottie's career was over, that she would probably never slay a dragon again. The idea of her being close, choosing one of our own towns, was enough. We all clung to that hope as the Thorskards put their affairs in order in the city and loaded up their lives into a fireproof moving van.

And then she moved to Trondheim, with her family in tow, and we got our very own dragon slayer.

OWEN THE WEEDY

When he's older, I'm sure, they'll sing songs of his bravery and his heroic deeds. Once he's filled out enough to merit a name like "Owen the Broad" or "Owen the Football-Shouldered," he'll be a legend. Right now, though, on top of being Lottie Thorskard's nephew and de facto town hero, he's reed-thin, weighs 150 pounds soaking wet, and I have to tutor him in algebra. And English. It would be embarrassing if it weren't so funny.

It's a family thing—the dragon slaying, I mean, not the bit where he's rubbish at school. His father slays dragons and his aunt used to, before that dragon's tail ended her career. His grandmother slayed them as one of the first members of the Pearson Oil Watch before that, and all the way back through the line. There's Viking in Owen somewhere, a broad euphonium and rolling drums and something else I haven't pinpointed yet, all buried underneath the crap life throws at adolescents. Before that day, though, I'd only ever seen it in hints and flashes. Usually he hid it so well you'd think he was just any other kid, trying to survive high school long enough to fill out his growth spurt.

It was a sunny day in early December when I first saw the Viking shine clear through in Owen. I was at his house and we were reading *Heart of Darkness*, which is a valid piece of literature, I'll admit, but still not exactly relevant to the interests of a small-town Canadian teenage girl, and I was trying to explain that European imperialism was not the answer to everything when the phone rang.

He answered it with a brief and businesslike "Hi, Dad," and squared his shoulders. He was still narrow and thin, more "Owen the Weedy" than anything else, but I could imagine him in his armor, with trumpets heralding his entrance, as he carried his shield in one hand and his broadsword in the other and didn't collapse under their weight.

There must have been a dragon close by for his father to call the house. The number of attacks had been steadily increasing ever since the family had moved to Trondheim, but usually they were concentrated more toward the lake. Owen lived with his dad and his aunts in a big old house outside of town. His mother had duties of her own that I wasn't comfortable asking about, so his aunts trained him in swordsmanship while his father traversed the countryside defending livestock and farmsteads. I sat at the kitchen table, worrying my pencil between my finger and thumb, and tried not to look like I was more interested in the phone conversation than I was in the book, but it was very nearly impossible.

When Owen came back to the table, he had a reluctant smile on his face. He looked different than he had before he'd picked up the phone. His skin was flushed with excitement, and his eyes sparkled with anticipation. His smile widened as he sat down, and he seemed somehow to take up more space. The overture to some kind of Nordic saga began to hum in my head.

"Dragon?" I said, no longer even pretending that I was paying attention to the homework.

"Just a small one," he said. "Dad thinks it's about the size of a bus, plus the wings."

"That seems big enough to me," I said.

"He's engaged the adult dragon," Owen said. "The little one flew off toward town. I'm supposed to go intercept it."

We had an algebra test tomorrow that he hadn't studied for. We were supposed to work on that after we finished the homework for *Heart of Darkness*. On the other hand, in the face of an inbound dragon, math was probably the least of our worries. One of the fringe benefits of tutoring a dragon slayer was that it occasionally got you excused from your homework altogether.

Most teenagers only ran afoul of dragons as a result of their own carelessness or inattention. It was not uncommon for a new driver to be stranded on a gravel road with a flat tire and an engine belching carbon. There were also stories of field parties ending badly when a dragon came out of the corn and closed in on the bonfire in the dark. Dragons didn't get much from carbon in terms of nutrition, but they came after it like candy whenever it was in the air, and since humans were usually located close by, they didn't exactly want for nourishment.

Owen, of course, was not most teenagers. He never had been. He didn't precisely chase dragons—that was his father's job—but he didn't run away from them either, and that made him unusual. And if Owen was unusual, then so was I. That's why I was sitting at his kitchen table, genuinely hoping he'd ask me to drive him to meet whatever kind of dragon was headed our way. I didn't let myself think about what my parents would say. They were nervous enough that I was hanging out at Owen's house. I was pretty sure they would not be at all sanguine if I arrived home with even slightly scorched tires. Maybe I had overestimated my use on a dragon slaying expedition, anyway. It wasn't like I was doing this professionally.

I wasn't sure how much longer I could cling to that excuse, though. I was hardly an amateur anymore. I'd been there when Owen's family slayed a couple of dragons, but his aunt Hannah usually insisted that I hide in the dragon shelter until after it was done, which, for the record, was fine with me. But I couldn't stay underground forever, not if I wanted to do my job.

I wasn't exactly in a hurry to face any of them, but I was hardly going to let Owen go off on his bicycle when my car was parked in the driveway. Still, I didn't want to push my luck. It was entirely likely that Owen would rather face this dragon by himself. I did my best to sound as neutral as possible, a steady chord waiting for the composer to push it to minor.

"I can lock up, if you need to go," I said.

Owen looked at me for a few moments, and when I didn't meet his gaze, he looked down at the pencil I still held in my hands. I could almost hear his mind putting things in place, shuffling his sense of duty with his sense of adventure. I was in and out of the house more and more now that Owen was training harder, even though he was doing better at school than he had been when classes had started in those first few weeks of September. Practically one of the family, Hannah liked to say.

When he looked up at me again, his smile was even wider, almost incandescent on his face. There were tightly wound strings shivering in the air as the overture began in full. We were definitely getting out of that math test.

"Wanna come?" he said.

That's not how it started.

FIRST DAY DETENTION

I met Owen Thorskard on the first day of grade eleven. He was lost, looking for English. Apparently the principal had decided that, as a future dragon slayer, Owen would be able to find the classroom on his own. When I found him, bouncing on the balls of his feet as though the first few bars of the National Anthem had rendered him incapable of walking, he looked a little bit shell-shocked. I stopped beside him because being caught in the halls during opening exercises was embarrassing, and I couldn't bring myself to walk past him. I didn't recognize him. The pictures we'd seen were mostly of Lottie and Aodhan, and Owen wasn't exactly what crossed your mind when someone said the words "dragon slayer."

Even though Trondheim had passed the summer in a state of near euphoria on account of miraculously acquiring a dragon slayer of our very own, Lottie had done her best to keep Owen and his other aunt, Hannah, out of the eyes of the media. It wasn't really that hard. Trondheim was hard up for news most days, it was true, but between following Aodhan around to dragon slayings and following Lottie around to see if she did anything interesting, our local reporters were pretty much spoken for. The city journalists had all gone back home as soon as they had assured themselves that we really were as boring as they had been suggesting all through the summer. After they were gone, we returned, more or less, to business as usual.

Anyway, that's how Owen managed to make it all the way to the first day of school without being instantly recognizable to everyone in the town. It's also how I ended up getting this job, but I am getting ahead of myself.

My name is Siobhan McQuaid, and I have lived in Trondheim all my life. My situation is not unique. It is more unusual to be from somewhere different and have moved to Trondheim, like Owen did, than it is to have never lived anywhere else. You might think that his newness would have been enough to set Owen apart, and any other year you would have been correct, but the year I started grade eleven was also the year that Trondheim Secondary amalgamated with Saltrock Collegiate. For one morning, there were plenty of new faces in the school hallways, and for one more morning, Owen fit in just as well as any of us.

"I don't suppose you have English right now?" he said to me in a hopeful tone when the anthem finished playing and we could move again without feeling that we were willfully betraying our country.

"Actually, I do," I replied. "It's this way."

As he followed me down the hall he matched my quick pace, not looking like he was entirely comfortable with how long his legs were. I knew, as Owen didn't, that our English teacher was merciless. There wouldn't be any slack for being late on the first day, even if he was new and I had miscalculated how many parking spots would be left in the school lot due to the influx of new students. I never for a moment that day thought they would sing songs about him. And I certainly didn't think that I would be the one who had written them.

"An excellent beginning, Miss McQuaid," Mr. Cooper said when I entered the classroom, Owen a few steps behind me. "Detention on the first day of school. At least you've nowhere to go but up."

I didn't say anything, mostly because I genuinely liked Mr. Cooper and couldn't really fault him for following school protocol, regardless of how I felt about an English teacher abusing prepositions. I slid into one of two empty desks at the back of the room and returned the sympathetic glances of my classmates who had gotten seats closer to the front. I was stuck under the vent, which meant I would be freezing in good weather when the AC was on and sweltering in the winter when they turned on the heat.

"And you are?" Mr. Cooper said as Owen took the seat beside mine. Looking back, this was probably one of the better moments of my entire life.

"Owen Thorskard," Owen said as quietly as he could, but it didn't make a difference. Everyone heard him, and the sudden silence was like a needle scratching vinyl (though I doubted that anyone in the room except for me, and probably Mr. Cooper, had ever actually listened to a vinyl record).

The expression on Mr. Cooper's face was priceless. Not only was he going to be Owen Thorskard's first teacher at TSS, but he was going to have to give him detention right off the bat.

The whole class shifted nervously, right on the edge of giggles. I felt the whole school year stretch out in front of me, a note held by a player who was running out of air. If they laughed, Mr. Cooper would never get control of the classroom back again.

"Detention." When Mr. Cooper managed to talk, his voice was level and balance was restored. "Miss McQuaid can show you the way."

"Yes, sir," Owen said.

From then on, the class proceeded as scheduled, with introductions and a slightly more interesting round of "What I Did on My Summer Vacation" than usual. Even though Owen only told a story about moving to Trondheim, several of the other students had stories of Aodhan valiantly defending their farms or houses. I wondered, for the first time, how much trust I could place in the truth of those stories. Dragon slayer or no, Aodhan Thorskard was still only one man, and he couldn't be everywhere at once. I knew that the Littletons had lost four fields, not to mention all of Chelsie's hair, to a corn dragon just last week. And Alex Carmody's cousin had died in Lake Huron after a *Draconis ornus* tried to carry off the car he and his girlfriend were "sitting" in. They had bailed rather than wait to be eaten by the soot-streaker, and while the girl survived the fall and the swim to shore, Alex's cousin hadn't been so lucky. Yet in the stories my classmates told, Aodhan was a giant, seemingly capable of leaping small drive sheds in a single bound, and left no dragon unvanquished.

Owen seemed to slump lower in his chair with each story, and by the time the bell rang, it looked like he was having second thoughts about his continued participation in public education. He followed me to history, which we also had together, without saying anything at all. This time, we were early and secured seats safely in the middle of the classroom. Owen would have sat up front where, presumably, he could just let people stare at the back of his head and not have to endure them turning in their seats to look at him, but I dragged him back a few rows.

"It's for safety," I explained, as the other students trickled in and took seats around us. "Mr. Huffman teaches with a meter stick in his hands. When he gets carried away, it can be dangerous in the front few rows."

Owen smiled at me then and sat up a bit straighter.

Mr. Huffman adapted fairly quickly to learning that he had a potential dragon slayer in his class. He'd skipped over introductions entirely and just launched straight into his lesson. "There's a lot of history," was his argument, "and we're going to have a hard enough time getting to it without dawdling at the start. I'll learn your names eventually." So he had no one to blame but himself when, after he made a comment about the legality of forcing all newly minted dragon slayers to join the Oil Watch, everyone who had come from English looked at Owen.

"You're him, then?" Mr. Huffman said, being more apprised of current events than Mr. Cooper, apparently. "Well, good luck to you."

I blinked, a bit surprised, but Owen only said, "Thank you," and kept taking notes.

Our school day was still split five ways: four seventy-six minutes classes and an hour for lunch in the middle. The school board kept trying to rework the schedule so that we had six classes instead of four, but ever since Saltrock Collegiate had closed last spring for the amalgamation and the school board had moved into their old building, there had been an unusually high number of dragon attacks. It was rumored that Aodhan had been called there almost once a week since his midsummer arrival. Whatever the circumstances, the school board had been too busy to worry about something as mundane as the educational welfare of their students, and so we still had just two long classes before lunch.

"Well," said Owen when the bell rang. "At least I know where the cafeteria is."

"We have detention," I reminded him.

"Yes, but it's lunch time," he said.

"That's when we do detention," I said. "If we did it after school, kids would miss their buses."

"I hadn't thought of that," he said. "Small towns are weird."

"Yeah," I said. "We kind of are."

"I do like it here, though," he said, closing his pencil case. He looked like he thought he might have offended me. "It's quiet."

"And our dragons are smaller." That wasn't true, exactly. Some studies claimed that dragons that preyed on cities and ate more carbon were bigger. Others theorized that it was easier to fight a dragon on open ground than it was to do it in an urban landscape. Even as I thought it, though, I realized that I wasn't sure if I had meant actual dragons or the more pernicious, high school cafeteria kind. It hardly mattered. After today, he'd probably disappear into a group of popular students, and I'd never get to talk to him again. I knew that was a stupid thing to think. Even with the addition of the SCI students, the school was still small enough that I'd see him every day. And, after all, we did sit next to each other in two classes. But we wouldn't be friends.

"There's that too," he said, apparently deciding to take me literally. "What do we do in detention?"

"I have no idea," I told him. "This will be my first."

Forty-five minutes later, I still had no idea what happened in detention. Or at least I assumed that not everyone had a detention like ours. Instead of writing lines or doing our homework, Owen had spent the whole time detailing his training regimen to Ms. Ngembi, our vice-principal. She coached soccer in the spring, and I knew she was already trying to determine if Owen would be able to play for the team.

"I don't really have a lot of time for school sports," Owen said, as lunch wound down. "But I could ask my aunts."

"You don't train with your father?" Ms. Ngembi said. Her tone was surprised, and I wondered why she thought someone like Lottie Thorskard couldn't train another dragon slayer.

"No, he's too busy," Owen said. "There aren't always as many dragon attacks out here, but he does have a very large area to patrol. He spends a lot of time driving."

"Of course," Ms. Ngembi said. "Your aunt must be inspiring to you."

"*They* are," Owen said. I don't think Ms. Ngembi noticed the difference in his voice when he spoke of his aunts to people outside the family. He wasn't cold by any means, but he was very professional, and sounded a lot older than he actually was.

"My goodness, look at the time!" Ms. Ngembi said, as the clock on her desk gave a quiet ring to indicate that we'd served our punishment and that she was legally required to let us go eat something. "Go have your lunches, and hopefully the next time we meet, it will be under better circumstances."

Once we were in the hallway, Owen looked down toward the cafeteria. It was loud enough that we could hear it all the way from where we stood, and I could tell that he wasn't looking forward to the hush that would fall over the crowd when he entered.

"They're all going to know who I am now, aren't they?" he asked, not sounding particularly hopeful.

"Yes, they are," I told him. "And they'll also know that you had detention. You're probably a rock star in there."

"Is there another place to eat?"

"I usually just eat by my locker, when I don't have music stuff to do," I said. "It's quieter, and so long as you don't make a mess, no one cares."

"Let's do that," he said.

I had music after lunch and Owen had gym, though he was decidedly morose at the prospect. I didn't see him again until fourth period algebra, where he secured me a seat at the front.

"Three out of four classes," he said when I sat down. He sounded like he'd won something "That would never happen in Hamilton."

"A lot of things happen here that would never happen in Hamilton," I told him as Mrs. Postma called for attention.

"I'll bet," he whispered. "So, what do you guys do for fun?"

To my credit, I managed not to laugh in his face.

OFFENSE/DEFENSE FRIDAY

The first time I saw Owen fight a dragon was in history class. It was the second Friday of September, and even though it had only been one week since Labor Day, and summer was hardly a distant memory, Thanksgiving seemed like an eternity away instead of a month. To make matters worse, it had been sunny and warm all week, and by Friday everyone was pretty much done with learning long before we even got out of English class. When we arrived in history, we could already tell something was up, because Mr. Huffman was rearranging the desks so that they faced each other in pairs. The desk pairs formed a snaking line from the back of the room to the front.

"Just sit down," he said. "Wherever you like."

Most of us took the seats that were usually ours anyway. Sadie Fletcher took the opportunity to sit across from Owen before I could get to my chair. I wasn't entirely surprised. I had been avoiding the cafeteria as much as possible, eating lunch as quickly as I could by my locker before heading to the music room to practice. Jazz and concert bands started next week, and after waiting for two years for Sarah Mommerstein to graduate, I really wanted my turn at the school's only bari sax. I knew that I had competition, though, as a couple of the kids from SCI also played, and I wanted to be sure I was the best option when we had auditions on Monday.

It meant that Owen had been on his own at lunch, since he didn't play an instrument, so he'd spent most of the week getting in with the popular crowd. Sadie was, I knew, probably more interested in saying she'd dated a dragon slayer than actually dating one. The look Owen shot me as I sat down beside him was a little bit panicked.

"Congratulations!" Mr. Huffman said. "You have all chosen sides for Offense/Defense Fridays. Which I shall call something else as soon as I come up with a better name." He gestured with his right hand, brandishing the meter stick. "Those of you facing the wall are dragons, those of you facing the window are dragon slayers."

It was difficult to say at that exact moment who was more mortified: Owen, who was staring past Sadie's head out the window as though he could will it to brick itself over, or Sadie, who had just realized that she was the dragon. Mr. Huffman was clearly having the time of his life, and I couldn't help but smile into my hand.

"Before you begin your battle, however," Mr. Huffman said, unrolling a large paper map and affixing it to the not-so-charmingly anachronistic blackboard, "I will give you some information. You will be reenacting this historic encounter."

Despite our confusion, Mr. Huffman had our attention, and we all stared at him as he talked.

"The year was 1956, October 29th," Mr. Huffman said. "The last Great War was finished, but things were not easy in the world. The dragon population, having gorged itself on the smoke over Europe for the better part of a decade, had never been higher or more ferocious, and they could smell the oil in the Suez Canal."

With a dramatic flourish, Mr. Huffman stepped aside to reveal a map of the canal, where Egypt and Israel kissed across the Sinai. We could see the English, French, and Israeli lines, and the noughts and crosses that marked their skirmishes with the Egyptians. I looked at the desks and realized that, though the classroom was too short for us to be in a straight line, Mr. Huffman had undoubtedly arranged the desks so that we mirrored the canal's path as closely as he could manage.

"Tensions were high," Mr. Huffman continued. "Dragon slayers were present in force, but they were still officially enlisted in their various armies and had loyalties only to their own countries and allies. They would not necessarily go to the defense of an oil ship from another nation. The canal was in danger of being overrun. With blatant disregard for safety and collateral damage, the Israeli forces decided to take advantage of English and French interests in the area, and attack the Egyptians for sole control of the canal."

The class shifted uncomfortably in their seats. The Great Wars had shown us that attacking one another, releasing all that carbon and lighting all those fires, only made the dragons more pernicious in their attacks. The non-aggression pacts that had been signed in the wake of World War II were tenuous, yes, but the literal threat of fire from on high was usually enough to keep rogue nations in line.

"The dragons responded in number," Mr. Huffman said. His voice was low now, but the room was so quiet you could have heard a pin drop. "Like moths to a flame, they swept down across the British and French lines, making straight for the oil tankers which belched smoke into the sky above the canal. For the purposes of this exercise, dragon slayers, you are each charged with getting your own oil ship safely from Port Said, the back of the room, to Suez, which is the blackboard. When it is your turn, you tell me your move and I'll tell if you were successful. You will find the details of your ships or your species of dragon on the cards I am passing out now."

We must have looked like idiots, gawking at him like that. Most of the kids were still confused as to the point of the exercise, having realized that this was a historical battle and we all knew the outcome already. I, on the other hand, had different concerns.

"But this wasn't a dragon battle," I said. "Not really, anyway. The oil ships fought one another to get clear of the canal."

At the back of the room, a couple of seniors who were repeating the class for better grades started to poke each other with pencils.

"You're right, they did," Mr. Huffman said. "The dragons were able to pick off the ships one by one, and they're not even capable of higher brain function. It was a messy week for the Anglo-French troops and dragons slayers."

"We need Pearson," I said.

"You mean *you* need Pearson," Sadie said in a quiet voice. My opinion of her rose a little bit just then. She clearly had a brain. She looked apologetically at Owen. "I might win if he doesn't show up."

"Yes, you get Pearson," Mr. Huffman said. "But by the time he shows up, half the boats are sunk and only a quarter of the dragons have been slayed. Every dragon slayer sitting behind Owen, you're dead. The four dragons at the back of the line are dead too. The rest of you, pick a surviving dragon slayer and pull up a chair."

"Nobody took a turn!" one of the seniors protested. "How can I be dead already?"

"Siobhan called for Pearson," Mr. Huffman said. "That was your turn."

There was considerable scraping and more than a bit of teasing as the dead dragon slayers got out of the way and the remaining four dragons picked a slayer to attack.

"Can we gang up, or do we have to fight evenly?" Sadie asked as all four dragons tried to sit around her, facing down Owen across the desks.

"Where are my UN reinforcements?" I demanded at the same time.

"Yes, you can, and they're on their way. Which means it's the dragons' turn again," Mr. Huffman said, passing out blue ribbons to the eight dead dragon slayers. "Congratulations on your reincarnation. You are now representatives of the United Nations. Please wait for orders."

"Orders from whom?" Alex Carmody said, wrapping the ribbon around his wrist.

"Orders from Siobhan," Owen said. "Unless you want to be Pearson."

Alex looked at me for a moment. "Not a bit."

I looked at the map we'd made, spread out along the canal in a thin line. Owen was the closest to Port Said, the last surviving ship in the inadvertent convoy, and Sadie used her turn to sic all five dragons on him. I would be upset if he died, I realized, but it was far more convenient for him to sink behind us than it was for the dragons to pick a target that would block our path to Suez.

"Reinforce the front of the line," I said to my blue-ribboned troops. They hesitated, looking at Owen. "Now!"

They moved to the front of the room and used their turns to shepherd the ships down the canal in a more or less orderly fashion, though we did lose two more tankers, with all hands, in the process. With their help, turn by turn, the oil ships started to reach Suez and the relative safety of open water.

"A little help, Mr. Pearson?" Owen said. His boat had taken significant damage. His detail card kept it moving forward, though at a limping pace. Sadie was merciless in keeping the dragons on him, and he couldn't hang on much longer. I checked my card again and remembered that my tanker was one of the old Egyptian models, and sparsely crewed. It was my turn and my call.

"I'm abandoning ship," I announced. "And lighting the oil on fire."

Everyone looked at me like I was insane, and perhaps I was. The dragons flinched; everyone knew that no matter what else a dragon was doing, it would follow the smell of burning oil for kilometers. I'd just made myself the biggest target in the Middle East. Mr. Huffman waved them on, and they all came to circle me.

"Do we have to?" asked Sadie, knowing that her turn was about to be wasted on something that was tactically unsound.

"You do," Mr. Huffman said. "Dragons can't think, and thank goodness for that."

"It's your turn," I said to Owen. "You have to get around me while the dragons are distracted, before the fire spreads."

"Where are your lifeboats?" he asked.

"Upriver," I told him. "I'm not stupid."

"You just lit yourself on fire in the middle of the biggest dragon battle since Vimy Ridge," he pointed out, but he moved past me and stopped to pick up the life boats. "I don't really think you're in a position to say things like that."

"So now what?" asked Sadie, from the center of the dragons who flocked around my burning tanker.

"What do dragons usually do when they're fighting over oil?" Mr. Huffman asked.

Sadie sighed. They would turn on one another. "Good job, Siobhan," she said. Then she paused. "Wait, if Pearson's dead, who writes the Oil Watch code?"

"Everyone, take a seat somewhere," Mr. Huffman said. He was holding the meter stick in both hands and swinging it back and forth like a golf club. By the time we were settled, it was in his left hand, and he was scratching his head with it. "Pearson was a great man, I am not gainsaying that, but do you really think that he was the only person on earth who was capable of codifying the Oil Watch? If Pearson had died, it would be called the Hammarskjöld Oil Watch, after the other man who helped Pearson write it."

"But Pearson didn't die," I said. "I did. This was just an exercise to see what we would make of a similar scenario. If it had been the actual battle, I wouldn't have been able to light my tanker on fire and Owen's would have gone down. I would have made it to Suez and written the articles, and the Pearson Oil Watch would still become the front line in the international defense of oil."

"Exactly," Mr. Huffman said. "These are models, thought experiments if you will, to see what you will do, what you can think of when you're in a tight spot. Although I must admit that I hadn't expected anyone to light themselves on fire the first week."

"You mean we get to do this again?" Alex said, excited.

"It is called Offense/Defense Friday," Mr. Huffman said. "I imagine there will be a Friday at the end of most weeks."

There was generalized laughter at that, and we moved the desks back into place.

"I'm sorry I took your seat," Sadie said to me, her voice low enough that no one else could hear her over the scraping of the desks against the linoleum floor. There was something about her tone that made me doubt her sincerity.

"I think it turned out okay," I told her, and smiled. She smiled back as the bell rang.

It wasn't until halfway through lunchtime, in the middle of a particularly intricate section of music, that I realized the cafeteria was probably abuzz with stories about the girl who lit herself on fire to save Owen Thorskard.

FIREPROOFING AND
PLANNING FOR THE FUTURE

Everything in Trondheim is fireproof, or at least as close to being fireproof as it can possibly be. Special care is, of course, taken around buildings like the hospital, the schools, and the hockey arena. Never let it be said that here in Canada we do not have our priorities in order. Most of the houses are made of brick with glass windowpanes fitted tightly against the frames for maximum heat retention. Stone houses with heavy slate roof slabs or stainless steel panels instead of shingles are becoming more common, but the expense is more than average people can afford. Most families in Trondheim just cover the chimney, block the fireplace, install gas heating, and hope for the best.

Saltrock Collegiate Institute had been an older school than Trondheim SS, with grounds that backed onto the bluffs along the shore of Lake Huron. It wasn't less safe than Trondheim Secondary was, but given the choice between a school that looked like something out of a Viking dare and a school that looked like a fortress, even the most loyal Saltrock alumni had admitted that if we were going to amalgamate, it was better to do so in Trondheim. It was worth pointing out that Trondheim was much more central, and therefore busing students to it would be cheaper, but both of those factors were mere footnotes in the final recommendation made by the Board of Education.

The high school in Trondheim had been built three times, not because parts of it had been burned, but because as more and more people moved to the area, the school required more physical space. The oldest part of the school was the most heavily fortified, three stories built of red brick, with the entranceway flanked by two guard towers. It had narrow windows and thick walls, and it housed the more flammable aspects of the high school environment, like the library and the art room. The second phase of building added the quad, four long hallways around a central courtyard that was mostly used to demonstrate to grade nine students how *not* to act during a dragon attack. These hallways were mainly for big classrooms: music, drama, and the various shop classes, along with the cafeteria and the administrative offices. The final phase of building had resulted in a second, slightly smaller, gymnasium that was mostly used for badminton and volleyball, as it tended to echo a lot, making basketball or floor hockey something of an exercise in auditory torture.

The population surge that had resulted in the building of all these extra hallways had more or less waned by the time I started grade nine, and that's when the whispers of amalgamation first started. Two years later, we were all one big happy family, and the Board of Education had moved into the old Saltrock CI building, where they could be attacked by dragons on a weekly basis, for reasons that were still unclear. The consensus, unofficially of course, was that this was probably what karma had intended.

Ever since the second week of September, when we had played at dragon slaying in history, Owen navigated the halls a bit less like he was completely lost. He had no problem making friends—not a big surprise—and every time I saw him, he looked more settled. We spent a lot of time together at school—with three classes in common we had little choice—but I was busy with music most evenings and weekends, so I didn't see him outside of school. By the end of September, he was at least managing to get to class on time on a regular basis, but I could tell by the amount of red pen on his algebra homework that his schoolwork wasn't going very well. I didn't think it was my business, though, so I didn't mention it. I figured that he probably had other things to worry about.

Even though we still had a whole other year after this one before we would be out in the world, there were a lot of decisions to be made. I had made mine with my course selections: English was required, history was sure to be a good mark on my transcript, I needed music to live, and algebra was a compromise with my father for not taking any of the business or accounting classes on offer. Next semester I had drama, French, and two free periods that I had already negotiated with my music teacher to spend in the music room, working on extra projects for university applications that weren't even due for another twelve months. I'm a planner, what can I say?

But at the same time, I was also unsure. I knew I could get a degree in music, but I wasn't sure what I'd do with it afterward. I loved composing, loved taking the streams of notes I saw around me and turning them into something that everyone else could hear, if I ever actually let another person listen to them, which I never did. But composition wasn't really a high-paying job, unless I somehow managed to become John Williams, and while I didn't mind the idea of teaching kids to play piano or training them with various band instruments, the idea of teaching at a high school made me want to hide under my bed.

As far as I was concerned, Owen had it easy. He just had to get through high school and then everything was decided for him. When they turned eighteen and finished high school, all dragon slayers were conscripted into the international dragon slaying force, called the Pearson Oil Watch after the aforementioned Lester B. Pearson, who had come up with the treaties that made it possible. The slayers served all over the world, wherever there was oil or some other natural resource that was a tempting target to dragons. The idea was to make sure that the dragon slayers were loyal to their comrades and their jobs first, and their countries second. After their four-year term of service was up, they were welcome to take any contract they liked, as Lottie Thorskard had done, or to retire and start training someone else, as Owen's father had tried to do before his sister's injury.

I suppose it crossed my mind from time to time that Owen might have appreciated a bit of freedom, or even that he was terrified of getting some sort of fiery death, but he never acted like it was something that kept him up at night. He had laughed with me, that first day, and seemed like a normal kid.

Ever since then, though, he had been weirdly professional at school. I figured that he just wanted to keep his distance from his rapidly increasing group of fans, or maybe that he wanted to focus on his studies and his training. He didn't owe Trondheim anything, after all, and there was a very real chance that after he left for his Oil Watch tour, we'd never see him again, except on the news when he did something brave enough to save people or to get himself killed.

As October began and Thanksgiving weekend loomed, I had more or less resigned myself to someday being able to tell my students that I had shown Owen Thorskard how to get to English class the first day of school and that this would be the limit of my anecdotal time with him. I wasn't even particularly upset about it. I had plenty of other things to worry about. But something pulled at me. And it meant that every day, three times, when Owen slid into the seat next to mine and smiled, I smiled back at him.

I couldn't for the life of me figure out what it was. I spent three days trying to tease it out on the piano, the notes pulling at me as I scratched them out on the staff paper I preferred to scribble on rather than letting the computer take dictation for me. The piano was all wrong for him, though. It was too big and complicated. There were too many tones at the same time. Owen wasn't shaped in chords. I knew the entire saxophone family was wrong without even picking one up, and the flute was out for sure. All of them were fine for support in the main piece, but the melody belonged to something else, and I couldn't identify it.

"Siobhan?" My music teacher's voice pulled me out of my speculation. She sounded concerned, and I realized that I was sitting on the floor with staff paper everywhere and half the woodwind section within arm's reach.

"I'll clean it up!" I said. "What time is it?" I realized that I was having this conversation backwards, and looked up to make eye contact. "Good morning, Mrs. Heskie."

I'd come in early today to play for a bit before classes started. Mum and Dad said they didn't mind when I did it at home, but Mum was on nights at the hospital this week, and I hated to wake up and start playing just as she was going to bed. Mrs. Heskie usually got to school by seven o'clock anyway, so it wasn't a big deal for her to let me use one of the soundproof music rooms.

"You just missed the five-minute bell," she said. She was definitely laughing at me.

"Shoot," I said, barely aware I'd spoken out loud. There was no way I was going to get all this put away before the final bell rang. I'd be lucky to get to my locker to drop off my coat as it was.

"You can leave it," Mrs. Heskie said. "You'll be back at lunch anyway, and none of my morning classes will need the practice rooms today."

"Thanks," I said, and grabbed my bag.

"No running in the halls!" she shouted after me, but I ignored her and made a dash for my locker.

By the time I made it to English, seconds before the bell, I realized that my problem with Owen was that he wasn't a woodwind at all. The woodwinds, single and double reeded, were my default after the piano because they were the easiest for me to play. I'd been playing the piano pretty much since I was old enough to sit upright on the bench, and when I'd started high school, I discovered that I took to woodwinds as naturally as if I'd been playing them all my life. But that wasn't going to be enough, apparently, if I ever wanted to get this song out of my head and onto the paper where it belonged. I was going to have to learn how to play the brass.

AN INVITATION TO DINNER

When I sat down at my desk in algebra, Owen was already waiting for me. His gym teacher must've let them hit the showers way earlier than my last gym teacher had.

"What are you doing tonight?" he asked, as soon as I was sitting down.

"Nothing," I said. I had what most people would call a boring social life, a classical holdout in a punk rock world.

"Do you want to come over for dinner?" he said. "Aunt Hannah's been asking all month if I've made any friends yet."

"Will they freak out that you've made friends with a girl?" I asked him.

"Will you freak out that you're having dinner with Lottie Thorskard?" he fired back.

"Fair point," I said. "Sure, I can even drive us so you don't have to take the bus."

Owen only took the bus in the afternoons. In the morning, he ran to school and Hannah waited for the school bus, so that she could put his backpack on it. Most days, he beat the bus to school by several minutes. The cross-country coach had been devastated when Owen told her he simply didn't have time to play school sports.

"Works for me!" he said, and then Mrs. Postma called for homework.

Owen grimaced as he looked down at his assignment, but then squared his shoulders and handed it over. Most people who said things like "I'd rather face a dragon than take upper level algebra" meant it figuratively, but in Owen's case it was the literal truth. He was only taking the class because you were more likely to be commissioned as an officer in the Oil Watch if you had maths and sciences on your transcript.

"I talked with some of the guys during gym," he said, as the paper shuffle went on around us. "They told me they'd never heard of Mr. Huffman doing anything like that before."

I thought about it for a moment. Our second Friday had been quite simple, just protecting a medieval castle, but it was still more exciting than regular class work.

"He did wish you good luck back at the beginning of the month," I reminded him, finally. "Maybe this is his way of teaching you specifically. It's not like it hurts the rest of us to learn it, and it definitely helps you, don't you think?"

"It takes a village to train a dragon slayer?" Owen said skeptically.

"Something like that," I said. I knew people were already starting to wonder if Owen would come back to Trondheim after his tour in the Oil Watch, or if he'd go where the money was, in the city. I hadn't given it much thought, to be honest. I wasn't sure he'd be able to take on a dragon until he stopped looking so scrawny, and I knew he had his own doubts. He didn't need my meddling. Also, I had that audition next week and we were probably going to have a pop quiz in algebra on Monday anyway, because Mrs. Postma was like that sometimes. "In any case, it was fun."

"Maybe next week, I'll get to rescue you," he said.

"Maybe next week, you'll be the dragon," I pointed out.

Whatever he might have said to that was probably more interesting than algebra, but since Mrs. Postma started to talk, I never found out what it was. For the next hour, there wasn't much opportunity to chat. When the bell finally rang, we headed for our lockers. They were in the same hallway as everyone else in the eleventh grade, and I was surprised at how many people called out to wish Owen a good weekend in a way that seemed more genuine than starstruck. If I was Owen's friend, I was clearly not the only one.

"Did you tell your aunts I was coming over tonight?" I asked, wondering if he was looking for an out.

"Aunt Hannah told me to bring someone home," he said. "She gets anxious when she thinks I'm not fitting in with the right crowd."

It dawned on me that Owen and I had been spending quite a bit of time together. None of it was particularly social, but my friendships had always leaned more toward "do you want to work on this English assignment" than "come over and meet my famous aunt." Now that such an invitation had been issued, I had to wonder if my relationship with Owen was developing beyond something I was prepared to deal with. Still, the opportunity to meet Lottie Thorskard didn't come along every day, even in a town as small as Trondheim. For that, I could at least try to be neoclassical for the evening.

"And you think I'm the right crowd?" I said. I wasn't exactly a crowd to begin with.

"You caught Pearson," he said, as if that explained everything.

"Everyone knows about Pearson," I told him.

"Yeah, but Mr. Huffman didn't make him part of the game. He waited until you brought him up." He stopped at his locker and I continued down the hall to where mine was.

I collected the books I would need for the weekend from my locker. I wondered briefly if I should sign the bari out for the weekend as well, if only to prevent someone else from getting it, but regardless of how much I liked the sax, I knew that it was just for fun. I needed to focus on the piano and my compositions over the weekend. If nothing else, it kept my parents from re-starting the university talk.

"Shall we?" I said when Owen showed up with his bag over one shoulder. Now that I was pretty sure we were friends, I decided I should probably be friendlier. Probably. Owen had a sense of humor, and it wouldn't kill me to try to be funny every now and then. I led the way into the parking lot, which was full of students doing their best not to maim one another in their rush to get home for the weekend. "I just want to drop my books at home on the way."

"Or you could bring them and we could do the algebra together," he said. "And maybe the English."

"You really know how to show a girl a good time," I said, but to be honest, the idea of not having to do my homework alone and getting most of it out of the way on Friday was kind of appealing. No wonder I was boring.

"Hey, being a dragon slayer isn't all glamour and commercial endorsements," he said. I had the key in the driver's side door, and I hesitated before I turned it. He must have seen me, though, because after we got into the car, he turned to me and said, "Aunt Lottie is a lot like me. And she knew before the first day she started training that she'd probably get injured or killed fighting dragons. It's what we do. You can talk to her about it. It's not like she's traumatized."

"She fell off the Burlington Skyway," I said, as the engine turned over and began to hum. "That's kind of traumatic."

"Yeah, but she spent her whole life preparing for something like that," he said. "She's not emotionally bereft. She no longer has to risk life and limb on a daily basis, and all it cost her was a limp and the distinction of being the highest-paid dragon slayer of all time."

"When you put it like that, it doesn't sound so bad," I admitted, pulling carefully out of the spot. I didn't really relax until we were on the street. Mum and Dad had been worried that my having a car would make me isolated on the road and more vulnerable to dragon attacks on account of the carbon emissions, but honestly I was more concerned that I would kill one of my classmates in the parking lot because they weren't looking where they were going.

Owen's house was surrounded by cedar trees, which blocked it from view if you were on the road, but also provided a lot of material for burning if a dragon ever decided the house looked tempting. Inside the cedar hedge, the two-acre lot was almost entirely free of grass. To the side of the house there was a shed with a wide doorway and a nerve-wracking amount of smoke issuing from the chimney. As we pulled in, however, the smoke thinned, and I knew that the fire inside the shed must have been banked.

"Aunt Hannah's work shed," Owen explained, off my nervous expression. I felt kind of stupid, because I'd forgotten until that moment that Hannah was a sword-smith and made swords for her wife, brother-in-law, and nephew. "She knows what she's doing."

I parked the car and killed the engine just as Hannah came out of the shed. She was quite tall, and had very broad shoulders. She smiled when she saw us, only a slight facial tick indicating her surprise that her nephew had brought home a girl instead of a boy, and we got out of the car.

"Aunt Hannah, this is Siobhan," Owen said, waving at me with one hand and swinging his backpack up with the other. "From school."

"Nice to meet you," Hannah said, offering her hand.

"Hi, Ms.—uh," I said, and then winced because I only realized after I said it that I didn't actually know what Hannah's last name was. "Thank you for letting Owen invite me over."

"Hannah, please," she said, and her smile let me know I hadn't offended her. "MacRae-Thorskard is such a mouthful. And you are quite welcome."

"Owen!" said a voice from the house. I looked up and saw another woman standing on the porch, all of her weight on one leg. The most famous dragon slayer in North America. "You failed to mention the part where your friend was a girl."

"Lottie," Hannah said. "Be nice."

"Where would be the fun in that?" Lottie said. I was, I imagine, quite pink, but I wasn't anywhere as pink as Owen. I decided that I liked her. She turned to me and raised an eyebrow at my car. "You drive that thing?"

"I took all the classes," I said defensively. My car wasn't much to look at, but it was as safe as a carbon emitting vehicle could be. "I'm Siobhan. I helped him find his classes on the first day, and now I can't seem to shake him."

"That happens," Hannah said, cutting off what I hoped wasn't another disparaging remark about my car. Owen looked at me like I had betrayed him absolutely, but Lottie laughed, and the awkwardness passed. "Lottie and Aodhan wandered into my father's smithy in 1985 and I haven't been able to shake them either," said Hannah. "You're probably stuck with us."

"Us?" I said, momentarily confused. I couldn't figure out why I would be stuck with all of them.

"You could have waited until dessert," Lottie said to Hannah with a fond smile.

"Come on in, Siobhan. This might take awhile to explain."

DRIVER'S ED.

Today, they tell you way too often in high school, is the first day of the rest of your life. It may also, if you decide to drive your car without taking driver's ed, be the last day of your life. They like to really highlight that in the brochures.

At the precise moment little Amelia was watching Lottie Thorskard plummet off the Burlington Skyway, I was standing in the driveway, gawking at the 1998 Toyota Corolla that my parents had bought me for my birthday. I was more than a little surprised, to be honest. I hadn't expected them to trust me with a car so early in my relationship with driving.

And yet there it was: four wheels, paint a color of greenish yellow not ever found in nature, late spring morning sun glinting off the windshield. My very own car.

"Go ahead and say it," my mother said. She has a healthy sense of the morbid, which I'd been told was typical of someone in the medical profession. I came by it honestly.

"You don't love me enough to buy me a hybrid?" I asked.

They'd probably had this conversation themselves and I wasn't entirely sure I wanted to know the details. To be perfectly honest, I was less than concerned with my own mortality at this particular moment. I was already wondering how fast my car could go.

"Don't press your luck," said my father. "Just make sure you always follow a truck and the dragon will go for it instead of you."

"Do you love me enough to pay for driver's ed?" I asked.

"Nope," said Mum with a careless smile. "You're on your own for that too."

"I did make French toast, though," Dad offered, as though that would save me from a fiery death on some deserted roadside.

"Best. Birthday. Ever," I declared, and we went inside for breakfast and to listen to the morning news.

Only some of that is true, of course. I wasn't wearing my watch, so I have no idea if the first time I saw my car was also the exact moment Lottie fell. It certainly makes for a better story that way, though. And it wasn't my best birthday, either. That came later.

But I did have to spend some of my precious summer holiday in driver's ed, if only so that I could save a bit of money on my insurance, which, given our rural locale, was already guaranteed to be higher than if I'd lived in a city where a dragon could go for a factory instead of for me.

After World War II, when automobiles became a staple of

Western culture and the dragon population boomed thanks to the glut of carbon emissions over Europe, the United States, and Japan, there were a bunch of car-related tragedies in rural North America. It wasn't so bad in cities or in Europe, where the population was concentrated and there were always more appealing targets for dragons to go after than a lone car. But in the countryside, a carbon-burning car was one of the most dangerous places to be. After a dozen years of debate on whether to allow teenagers to drive, the government finally implemented an education program to teach young drivers how to drive defensively, providing the basics of what to do in case a dragon tried to make off with your car while you were in it.

To be honest, I was kind of excited to take the class. Trondheim had seen several cases of a car being carried off in the last decade, and more than a few people had been scorched while driving on the many unpaved side roads in the region, but it wasn't as bad as it might have been. This was primarily for two reasons. First of all, a dragon was far more likely to go after a tractor than it was to go after a car, and we had nothing if not tractors aplenty. Second, as the mines in Saltrock grew in size and production, they presented a far more tempting target. Still, the class promised to be entertaining, and at the end of it there was the promise of independence from my parents—not to mention arriving on time for band rehearsals, since between my mother's crazy schedule and my father's lack of get up and go at six o'clock in the morning, my tardy record was a bit well spotted.

"First thing's first," said the instructor on the first day of the four-day course. "How many of you are driving hybrids?"

She sounded hopeful when she asked it, but she had to

know that there was a chance that no one in the class would have one. The government had been pouring money into the development of electric cars for almost two decades now, and though they were effective in preventing dragon attacks, the jury was still out on how effective they were at not stranding their drivers in the middle of nowhere. Again, not a big risk in the city as there wasn't a lot of nowhere to be stranded in, but around here it was something of a more pressing concern. They were also apt to throw a fit if driven on gravel roads. Since most of the kids in the area lived on farms, hybrids simply weren't practical. Not to mention they were still quite expensive. Indeed, only two kids raised their hands. The instructor deflated a little bit but pressed on.

We spent most of the morning learning about the more banal aspects of safe driving: four-way stops, three-point turns, small dragon evasion, and the like. By the time the afternoon rolled around, everyone was really, really bored. The instructor must have sensed that she was losing us, because after lunch we got into the real dangers. There was a video on fire suppression and another on how to evade an attack from the air (though this was, the instructor admitted, mostly useless if the dragon caught you on a gravel road).

Then we got to the meat of the lesson: dragon identification. There weren't a lot of different species of dragon in the Trondheim area, but there was enough variation that a refresher never went amiss. Also, as our instructor pointed out, there were some differences when it came to avoiding a dragon while driving.

Draconis lakus was first, as it was the most common dragon in the Trondheim and Saltrock area. It hunted primarily along the shoreline of large bodies of water, but was making forays further and further inland. It was slow, though, and once it landed, it didn't always get back into the air quickly. If you were in a car, it was fairly easy to drive away from it. A grounded *lakus* couldn't even catch you if you ran. Next was *Draconis siligoinis*, the smallest dragon native to Canada. It was fast enough to catch a car, in theory, but it was also pretty stupid. It got its name because it like to hide in corn fields, which it did at all times of the year, including when the corn was not high enough to conceal it. It was also stupid enough that sometimes it couldn't tell corn from beans, making it easier to track. If you were attacked by a *siligoinis*, the key was to get off the road, leave your car, and hide.

Draconis urbs was, like the *lakus*, big and slow. It had once been predominantly associated with cities. The *urbs* was cause for concern in that it had previously stayed in urban areas but was now encroaching more and more into the rural parts of the country. Trondheim, set in from the coast of the lake and a two-hour drive from the closest city with more than a million people in it, was slowly being sandwiched between the *urbs* and the *lakus*. Fortunately, *urbs* could be evaded the way the *lakus* could.

The most concerning dragon, however, was the *Draconis ornus*, the soot-streaker. This was the dragon that had brought down Michigan, and until a decade ago, it had never been seen in Canada at all. It had been content to plague Michigan and then to pester the other industrial states that took Michigan's place after it was abandoned. *Ornus* had crept across the border at last, to harry Hamilton and Toronto, and was even encroaching on the paper mills and nickel mines in Sault Ste. Marie and Sudbury. And, of course, it was also making its presence known at the mine in Saltrock. The *ornus* was big enough to make off with a tractor, and our instructor explained that if you were beset by an *ornus* on the road, your best chance was to find something that was emitting more carbon than you. There was, apparently, no honor in driver's ed.

By the time the afternoon wore out, a few members of the class were clearly having second thoughts about the whole driving thing, but I was not one of them. My car, after all, looked so desperately unappetizing that I was pretty sure no dragon in its right mind would go for it, no matter how much carbon I was emitting.

After class got out for the day, I walked down to the clinic where my mother worked most Saturdays when she wasn't on call at the hospital. We'd driven into town together that morning in my car, since I still had to have an adult drive along until I passed driver's ed, and then gone our separate ways from the clinic parking lot. I guessed that she'd probably spent her whole day as bored as I had been that morning, since if there had been an emergency we would have seen the ambulances go past the driving school. At least I'd gotten to watch mildly entertaining videos all afternoon. She likely spent the day assuring various denizens of our aging population that their medication was, in fact, necessary and would not, in fact, make them more attractive to any dragon that happened to pass by.

After class, I drove us all the way home, with only one stall and not so much as a dragon-scale sighted in the distance. By September, I was driving myself everywhere with minimal oversight from my parents, which is how I managed to get all the way to Owen's house for dinner and back before they realized I was friends with a dragon slayer.

DINNER WITH
LOTTIE THORSKARD

We didn't wait for Aodhan to get home before we ate. Instead, Hannah and Lottie moved around one another in the kitchen putting the finishing touches on spaghetti while Owen and I set the table. Watching them, I could tell that they had an easy system working with each other, even though Lottie's injury probably changed their patterns a little bit. Still, they were both in good spirits and poked fun at one another as they did their best not to burn the garlic bread.

"She burns everything," Hannah explained, planting a kiss on Lottie's cheek.

"That is not true," Lottie argued.

"It is true," Owen pointed out. "Though since that's the point of crème brûlée I'm not really complaining."

"Thank you, dear," Lottie said sarcastically. "Your good opinion of my desserts means ever so much."

"It's because Lottie doesn't understand fire," Hannah said,

looking directly at me. "She views it as the enemy."

"And Hannah knows how to control it," Lottie added. "Or so she likes to remind me. Are you two nearly finished? We're about done here."

"Yes," said Owen, placing a stack of serviettes in the center of the table. "Have you heard from Dad at all today?"

"He's up somewhere around Kincardine," Hannah said. "Something about an infestation, though the cell phone kept cutting in and out so I'm not sure if he was talking about the dragons or the sheep. He probably won't come home until Sunday."

"I'm sorry he's gone so much," I said. "It's really appreciated, though."

Lottie looked at me and smiled. She didn't look anything like she did on the television, I realized, and it wasn't just the make-up and the clever lighting. On camera, she was a dragon slayer, a professional warrior to the core. Even though she could no longer slay dragons in the field, on TV she was all flash and fire and sound bites. Standing in the kitchen, she was kind of smaller, as if she were a trumpet with a mute in the end, playing all the same notes but at a more personal volume. It was like she was real—all of her persona made genuine in a way it couldn't be on film. She was no longer larger than life, but she was no less full of it. I squinted at Owen, trying to make the same changes in him, but I couldn't see it yet.

"Trondheim has been an easy place to live," Hannah said. "And Aodhan likes the travel."

"And honestly, in Hamilton it was just as bad," Owen said. "With Aunt Lottie's commute and city traffic and all the special events she had to go to, it was like we barely saw her."

"I can't say I have any complaints," Lottie said, limping to her seat at the table and ladling sauce onto the noodles Hannah had served out for her.

"You haven't had to deal with the snow yet," I pointed out, passing the marginally singed garlic bread to Owen.

"True," she said. "But it's quiet enough to think here, and I appreciate that."

I was dying to ask what she spent her time thinking about. She'd continued to do speaking engagements and the odd commercial for TV or radio, but for the most part Lottie hadn't done a lot to rate national news coverage since moving to Trondheim. I'd thought at first that she'd simply retired, but now that I'd met her, she didn't strike me as the type for inactivity. Training Owen couldn't possibly take up all her time. I didn't ask, though, because I wasn't sure how it would be received. Plus, the "stuck with us" from earlier was still hovering over me, and, given the choice, I'd rather they explained that one first.

"Owen tells me you're good at school," Hannah said conversationally. She twisted the spaghetti against her spoon and formed a perfectly sized bite.

"I get by," I said, which was the truth. I wasn't that far from the top of the class, but that was mostly because there were only about fifty people in it, even with the addition of the students from Saltrock. I had good grades, but not through any concerted effort.

"I'm more interested in the music," Lottie said. I began to wonder how much of their surprise at my arrival had been genuine. It seemed that Owen had told them more about me than I'd thought, given their reactions. Maybe they'd just been trying to set me at my ease.

"That I'm quite good at," I said. There was no point in false modesty. I had a wall of trophies and certificates to back me up, and I'd long since given up pretending that my attachment to my music was a passing fad.

"It is good to have useful hobbies," Lottie said, and I couldn't help looking at her questioningly.

My music had been described as nice or even worthwhile, but certainly not useful. Perhaps if I'd been a better singer or at least pretty enough to bank on my mediocre vocal abilities, I'd have been more optimistic as to my future in the business. As it stood, the best I could hope for from a composition major—even one from Laurier, which had the best program in Canada—was a life of teaching music to kids during the day and scraping out tunes for fun at night.

"What Lottie means," Hannah said, "is that she has a bandwagon to fill and she's hoping you'll jump on it."

"I still think we should have waited until dessert," Lottie muttered.

I looked at Owen, who was determinedly staring at his plate, and wondered what in the world I had agreed to by coming over for dinner.

"Could one of you maybe explain what you keep hinting at?" I asked. "Because this is starting to get a bit creepy."

"What do you know about the history of dragon slaying?" Lottie asked, just as I took a forkful of pasta. It seemed like an easy enough question, but the way she asked it made me realize that she probably wasn't asking for a recitation of the Oil Watch Articles. I took my time chewing to think of an answer.

"Not much, I guess," I admitted, after swallowing. "I mean, I know what they show us on TV and teach in history, but I don't think that's what you're talking about."

"You're right, it isn't," Lottie said.

"Please feel free to continue this by talking with your mouth full," Hannah interjected. "Or else your dinner will be cold by the time you're done."

"Before the Industrial Revolution, dragon slayers were tied to the towns they were born in," Lottie said. "It had nothing to do with money or fame, it was a matter of loyalty and honor, and every small town could count on a dragon slayer's protection."

"What happened?" I asked, because I could remember the Prime Minister saying pretty much the same thing during the last election, promising that dragon slayers would be more available to small towns. It had been enough to get him elected with a majority government to back him, despite his complete failure to carry through on any of his other campaign promises so far. Trondheim had simply gotten lucky, and we knew it. But the way Lottie spoke suggested that she could see an easy solution to the problem, albeit one that the government wasn't going to like.

"Factories happened," Hannah said. "Cities became the centers of more than population. Carbon smoke started belching into the skies over Europe and Asia, and Africa and North America took to mining and drilling with a new intensity to support the demand."

"And then the wars," I said.

"And then the wars," Lottie confirmed. "And between the wars, the rise of Fordism, which, in addition to ensuring that nearly everyone in North America could afford a car, set in motion a higher state of industrialization that promoted even more carbon emissions."

"I'm not sure what that has to do with dragon slaying," I said. "Well, aside from the fact that there are more dragons now than before the wars, and more cars."

"But not more dragon slayers," Hannah pointed out. "It's still a family business. No one ever becomes a dragon slayer without being born to it, even though the days of not being able to afford a sword and shield are mostly over."

"And with men like Ford offering dragon slayers money, lots of money, to come and work specifically for them," Lottie added, "small towns, and even some small cities that didn't have any wealthy industries, lost their dragon slayers. Governments responded quickly, for the most part, implementing mandatory military service for all dragon slayers. That's how we got through World War II. No one wanted to go into the field having lost their dragon slayers to corporations."

"So the army had dragon slayers and the corporations had dragon slayers, but no one else did?" I said.

"Particularly after the Oil Watch Articles codified everything, putting the protection of world oil reserves at the forefront of dragon slaying." Hannah said. "A dragon slayer went straight from school to the Oil Watch, took a tour abroad or served in Alberta, and then came home to a contract somewhere, or ended up in the Royal Canadian Mounted Dragon Slayers."

"Which is what you did," I said to Lottie. She nodded, and something occurred to me. "Are we paying you?" I asked. "Are we paying Aodhan, I mean?"

"No," Lottie said. "You're not."

I looked at Owen, and suddenly I was in the middle of an unfamiliar symphony.

"You want to encourage dragon slayers to come back to small towns and stay there," I said, finally getting some sense of where the conversation was heading, even though I didn't understand my own part in it yet, like everyone else had been practicing for weeks, and I was sight-reading the sheet music. "Without a contract or being in the RCMD."

"See, I told you," Owen said, in the same tone he'd used when he pointed out that I had thought of Pearson.

"You did," said Lottie, and I knew that she understood his doubts and fears, even if they hadn't talked about them yet. "And yes, that's what I would like to see happen. The cities can take care of themselves, but there has been a steady increase in rural dragon attacks, and concentrating dragon slayers in the cities, the way we have been, will only lead to disaster."

I thought about the school board office, how it been under attack so often lately. I thought about Saltrock in general, and how much it needed the salt mines and the grain elevators. Our local economy depended on the oil-burning heavy tankers that came in and out of the harbor every day, belching carbon into the air. I had never given consideration to the politics of dragon slaying before. I felt like I'd suddenly discovered more pieces to a puzzle I had thought complete, and I wasn't sure what to do with them. What Lottie was talking about was huge, the biggest thing that had happened in dragon slaying since the Pearson Oil Watch was founded. And for some reason she needed me to make it work.

"So you're setting a precedent," I said slowly. "And you're going to use Owen to set it too. But why do you need me?"

"Well, to begin with, Owen can't fail algebra," Hannah said lightly. "That would set a dreadful example."

"You want me to tutor him?" I asked.

"Yes," Owen said. "I do. But it's more than that."

"Just tell me," I said, setting my cutlery down on my plate. It was time to catch up with the rest of the orchestra. I had never liked the feeling of being half a measure behind.

"Every dragon slayer used to have a bard," Lottie said. "Someone who records the dragon slayer's actions. They did it two ways, actually, first to present the slayings to the public, but also in a more prosaic way, so that the dragon slayer could learn from his or her mistakes. But now it's all covered on the news or TSN like a sport. There's no soul, no personal attachment between dragon slayer and bard."

"You want me to be Owen's," I said.

"Times have changed," Hannah said. "But we need more than press releases and idiots with smartphones who don't know when it's time to run away."

"And you can write music," Lottie said. "Like the old bards did, back before everyone could read. Dragon slayers don't have an oral history any more, just a million hits on Google. If you could make Owen popular in music, it would catch people's attention."

"You've never even heard my music," I said. "And I've never written music with lyrics."

"Owen says you're good," Lottie said. "That's enough for me."

"Owen's never heard my music," I pointed out. "He's just heard me play."

"You don't have to decide now," Hannah said. "Just think about it."

I looked down at my plate, at the burnt crust of my garlic

bread. I thought about Aodhan, out driving around on his own in the middle of nowhere because his sister had a crazy idea. I thought of Owen, who seemed quite willing to toe the family line, rounding out the orchestra of Lottie's vision. I thought of Trondheim, and the rest of the county, which had only lost a dozen buildings and four people to dragon fire since the Thorskards had arrived in town.

"No," I said. "No, I think I'll do it. I mean, I'll do it."

I looked at Lottie when I said it, but I could see Owen sit up straighter out of the corner of my eye. Lottie smiled, and when I glanced at Hannah, I saw that she was smiling too. I wondered briefly if I should maybe have asked my parents before agreeing to become an accessory to dragon slaying, but then I decided that at least this might provide something interesting to discuss when the inevitable "What do you mean you're not sure about university?" talks began again.

"Great!" said Owen. "Of course, this means that now we have a pretty big problem to overcome."

"What exactly?" I asked, trying to remember if there was some sort of government policy I should have taken into account before signing up to do this.

"I'm really bad at math," he said, and started clearing the table.

THE STORY OF MODERN MUSIC

Most postmodernists blame the decline of the dracono-bardic tradition on the sudden and soaring popularity of the Beatles. The Lads from Liverpool were exactly that: four guys with accents who sang about love and truth, and never once mentioned a dragon slayer. The world split around them. There were many who loved the simplicity of the music, the harmonies and the earnest quality of the lyrics. And there were many who were afraid of the example they were setting.

For the first time since Shakespeare, who had also ignored dragons for the most part and set his plays in bizarre alternate universes where dragons were imaginary creatures of significant rarity, the English-speaking world was confronted by a cultural phenomenon that was insanely popular and entirely bereft of danger. An entire generation of young people (my parents included, though both will deny it unless under threat or blackmail), threw themselves at the Beatles, much to the concern of their elders, who worried about the effect listening to the Beatles' music might incur.

And that was before you got to their hair.

The end result was, of course, the British Invasion, which saw other bands with varying musical styles become popular in North America, drowning out the screams of the traditionalists, who insisted that too much music and not enough dragon slaying could only result in long-term damage to social order. If only, was the common lament, Buddy Holly's airplane had not been beset by dragons while he and a few other bards and their dragon slayers were flying over Iowa. Then, just maybe, the American music scene would have been strong enough to stall the Brits.

As is often the case, the postmodernists were almost entirely incorrect.

The true decline of dracono-bardism was not the result of the Beatles or the Stones or the fact that Buddy Holly died a few years before anyone in North America heard of John Lennon. It was the not the fault of any one thing, though history is a sensational medium that tends to latch onto one idea and pretend it is responsible for everything. By the time the Beatles appeared on the Ed Sullivan show in 1964, the traditional relationship between a dragon slayer and his or her bard was already under significant strain.

"And if anyone ever argues that point with you," Lottie said, "Ask them the name of Buddy Holly's dragon slayer."

It took me more than fifteen minutes to find it on the Internet, and even then, no one seemed to be in agreement over how the dragon slayer's name was spelled.

Anyway, what really happened was that in 1897, Irish author Bram Stoker published a story that almost everyone knew but few people had ever actually read. *Dracula* and the various sparkling and over-romanticized versions of it that followed, was written in the style of a bard even though Stoker himself had no connections to the dragon slaying world. The popularity of the book, coupled with the already infamous story of Vlad the Impaler, served to foment distrust between dragons slayers and the general public—and also resentment, as, for the first time, the bards started to operate separately from their subjects. The end result was an entirely new canon of dragon slayer stories where, instead of being the hero or heroine, the dragon slayer was relegated to being at best a creepy stalker, if not the outright villain.

There were a few exceptions. Canada managed to retain a portion of its traditional music, largely thanks to a statute that mandated 40 percent of everything on the radio had to be written by a Canadian or feature a dragon slayer. This allowed for the success of songs like "The Wreck of the Edmund Fitzgerald," which told the story of the attempted rescue-by-dragon-slayer of a tanker's crew after they were attacked in the middle of Lake Superior. Even though the tragedy resulted in the death of everyone involved, and Gordon Lightfoot, the composer of the song, was no more a bard than Stoker was, it still clung to the old heroic style.

The other exception was, of course, Lottie Thorskard. She had been the first dragon slayer in more than half a century to actively play up her ancestry (Norwegian) instead of focusing on the country of her birth. Her critics said that this could only damage the reputations of Canadian dragon slayers, but the effect was that, thanks her enormous success and fame, stories and songs based on Beowulf and his ilk grew popular again, though never quite eclipsing the popularity of the Stoker knockoffs, largely because Americans had more buying power.

This was the landscape as I entered it: unbalanced and fraught with the potential to blow up in everyone's faces. There had already been some casualties. In 2003, the Dixie Chicks had been eviscerated for their stand against American dragon slaying policy, though they, like Lightfoot, were not actual bards. A few years later, Lady Gaga, also not a bard, had taken to the stage with elaborate shows and over-the-top music videos that incurred the wrath of pretty much everyone over the age of forty, until halfway through her second album when the subversively brilliant, pro-dragon slayer nature of her music became apparent. Still, I didn't exactly want to follow her model either. For starters, I can't walk in regular platform shoes, and Lady Gaga's shoes are typically closer to architectural features than they are to footwear.

The more I thought about it—and I thought about it rather a lot after I kind of impulsively accepted Lottie's offer—the more I realized that for more than a century, and probably longer, dragon slayers and bards hadn't been working together, and that was the problem. I still didn't know exactly how I could help Owen, or if I could write songs with lyrics, but I was starting to understand that *the idea* of teamwork was more important than anything I might write about us. It was the image of it, dragon slayer and bard, that we were going to restore. Sure, it would help if the actual content was good, but the fact that the songwriting was secondary went a long way toward bolstering my confidence.

Almost none of that helped me explain it to my parents.

PARENTAL CONCERN
AND SWORD LESSONS

Dinner at Owen's became a weekly event. Well, eventually. The next Thursday night, when I told them I was going out again on Friday, I was surprised when Mum put on her most serious "we need to talk about your prognosis" face.

"Siobhan," she said. "Your father and I have talked, and we're not entirely comfortable with this decision."

"To go to a friend's house for dinner?" I said. "You've been shoehorning me out of the house for years."

"We meant to a dragon slayer's house for dinner," Dad said.

I looked at him with confusion. "I'm pretty sure I'm not on the menu, dad."

"Maybe not *their* menu," Mum said. "But you've only been there once and you already volunteered to fight dragons with them. I just think we should talk about that."

"I'm not fighting dragons!" I said. "I'm pretty sure they're not even going to let me watch until I'm older. They're just planning ahead."

Mum and Dad exchanged a glance, and I knew I'd stepped in it. They were all for me planning ahead, but they preferred it to be more along the lines of picking a university, or something equally unlikely to get me set on fire.

"Siobhan," Mum said after a long moment. "You know your father and I support you and your music. And I know you think that the Thorskards have the best intentions, but we're your parents. It's our job to think about your safety."

"Believe me," I said. "I am thinking about my safety. And it's just dinner tomorrow."

In the end, Hannah had to call them and tell them that she and Lottie would be supervising us. My mother somehow managed to get her to promise to teach me how to use a sword as part of the bargain, which was not something I would ever have anticipated. Mum and Hannah took a more or less instant liking to one another, by virtue of the fact that they were both possessed of a goodly amount of common sense. Once she got over being starstruck, Mum got on well with Lottie too. I don't think she anticipated spending afternoons having tea with one of the more famous married couples in Canada, but when it became apparent that Hannah and Lottie had adopted her, Mum more than rose to the occasion. For his part, Dad only insisted that Owen come over to our house for dinner a couple of times as well. I think Dad was more worried about teenage hormones than he was about the dragon slaying, which Owen thought was terrifying and I thought was actually kind of funny.

And that's how I went from Siobhan McQuaid, unassuming music lover, to Siobhan McQuaid, dragon slayer by proxy. It's not a particularly epic tale, though I could make it into one if you would rather (and I probably will, if I am ever asked to write an autobiography), but it's what happened.

The sword fighting turned out to be quite a bit of fun, once the agony of muscle development produced actual muscles. I'd never been much for sports before, preferring music to running around, but at least carrying a bari sax around prepared me for the weight of a sword. I was shorter than Owen was, and a bit stockier so my balance was good, but he had several years of practice on me. He trained with a sword that was nearly as tall as he was. Even with both hands on the hilt, I couldn't hold the tip up off the ground for very long. His actual sword was shorter and a bit lighter, but by training with the heavier one, he built up more stamina. The sword Hannah gave me was one she'd made for Lottie's physical therapy. It wasn't exactly light, but it was manageable, and by the end of October, I'd gotten used to carrying it around when I wasn't at school, strapped to my back so I wouldn't trip over it (but where it could whack me in the head with the pommel if I turned too quickly).

Before Owen, I'd spent most of my Saturday afternoons playing piano or poking away at my compositions. Now, rain or shine, I spent them in the practice ring in Owen's yard, facing off against Hannah or Lottie, or more rarely Owen himself, with Lottie's old broadsword in my hands. I'd probably never actually get close enough to a dragon to use anything I was learning, but it made my parents feel better, and it meant that when I watched Owen drill, finding rhythm and rhyme in the growing symphony of his motions, I could more accurately describe what he was doing. The axiom "write what you know" was a bit forced in my case, but I didn't really mind, once my arms stopped feeling like lead weights while I played the organ on Sunday mornings.

The last week of October was bright and sunny. Children prepared their Hallowe'en costumes two sizes too big in case the weather turned, and the farmers collected the last of their crops, one eye on the ground and the other on the sky as they sat in the high combine seats or drove the gravity bins between field and silo. Hannah was taking advantage of the chilly air to work in the smithy in the mornings, and so I watched while Owen trained with Lottie. The sky was absolutely clear, except for the smoke from Hannah's forge, and I was so used to seeing it now that it didn't make me nervous anymore. Fortunately for me, Lottie was always on guard, even when she was crossing swords with her nephew, and so when the dragon decided that Hannah's smithy looked like a good target, Lottie was the one who saw it coming.

The dragon came down on us from the west, which meant it must have flown over Trondheim on its way. Since Lottie had spotted it with enough time to spare, she sent Owen racing for their real swords and yelled for me to run and get Hannah out of the smithy. I was in such a rush that I forgot my backpack on the ground by the training ring. Dragon drills at school had left me with the habit of dropping everything when the alarm was given, and it wasn't until Hannah had smothered the flames in her forge with the water she typically used for quenching and locked us both in the dragon shelter just outside the smithy door that I even missed it.

"How are you so calm?" I asked her. She was sitting on the old red chesterfield that Lottie had put in the shelter, but I was too anxious to sit. This was the closest I'd ever been to a dragon attack, and I knew that, outside, Owen and Lottie were using their swords for real and that there was nothing I could do to help them.

"Practice," Hannah said. I looked at her and realized that even though she looked at ease, her fingers were laced together and white at the knuckles. "I do this a lot, you know."

"Do they usually make you go in the shelter, or is that just because I'm here?" I asked. I wanted her to talk more than I've ever wanted anyone to talk in my whole life.

"It depends," she said. "If it's just Lottie and me here, then I stay with her. She's not as fast as she used to be, but she refuses to hide if a dragon comes. If Owen or his father is here, then I'm down here by myself. Frankly, it's nice to have company."

"You're welcome," I said, and wished I had my backpack so I could scribble dissonant and nonsensical notes onto the staff paper I always carried in the front pocket of it. It might stop them from skittering on my skin.

There were a few moments of silence, until the tension got the better of me again.

"How did you and Lottie meet?" I asked. "For real, I mean. Did she really just walk into your dad's smithy?"

It wasn't unheard-of for a dragon slayer to have his or her own smith, though most of them had company connections that took care of their swords and armor. Dragon slaying wasn't as expensive as it had once been, but having a legacy helped. I knew from magazines that Lottie and Hannah had been together since before their time in the Oil Watch, but they had kept the bulk of their relationship deservedly private. I felt awkward asking and was about to rescind the question when Hannah answered.

"I was sixteen when Lottie and Aodhan came to my father's smithy in Ohio for the first time," Hannah said. "They were fourteen and twelve. Their mother had come to commission a sword from my father, who was quite famous in his own right, and we hit it off immediately. I knew I was going to be a smith, and I wanted to serve my country, but they didn't want me. When I met Lottie, I saw another way."

"I didn't know you were American," I said. That was quite a piece of gossip for the magazines to have omitted, and I wondered how that secret had been kept.

"It was big news before your time," she said. "And I'm not. Not anymore, anyway. I defected when I was eighteen. The Canadian Forces sponsored my entrance based on my merit and reputation as a smith."

I thought about it for a second. There was no law that said a Canadian dragon slayer couldn't have an American smith. In fact, our armies usually cooperated in that regard anyway, since Canada had a smaller talent pool. And defecting was a very serious decision.

"Oh," I said softly as realization dawned. Hannah had chosen not to join the American army because of the policies that led to Don't Ask, Don't Tell. The Americans had lost a perfectly capable smith, and we had gained another piece of Lottie's legend.

"Times change, thank goodness," Hannah said, a not entirely happy smile on her face, "but yes. I joined your army because I couldn't be in mine and still be myself. Two years later, Lottie went on her tour in the Oil Watch, and I was good enough to get myself assigned to the Middle East with her. The rest you know."

"I'm glad you're here," I told her. "Even though it must have been hard."

"Most worthwhile things are hard," Hannah said. "But thank you."

I sat beside her on the chesterfield, calm enough to stop pacing, and she reached out to squeeze my hand. Her fingers were calloused and burned from decades at the fire, and I was pleased to see that my own hands were starting to pick up callouses of their own, rough spots that showed where work had been done and muscles had been earned. I squeezed back.

"You want to know the real reason I can be so calm when they're out slaying dragons?" Hannah asked.

"Yes," I said. I really, really did. Anything that would help to silence the discordant notes that ran up and down my spine.

"I'm calm because I know I've done everything I can," she explained. "I've spent hours making sure their weapons are perfectly suited to their use. I know what they've eaten for breakfast. I've watched them train until they can't stand up anymore, and I've watched them stand up anyway and start again. I know that they are the best at this, and that sometimes they just need me to get out of the way."

"What did Owen have for breakfast this morning?" I asked, without really thinking about it.

"Lucky Charms," Hannah said. She giggled. "And bacon."

"I'm not sure that makes me feel any better," I said, laughing too. "But at least I know he had something healthy for dinner last night."

"That's the spirit," Hannah said.

There was a terrific crash directly above us, and I flinched in spite of my best efforts. Hannah still had hold of my hand,

and she tightened her grip at the noise. The shelter was underground, adjacent to the garage and across the yard from the smithy. I hoped that the house was still intact.

"Don't worry," Hannah said, guessing from my expression what I was thinking. "Lottie will have made sure that Owen drew the beast away from anything too flammable before they engaged it on the ground. The house will be okay and the smithy probably will be too."

"This is my first real dragon attack," I admitted. There had been a lot of drills at school, and nights spent in our dragon shelter. One time when we were driving home from London we got diverted off of Highway 4 because Exeter was on fire, but this was the closest I'd ever come.

"I think you're doing well," she said. "I was an absolute wreck for months after Owen was born, even though Lottie and Aodhan had the whole Oil Watch, and then the other dragon slayers in Hamilton, as backup."

There was a knock on the heavy metal doors of the shelter—a sound so unexpected that I jumped. When I realized what the sound meant, I collapsed in relief against the cushions on the chesterfield. It was over.

"Let's go see the damage," Hannah said lightly, but I could tell she was a little bit on edge.

We climbed the stairs and unlatched the doors. Presumably, the shelter had once been a root cellar or some kind of basement access, but the Thorskards had reinforced the entryway to make it as dragonproof as possible. With the latch undone, Hannah was able to push one of the heavy doors open, and I squinted against the bright autumn sunlight.

Lottie's face was red and she was breathing hard as she

leaned on her good leg. Owen was winded too. In one hand he held his sword, stained black with dragon's blood, and in the other was the smoking ruin of my backpack. I deflated a little bit. So much for the essay I'd spent two hours outlining by hand, because Mr. Cooper was a traditionalist who believed in good penmanship.

Behind them, dead on the ground, was the dragon.

Lottie followed my gaze from her to Owen, to the dragon, and to my backpack, and she smiled when I sighed.

"Don't worry, Siobhan," she said as if this happened all the time. I got the feeling it was probably going to. "I'll write you a note."

OF MEETINGS AND
NERVOUS BREAKDOWNS

I met Aodhan Thorskard ten minutes after the first time I touched a dragon. I'd seen pictures of Aodhan before, of course, and had even spoken with him on the phone a few times when I'd called to talk to Owen, but this was the first time we had ever met in person. He arrived in the driveway in his beat-up old Volkswagen minivan just as Lottie and Owen finished cleaning their swords and Hannah finished checking the pair of them over for injuries. I wondered at first how he had managed to show up so soon after the dragon's defeat, but then I saw the flashing lights on the roof of the van and realized that he must have been tracking the dragon himself when it made for the smoke pouring out of Hannah's smithy.

"Dad!" Owen said when Aodhan killed the engine and the lights and got out of the van.

He was tall, like his sister, and significantly broader. He looked like he could wrestle a dragon, not just slay it, and win handily. His shield, which he had pulled out of the passenger seat as he climbed out of the car, glinted silver in the afternoon sun, but I knew it was made of titanium. It was enormous, and it still covered less than half of his body when he held it. His sword was strapped firmly to the roof rack of the minivan because it was so long that if he'd carried in on his person for any length of time, he would probably trip himself up on it. He didn't match the voice I'd spoken with on the phone in the least, all cello where he ought to be bassoon. Or possibly bulldozer.

"Owen," Aodhan said. He didn't speak loudly, but he had the sort of voice you couldn't help hearing. Probably because he actually sort of was a giant in real life (though likely not quite tall enough to jump over drive sheds of any size), and people tend to pay attention to giants, even the ones who don't drive around with large swords strapped to the roofs of their cars. "I see you managed it."

"Owen was great, Aodhan," Lottie said.

"I was the bait, Aunt Lottie," Owen pointed out. "You're the one who got it."

"True," Lottie said. "But I'm not as fast I used to be and you made sure the beast went exactly where I needed it to be. Plus, I only snagged its first heart. You got the second one."

"It was already dead," Owen said, so quietly I think I was the only one who heard him.

"I'm sure it was an epic battle," Hannah said. "But can I go back to work now? I was right in the middle of something when I was interrupted."

"I'm not sure that's a good idea," Aodhan said. He gestured over his shoulder at the dead dragon. "I slayed that one's partner not too far from here, and there may be more in the area. I think you should lay off anything that makes a lot of smoke until we get the bodies cleaned up."

"Bollocks," said Hannah.

"Oh, cheer up," said Lottie. She rolled her neck and it cracked with distressing volume, though it didn't seem to bother her. "I haven't gotten to do that in weeks!"

"I'm so happy for you," Hannah said sarcastically, but there was a smile on her face that belied her tone. "I do love hiding in the bunker while you have all the fun."

Lottie grabbed Hannah's hand and pulled her in for a kiss. She was happier than I had ever seen her, and I realized that even though dragon slaying had been Lottie's job, and a dangerous one at that, she had genuinely enjoyed her profession. I wondered what it would be like—to lose something you love so much and have to live surrounded by constant reminders of it. I hoped that I would never find out.

"And Siobhan!" Lottie said, her arm still around Hannah's waist. "Are you all right?"

"Yes," I said. "I mean, there wasn't much to be afraid of in the shelter. And yours is a lot more comfortable than the one at my house."

"We built it knowing that we might have to spend a lot of time there," Owen said. "On account of the smithy."

"I picked out the chesterfield," Aodhan said. "I thought it was bouncy."

I had a sudden vision of Owen's gigantic father jumping up and down on the sofa, waving his ridiculously large sword around while a dragon tried to claw its way into the bunker, and started to laugh somewhat hysterically. I tried to stop, but every time I thought I was regaining control, my giggling would start up again.

"It's all right, honey," Hannah said. "That happens to everyone their first time. Let's go have some tea while Aodhan calls the disposal unit."

One of the other effects of having a dragon slayer move to town was that Trondheim also got its own dragon disposal unit instead of having to rely on the province. Dragons couldn't just be buried or burned, they had to be taken care of properly, beginning with the killing stroke. This was one of the first things I'd learned when Lottie started teaching me to use a sword. You can't just hack at a dragon. For starters, its scales are very hard, so if you whack its spine too many times, you'll end up with a dull sword and your hair on fire. The best idea is to stab the dragon's softer underbelly close enough to its hearts that you can kill it with a single blow.

In the old days, dragon slayers used lances from horseback to do this, but pavement and subdivisions aren't really practical for horsemanship. Even the rural areas around Trondheim didn't really have enough space to make it work, and so the broadsword has become the most common weapon for the modern dragon slayer. The exception to this was in the prairies in Canada and the US, where wide-open spaces allowed for old-style jousting tactics. The federally employed BB—or Mounties, as they were more commonly called—favored the lance tactic because they had so much ground to use in a fight. Occasionally, dragon slayers have been known to use longbows or crossbows, but the precision required, not to mention the size of the arrowhead, makes the weapon impractical in most locations. The broadsword is made long enough that the dragon slayer can maintain distance from the dragon, and sharp enough that it can slice one or both hearts cleanly.

A botched dragon slaying can be something of a disaster. Since dragons enjoy feeding on carbon emissions and do so whenever possible, a messy dragon slaying with multiple leaks can cause upheaval in a local environment. After Rome defeated Carthage, for example, the legionnaire dragon slayers went out of their way to butcher dragons improperly in the area around the fallen city. The resulting desert eventually spread to cover most of North Africa. Sometimes, an uncontrolled slaying is unavoidable given the severity of the dragon attack, but for the most part, dragon slayers try to be as particular as possible when slaying dragons. Broadswords require some degree of closeness to use, but if dragon slayers switched to heat-seeking missiles or some other kind of ballistics, the results could be catastrophic.

Trondheim used to rely on the army or the RCMD for dragon disposal before the Thorskards moved to town. It took days, sometimes, during which further environmental damage could occur. When the town and county councils realized that having a dragon slayer would result in more dragon carcasses, they started discussing options. They got bogged down in the bureaucracy characteristic of municipal cooperation, until the volunteer firefighter chiefs stepped in to assume the responsibility. This was deemed practical by all the councils on the grounds that, more often than not, fighting fires and disposing of dragons ended up happening simultaneously. Also, it was cheaper. Our local disposal units were therefore relatively new to their jobs and made up predominantly of farmers and local business owners. No one could fault their effort, though. My dad thought that it was probably because it was their own fields and homes they were protecting, and he was probably right.

Their response time was also very good, and they pulled into the driveway with a large flatbed truck and a small crane before the kettle had even boiled. We stayed inside with our tea while Aodhan went outside to supervise. Dragon slayers working with civilian backup wasn't terribly commonplace. It had been once. There were clear historical examples in Greek and Roman times, but during the Middle Ages a Transylvanian dragon slayer named Vlad III Dracul had taken to impaling local peasants as dragon bait, which kind of soured the dragon slayer/villager relationship. The situation was improving, but some less progressive individuals still saw the *Dracula* novel as a cautionary tale of what happens when a dragon slayer goes rogue. It was nice to see Aodhan getting along so well with his support crew.

"You really are okay, Siobhan?" Lottie asked. She still hadn't let go of Hannah's hand. I wondered how much of her euphoria was related to adrenaline.

"I didn't do anything," I reminded her. "I didn't even see the dragon until it was dead."

"She was a champ, Lottie," Hannah said. "We just talked while we waited, calm as you please. And still asking intelligent questions to boot."

"Eventually you'll get to watch," Lottie said to me.

"I figured as much," I replied. I wasn't exactly looking forward to it, but after today I knew that I'd much rather watch than be stuck belowground waiting for news. "It would be hard to describe something I haven't seen."

"Exactly," Lottie said. "Though that shouldn't stop you, once you get really good."

"You mean I get to just make things up?" I asked. "Doesn't that defeat the whole purpose of keeping track of how Owen does?"

"No, that's for real," Owen said. "But you can make things up when you talk to other people. Feel free to make me sound cooler than I am."

"That's not very hard, dear," Hannah said, but she was laughing when she said it.

"For example," Lottie said. "When you get home and your parents say, 'What did you do today at Owen's?' you could tell them a story about how fabulously brave we were while we fought. Eventually, you'll understand Owen's fighting techniques well enough that you won't actually have to watch him to know what he's going to do. It's all a question of style."

There was clearly more to being a bard than I'd originally thought. I have to admit, I kind of liked the idea of embellishing stories and learning to tell where embellishments had been made. Hannah had already explained a bit of it to me, in the bunker, though I hadn't realized it at the time.

The door opened and Aodhan came inside. Owen got up to get his father a mug of tea, and I was struck again by how tall Trondheim's Own Dragon Slayer was. If Owen grew up like that, we were going to be very fortunate indeed. The dragons would probably hide from him, if only they were smart enough to learn fear.

"Hello, Siobhan," Aodhan said as he took a seat at the table. "It's nice to finally meet you face to face."

He held out his hand and I extended my own to shake it. I

was only slightly afraid that he was going to crush my fingers, but his grip was gentle as he shook my hand.

"Likewise," I said.

"How is Owen's schoolwork coming along?" he asked.

"He's doing much better," I said. I was never particularly comfortable talking about Owen when he was right in the room with me. It made me feel awkward. "We're about to start *Heart of Darkness* in English and we have an algebra test coming up, but aside from that we're pretty much clear."

"And history?" Aodhan asked. I was starting to get the impression that he really didn't like being an absentee father, but it was the nature of his job so he caught up whenever he could.

"That I'm actually good at," Owen said. "Or I will be until Mr. Huffman moves on from dragon-related topics, anyway."

"Oh, that reminds me!" Lottie said, finally relinquishing Hannah's hand to reach for the pen and paper that sat underneath the phone. She scrawled a quick message and handed it to me. "There's your note for what happened to your backpack. Owen will bring you a new one on Monday. We'll replace anything you lose to the cause."

I looked at the note in my hand and read the hastily scrawled words: *Please excuse Siobhan McQuaid from this essay, as it was burned up by a dragon. L. Thorskard.* I looked up with a smile on my face. "You realize that Mr. Cooper is going to keep this forever, right?" I said. "The other teachers will probably be jealous."

"Don't worry too much about that," Aodhan said. He laughed, rolling broad and deep, finally a sound that matched his appearance. "Dragons tend to be equal-opportunity homework burners. There will be plenty of other notes."

He was right about that.

THE FIRST LIE

It went almost exactly the way Lottie said it would. I arrived home, safe and sound, and short one backpack, which, to my surprise, my mother did not notice right away. Her eyes scanned me quickly, checking for burns or other signs of impending dismemberment, as she always did when I got home from Owen's house, and when she found none, she hugged me and asked me about my day. My father, who was finishing dinner in the kitchen, yelled that I should wait until we were all seated so that I could tell them at the same time, and so I did.

This is the story I told my parents.

"I was practicing with Lottie, like she promised," I said.

"What is she teaching you?" asked my father.

"Today it was mostly evasion," I told him. It had the benefit of being more or less true. "That will be my main job if I ever get stuck with Owen and a dragon. I am supposed to get out of the way."

"I don't mind that at all," said my mother, and I nodded. I

was no dragon slayer, and I didn't ever intend to be, but learning to run away properly was definitely a skill that might come in handy.

"Me neither," I said. "Anyway, she was teaching me to dive and roll, and then to do it holding a sword. I'm pretty sure the goal is to not cut off my own head while I do it."

They laughed at that, and Mum passed me the peas. Getting them to laugh was key. If they were relaxed, they were far less likely to panic if they thought I had narrowly evaded death.

"Owen was doing his own drills separately with one of the dummies," I went on, "and Hannah was in the smithy."

"I really don't know where Hannah finds the time for everything," my mother said. I laughed and tried not to choke. I had no idea what my mother and Hannah talked about when they met for coffee, but I doubted it was knitting patterns and recipe swapping. She probably had almost as good an understanding of the family as I did.

"It's not that bad," my father said. "If you're going to have a smithy, you might as well have it in the backyard of a dragon slayer! It's probably the safest place in town."

That wasn't true either, of course. Ironically, the safest place in town was the office where my father worked as an accountant. It had burned down just before the Thorskards had moved to town, and was rebuilt with all the best and newest anti-dragon materials. Mum said that the only thing that really needed to be changed was the sign, which used to have a picture of a stack of coins on it, to represent people's investments, and now just had the name of dad's firm. Most dragons don't know treasure from dirt, but there's one breed that does have an affinity for gold, and of course that's the species of dragon that burned Dad's office to the ground.

"You're right, Dad," I said. This was going to be the hard part. I mustered up my most confident voice. "Which is why when I saw the dragon coming, I wasn't afraid."

"You saw a WHAT?" my mother spluttered. Dad just gaped at me.

"A dragon," I said, hoping my voice was level. "It came for the smithy. It was like nothing I'd ever seen before, so different than it looks on TV or in the movies."

I hadn't actually seen the dragon arrive, of course, but they didn't know that and I figured that it was probably sounded safer if I'd actually seen it instead of being warned at the last moment.

"There was so much smoke!" I said. "I don't know how a dragon ever manages to sneak up on anyone. This one was billowing so much we could see it long before it arrived. Owen had more than enough time to alert Hannah and fetch his sword and Lottie's."

Whatever I was doing was working. I had my parents' complete attention, and they didn't look too worried. It probably helped that I was obviously okay, but I figured that was no reason to squander a perfectly good opportunity to practice.

"Hannah and I stood clear while Owen and Lottie prepared to battle the dragon," I said. In my mind's eye, I could see the Thorskards' yard. I remembered what Owen had said about being the bait, and luring the dragon to a place where Lottie could slay it. All I had to do was fill in the blanks. "By the time it finally arrived, the fire in the smithy was out and the smoke was dissipating. The dragon had to look elsewhere for entertainment."

Though dragons are attracted to carbon emissions and do prefer to eat them, they get their real nutrition from protein. They will choose a cow over a human most of the time—and believe me when I tell you that I have no idea how that was scientifically determined—but they still go after humans more often than I like to think about. With the fire out, Owen probably looked like a tasty snack, which was what Lottie had counted on.

"But Owen was ready for it," I said, a clear picture in my head. "He was by the smithy, where the smoke had been, because that's where the dragon would go first. And then he ran. He runs all the time, you know, and he can run forever if he has to, and fast when he needs to. He ran faster than the dragon, which made it angry. It chased after him, half flying and half lumbering on the ground. Owen ran around the corner of the house, forcing the dragon to land completely. It couldn't make the turn moving that slowly in the air, so it had to be on the ground."

I had them. I could tell.

"And when it did finally round the corner," I said, my tone hushed. My parents leaned forward. I'm not even sure they remembered that their dinners were on their plates in front of them. "When it came around, the dragon found Lottie Thorskard waiting for it."

They smiled. They had read the articles and seen the stories on the news. They knew what came next.

"Lottie held her sword over her head and braced her feet on the ground," I said. "Even though she's injured now, she wasn't scared. She had the dragon right where she wanted it. All she had to do was land the blow, and she did, clean between the beast's ribs.

"And that was the end of that dragon." I finished with a flourish and took a bite of my rapidly cooling potatoes.

"That sounds much more interesting than my afternoon," said my father. "For which I'm grateful. One complete office burning in my life is more than enough for me, thank you very much!"

"Wait," said my mother. I held my breath. "What happened to your backpack? I'm sure you had it with you when you left this morning."

"Oh," I said, trying to be as nonchalant as possible. "The dragon got it. It's burned to a crisp. But Lottie wrote a note for Mr. Cooper explaining what happened to my essay outline, and she said Owen will have a new backpack for me on Monday."

"Why wasn't that in your story?" Mum asked. "Were you near your backpack when the dragon lit it on fire?"

"No," I said. "I had left it near the practice circle." I realized my mistake as soon as the words left my mouth.

"But the practice circle isn't between the smithy and the house," Mum went on. "You said that—"

"Oh, you know how it is with dragon battles," my dad said. "She probably got excited and mixed up a few of the details. The important thing is that everyone is safe."

Mum looked at me for a long moment, and I tried my best to look innocent.

"I'm glad they're going to replace your backpack," she said finally.

"Lottie said they'll replace anything I lose." I said it before I thought the better of it and waited for my mother to say something about how that was all very well, but they couldn't replace any of my limbs. She didn't, though. I decided to take advantage of the opportunity to change the subject. "I got to meet Aodhan, finally. Face to face, I mean."

"He always looks so lovely on television or when I read about him in the paper," Mum said.

"He's a giant," I said. "But he's a nice one."

"I think it's only proper that we get our dragons slayed by giants," my dad said. "Hopefully Owen will grow up to be one too."

"He's working on it," I said a bit carelessly and plowed on. "What did you guys do today?"

They hadn't really done anything exciting, but they proceeded to tell me about it in exhaustive detail anyway. I was relieved that my dragon encounter had gone over so smoothly, so I didn't really care, but I was still glad when I got to excuse myself to go upstairs.

"It's the essay," I said. "Mr. Cooper might let me out of the deadline, but I'll still have to hand it in. I might as well get started on it while I have a free evening."

"You live on the edge, Siobhan," my mother said as I scraped my plate in preparation for the dishwasher. If only she knew.

In my room, I went back over the story I'd told my parents. If it weren't for the backpack, I might have gotten away without any questions at all. I needed to remember that for next time, to focus on the details and make sure I didn't leave any holes. It was important to maintain my credibility if I was going to boost Owen's image.

I sat down at my desk and prepared to rewrite the essay I'd lost. Maybe this time I would type it. I booted up my computer and began to type, but I wasn't really thinking about comparing the short stories we'd read in class that week. I was thinking about swords and dragons and flaming backpacks, a brass ensemble supported by half a dozen kettle drums, and I was thinking about how else I could have explained what happened to my parents, how I might have cast it in meter and rhyme.

Even though I had lied, which was not something I usually did when talking to my parents, I was pleased with my first story.

MOSQUITOES AND
THE BRASS SECTION

Going back to school the Monday after my first up-close-and-personal encounter with a dragon was something of an anti-climax. The attack had been on the news, though the relatively secluded nature of the Thorskards' house and the speed with which Lottie had dispatched the dragon meant there was limited coverage. Also, an *urbs* had made a run at the ACC during a Leafs game, resulting in injuries to the general manager, who'd been in the parking lot at the time. Beyond the local media, no one really cared what had happened in Trondheim. I was pleased with the lack of notoriety for two reasons. First, I wouldn't be on-screen anywhere and second, Mum and Dad would never know that I had totally fabricated everything I told them on Saturday night. There was plenty of footage of Aodhan, though, and each replay of the report ended with the newscaster reminding us that the dragon slayer's own house had been attacked as well, though no damage was done.

I handed my note to Mr. Cooper with a reluctant smile on my face. The outline was about half completed in my brand new backpack if he chose to make an issue of it. It wouldn't exactly be my best work if I had to hand it in right on the spot, but it would be better than a zero. He read the note and looked at where Owen was sitting. Then he sighed.

"Can you have it done by Wednesday?" he asked.

"Yes," I said. "Not a problem."

"Good," he said. "Try not to get your homework lit on fire again unless you can't possibly avoid it."

"It's on my list," I said, because I was usually wearing my backpack, and death in a fire was not my idea of a good way to go.

I went to the back of the room and sat next to Owen while my classmates filed in. The stack of essays on Mr. Cooper's desk got higher.

"How many times do you think the 'a dragon ate my homework' excuse is good for?" Owen whispered to me.

I rolled my eyes. "Let's not try to find out."

I did my very best not to think of dragons again until lunch. This was easier said than done, because while Mr. Cooper insisted on telling us the life story of Joseph Conrad, which did not involve dragons, all Mr. Huffman talked about when we got to history was road building in Roman Britain, which brought up dragons as a matter of course.

A Roman emperor called Hadrian had wanted to build roads as far north as Scotland, but the presence of a hatching belt that stretched from what is now Nottingham to Newcastle had impeded his progress. I'm sure the Scots were thrilled, though. They got to carry on without interference from outside countries until Queen Victoria, who mustn't have been afraid of anything at all given what she'd done with Ottawa, decided that the hatching ground was inconvenient to her vacation plans. An entire Commonwealth's worth of dragon slayers was employed to push the dragons back until they were confined mostly to West Yorkshire. It wasn't the safest train ride, from London to Edinburgh, but with careful rail maintenance and a slight detour to Hull, it was workable.

Mr. Huffman turned the discussion to our own hatching belt, and what we did to traverse it to get to Northern Ontario. He argued that if it weren't for all the nickel and other metals north of the hatching belt, we wouldn't ever risk going there. Instead, we'd go down into the US through Buffalo, and go all the way around to Saskatchewan by way of Montana. Canada would be cut in half. The presence of metal north of Sudbury, he suggested, was the only reason that Manitoba even existed.

"Though, ironically," he concluded, the meter stick waving around his head so quickly that the front row flinched in unison, "we'd all be a lot safer if we lived in Manitoba, given the fact that dragons have very sensitive hearing, and therefore a great dislike of the constant whine produced by mosquitoes."

Manitoba: You'll be itchy, but you probably won't catch on fire. I'm surprised it wasn't on their license plates.

"In any case," Mr. Huffman went on. "No one has tried to move a hatching ground since Queen Victoria ordered it done in the mid-1800s. It's entirely possible that without the strength of the British Empire, there is simply no nation that can execute such an enormous task."

"But, Mr. Huffman," said Sadie. It was usually pretty pointless to wait for Mr. Huffman to call on you. If you sat there with your hand up, you'd lose all feeling in your arm before he saw you. "Dragon slayers aren't supposed to be loyal to countries first. They're supposed to be loyal to their profession."

"In theory, yes," Mr. Huffman said. "But how many dragon slayers have you ever heard of who went to a country other than their own home after their tour in the Oil Watch was concluded?"

There was a long silence. I racked my brain, trying to think if I'd ever heard of anyone doing that. From habit, I looked at Owen, figuring he'd know if anyone did. There was a very strange expression on his face, and I felt the overwhelming urge to change the subject as quickly as possible.

"Why should we bother with moving the hatching grounds?" I said. "Why don't we just weaponize mosquitoes?"

"That, Miss McQuaid, is an excellent idea," Mr. Huffman said. "I can't believe no one has ever thought of that before."

The class laughed, and the discussion meandered back in the general direction of the original topic. I looked at Owen again. His eyes were still strained, but his face had relaxed a little bit. When he made eye contact with me, he gave me the ghost of a smile and turned toward the front of the room.

By the time the bell rang, Owen was back to his old self, and he ended up heading for the cafeteria with Sadie while I went to the music room for lunch. We'd reached a wordless impasse on that topic. Owen would eat with the popular kids, and then come and watch me poke at the piano for whatever was left of lunch period. I can't imagine that it was very interesting, and I know it confused the hell out of Sadie, with whom I now seemed to speak about subjects other than schoolwork on a daily basis. I guessed she was operating under the "enemies closer" theory of high school politics, which I found exhausting. Fortunately, she turned out to have decent taste in music, so at least we had something to talk about instead of awkwardly not talking about Owen. Sadie asked endless questions about my sword training with Lottie and even took to calling me in the evenings, which my parents viewed as an immense success. More important than my newfound quasi-popularity, both Owen and Sadie understood that if I was in the middle of a song, I was not to be bothered. They never interrupted me when I was on a roll.

I'd spent most of the month trying my hand at various members of the brass family. The trumpet was first, and while I could manage it well enough, I decided that it was entirely too yellow for the music I wanted to play. I spent a long time with the euphonium, which was similar in sound to the bari sax and usually got the same part in band arrangements. I gave it up in the end, though, because it was so similar to the bari, and therefore wrong for the same reasons. We had a piccolo trumpet that I knew would be wrong before I picked it up, but I was tempted by the range anyway and gave it a go. It was a fluorescent disaster. I ruled out the tuba as too comical and too difficult to feature, and the trombone for being too stretchy, after only a few days of playing them.

I feel I should mention here that I was by no stretch of the imagination competent at any of these instruments. I could make them make noise, and after a couple of days, I could make them make noise on key, but I lacked any finesse. I didn't even take any of them home to practice, not because I didn't want to carry them to my car, but because I wanted to play them exclusively in soundproof rooms where no one could hear me making a fool of myself trying to play something I was new at. I did have my pride.

The day Mr. Huffman told us about Scotland was the day I cracked open the case with the French horn in it. I'd left it until last because I knew it was the hardest in terms of technique, but as soon as I picked it up, I knew that I was a little bit in love with it. Even if it was wrong for the music I wanted to play, and even if I never got past the "distressed duck" stage of playing it, I loved its coils and slides, the way it fit on my lap, and the way the bell glinted, catching the light as I spun it end over end to empty the spit valve.

I had just mastered the C Major scale when Owen arrived in the practice room. He had his algebra textbook with him, ostensibly to finish his homework, but I knew that he was far more likely to just sit there and listen to me fumble my way through. I wouldn't have let anyone else sit there and listen, but I thought that since I got to watch him learn to use a sword and do all sort of ridiculous drills with it, letting him listen to me butcher "The Old Gray Mare" over and over again was probably fair enough.

"What is that?" he said when I stopped to catch my breath.

"It was 'Frère Jacques,'" I told him. "I didn't think it was all that bad."

"No, I recognized the song," he said, smiling. "I meant what instrument is that."

"French horn," I said. "From Germany, of course."

"So why is it called the French horn?" he asked.

"I have no idea," I told him. "I think professionals just call it the horn, but I like the 'ench.'"

"It looks complicated," he said.

"I think it is," I told him. "Or it will be, if I ever get good at it."

"Why all the brass lately?" he asked. Apparently he'd been listening while I talked, because he was getting the family names of all the instruments right now. "I thought you were trying to focus."

That was the other reason I'd avoided taking the brass instruments home for practicing. Mum and Dad still hadn't given up on my going to university and getting a degree in theory and composition. If I started bringing home a bunch of different brass instruments, that might lead to discussions I wasn't really ready to have yet.

"I'm supposed to tell stories," I said. "And I need brass to do that."

"That makes sense." From anyone else, that would have been patronizing, but since the stories I was going to tell were about Owen, I thought he might appreciate not being left to the mercy of a woodwind narrative.

"It takes a village," I said, and he smiled.

"So long as you don't expect me to sing," he said.

"No fear of that," I told him and went back to torturing the horn.

GIRL TALK

When the phone rang that night, I didn't pick it up. I had a long and storied tradition of not picking up the phone, or at least I would if anyone ever told stories about me, but had I known of the events that would transpire because of the phone call, I might have answered it. I think it makes for a more active beginning.

"Siobhan!" Dad called up the stairs. "The phone's for you!"

The phone was almost never for me. That's mostly why I so rarely picked it up. I did have a phone in my room, a birthday gift from my grandmother when I turned thirteen because, as she said, now that I was a teenager I might need some privacy. It was enormous and pink and it didn't get a lot of use, but I had to admit it was easier than walking downstairs. Of my for-emergencies-only cell phone, which I had inherited from my mother shortly after getting the car, and which had only spotty reception at best thanks to our living in the middle of nowhere, little can be said.

"Got it," I said, after I'd picked up. "Hello?"

"Hi, Siobhan," said a bright voice. "It's Sadie."

"Hello," I said again. Then I felt stupid so I added: "How are you?"

"Great, great, thanks," she said. "Anyway, a bunch of us are going to the Taggerts' on Saturday night for a party. Do you want to come with?"

"Pardon?" I said, entirely surprised.

Sadie did me the courtesy of repeating the question in exactly the same tone, without dumbing it down to monosyllables.

"Um, I'll have to ask my parents," I said, stalling. I knew they'd be thrilled.

"Great!" she said. "Tell me tomorrow, and then I can come and get you on Saturday!"

"Okay," I said. I felt really awkward again and heard myself say, "Hey, thanks for inviting me."

"No problem," said Sadie. "I'll see you tomorrow!"

"Bye," I said, and we hung up.

It was, I thought, one of the weirdest things that had happened to me. At least, so far this week. And it held that distinction until Saturday at six o'clock when the doorbell rang.

"Sadie Fletcher!" my mother said very loudly when she opened the door. I was sitting at the table in a nest of staff paper, and I jumped. "I don't think I've seen you since you girls were in preschool."

That was entirely not true. Before the amalgamation, there had only been about six hundred students at TSS. Mum saw Sadie every year at commencement, when I played in the band and Sadie won several awards, despite not being a graduate. Also, Sadie's dad was an orthodontist, and there was an unspoken camaraderie among all the medical practitioners of Trondheim, largely on the grounds that, including the nurses and the dental hygienists, there were exactly twenty-three of them. It was possible that Mum hadn't spoken with Sadie since we were five, but not seeing her just wasn't an option.

"Oh, you know how it goes," Sadie said easily, kicking off her shoes and lining them up on the mat. "Siobhan and I just got so busy."

That was one way of putting it.

"Siobhan's in the kitchen," Mum said. "Go on in. Have you eaten?"

"Oh yes, thank you," Sadie said.

"Well, there's pop in the fridge," Mum said. "Siobhan can show you where the glasses are."

By now, Sadie was all the way across the front hall and halfway through the living room. When she saw me, her smile faltered a little bit.

"Hi," I said. "I'm sorry I'm not quite ready. I thought we would be going a bit later."

"Oh, no, we are," Sadie said. "Am I interrupting you? I didn't even think about that."

"It's fine," I said. I had already filled the last measure with rests, a sure sign that my muse was gone for the night. "I'm at a good place to stop."

"That's so cool," Sadie said. "Anyway, I'm here because I realized that I don't think you've ever been to a party, and I thought maybe you'd want some help picking what to wear."

Until that precise moment, I had planned to wear the jeans and polo shirt I already had on, with whatever coat was hanging by the door on my way out. Sadie was wearing jeans, but she had clearly put some effort into the rest of her outfit. I quickly decided that I was on alien territory, and it was probably best to take whatever advice the locals were willing to give me.

"That would be great," I said. "Let's go upstairs and assess the damage."

She laughed, and we headed for the stairs. As I walked past the TV room, Mum gave me a thumbs-up and a huge grin. I did my best not to roll my eyes.

"It's too bad Owen can't come," Sadie said, settling on my bed and picking up one of the pillows to fiddle with it. I stepped into the closest, which was a walk-in, and hoped that I was not about to embarrass myself too badly.

"Yeah," I said. I had hoped to have some backup. "His dad tries to be home on Saturday nights. They don't get to see each other all that much, with school and his dad's patrolling."

"Have you met him yet?" Sadie asked.

"Yes," I told her. "Will it be cold? I mean, should I be looking at sleeves or what?"

"Sleeves for sure," Sadie said. "It won't be freezing, but it is an outside party in November. What's Lottie like?"

"She's fantastic," I said, pulling off several hangers at once. "She's much more herself in person than she is on TV. Of course, she's herself on TV, but she's real in person. She can't cook very well. What about these?"

Sadie made me hold up each shirt in front of myself while she looked at me with a pursed smile, her head cocked to one side. When I got to the wine-red poet shirt Mum had bought me for a Mozart revue a few years ago, Sadie squeezed the pillow in glee.

"That one, for sure," she said.

"Really?" I hadn't even picked it up on purpose. "It's practically a costume."

"It's perfect," Sadie said. "And I don't think you've ever worn it to school, so it's essentially new. You'll look like an artiste, with just the right amount of pirate, plus you can wear a thermal underneath it and be warm."

"I didn't know that was the style of the time," I said, somewhat dryly, but I stepped back into the closet to change.

Sadie cracked up laughing at that. "You are something else," she said. I was pretty sure she meant it as a compliment. "Now, what were you planning to do with your hair?"

In the end, I sat in front of her on the bed while she did something involving twists and every hairpin I could scrounge. She talked the whole time, about the kids from school who would be there, and how there would probably be a fight if any of the Saltrock kids showed up, which was inevitable, since news of the party had been all over school for half a week. It was almost 7:30 by the time she was satisfied with my appearance.

I would like to add at this juncture that it's not that I am sartorially deficient in some way. I am perfectly capable of dressing myself for concerts and school, though I do tend toward the simple end of the scale of fashion. I might not ride the cusp of trendiness, but I wasn't exactly a candidate for *What Not to Wear*. Sadie was determined that I was going to make an impression, though (which I knew because she told me, halfway through the hair-pinning), and for reasons passing my own understanding, I let her. It's possible that I was in shock.

Anyway, I went to look in the mirror and Sadie produced a curling iron from her purse, which she plugged in and turned on herself. I had to admit, Sadie was good at this. I looked different, but I didn't look like a doll.

"I don't think either of us should bother with makeup," Sadie said, wrapping her hair around the iron. "It'll be dark."

"Works for me," I said. I did not get along with makeup on the best of days. "Thanks for this. I look much better than I'd planned to."

"You're welcome," she said.

I came back to sit on the bed and watched her finish her hair.

"Have you met Hannah as well?" she asked after a moment.

"Oh, yes," I said. "Hannah is amazing too, but in a different way from Lottie. She's a lot more practical. She was the one who convinced my parents that it was safe for me to hang out with Owen so much. And it was her idea that I learn to use a sword."

Something flashed in Sadie's eyes. At the time, I thought it was the lamplight reflecting on the metal tube of the curling iron, and I didn't think any further on it.

"That sounds like a lot of work," she said, voice neutral.

"It really is," I said. "My arms and legs are killing me, but I think I'm developing actual muscles."

I rolled up the belled sleeves of my shirt to show her. The muscles were still mostly in my imagination, but we both pretended we could see results. I could certainly feel them.

"I think I'm done," she said, reaching for the plug. She gave the iron a few minutes to cool down and then packed it back into her bag.

We headed downstairs to say goodbye to my parents. Mum made a lot of noise about my hair, and Sadie was modestly appreciative of the praise. Then Dad admonished us not to do anything stupid, like leave the car idling for warmth or light a fire or drink and drive, and we promised to do our best to survive the evening.

"Be home by eleven, please," Mum said. "And give us a call if you need anything, no questions."

"Your parents are pretty cool," Sadie said, as we headed for her car.

"They're thrilled I'm socializing," I told her. I pulled the shrug Sadie had insisted I bring in place of a coat around my shoulders. I was probably going to freeze to death. "They'd probably be okay with this even if we were going dragon baiting."

Sadie laughed again, and for the first time I genuinely began to wonder why she was doing this. She had been disappointed when Owen had told her he couldn't come, but her enthusiasm hadn't flagged at all when it came to going to the party with me. I had originally suspected that she had invited me as a courtesy to Owen, but her actions since finding out it would just be the two of us indicated otherwise. I had a moment of irrational fear that once we got the party she would ditch me.

The Taggerts lived one side road out from Trondheim toward Saltrock, in the opposite direction of the Thorskards. I had never been there—well, not since I was young enough to go trick-or-treating (there's always better candy in the country), but you could see the house, barn, and drive shed from the highway, so I knew roughly what I was getting into. About a dozen cars and trucks were parked in the driveway, and I could feel the bass in my chest, even though we were still a few hundred feet from the shed.

Bass emanations always made me feel a little bit ill, so I was pale when Sadie turned off the car and opened her door. She reached out and shook my shoulders.

"Siobhan," she said. "It'll be fine. You look great, you're with me and you're friends with Owen Thorskard. You have absolutely nothing to worry about."

I took a deep breath and smiled at her. She was, after all, correct in all of her assertions except for one: I did have something to worry about, because behind the drive shed, some idiot had already lit a fire.

BONFIRE OF THE INANITIES

The account was never particularly clear. The kids from TSS blamed the kids from Saltrock, and vice versa. All I knew for sure was that by eight, there was a sizable smoke plume, and since Jerry Taggert's parents were out of town for the weekend (hence the field party) and cell phone reception was notoriously poor this close to the Saltrock bluffs, we were on our own. There was a keg next to the bonfire. I stepped on at least three red plastic cups, crushing them under my running shoes, before I reached the edge of the fire.

"Well, I guess it's a good thing I didn't make you borrow my other boots," Sadie said, reaching down to scrape the mud out of her heel. "But if we ever do this inside, you totally have to. They'd look perfect with that shirt."

I looked at her like she was out of her mind, and then went back to measuring the fire. It was in a pit, thank goodness, and therefore relatively contained, but it was still going to take some doing to put out. It had probably been lit to provide some heat.

I had never understood why my schoolmates chose to spend their Saturday nights outside in the cold. Even the drive shed would have been moderately warmer, but for some reason, they were all standing around the keg pretending they weren't cold, or running into the drive shed for a few moments to warm up before coming back outside.

"Hey, Sadie!" shouted Alex Carmody, even though he was well within earshot. "Who did you—oh! Hi, Siobhan!"

"Alex," I said, nodding. "Do you happen to know if there's a hose around?"

"Um, I've never actually been here before," Alex admitted. "I just came because—well, I heard you were coming."

This whole thing just kept getting more and more ridiculous.

"You'll have to forgive Siobhan," Sadie said. "She's never done this before, and some idiot decided to ruin her first field party by lighting a fire. They'll probably kill us if we use the keg to put the fire out, don't you think?"

"Doesn't alcohol burn anyway?" Alex asked. "I'll find a hose."

He wandered off, and I turned to Sadie. I decided that I needed answers, whether we were about to get eaten by a dragon or not.

"What the heck is going on?" I said. "First you call me, then you invite me to a party, then you tell everyone I'm coming, and somehow that makes them all excited? Have I fallen into some kind of bizarro world?"

"It's because you're friends with Owen, Siobhan." Sadie said it as gently as she could. "People want to ask you questions about him."

"So you're just using me?" I said. "Not that I'm completely averse to that, mind you. Fire aside, this has been weirdly fun."

"I know, eh?" Sadie said. She didn't answer my question, though, because Alex came back with a bucket that was mostly full of water. I suspected he had dumped some of it as he ran back.

"I can get more," he said. He wasn't even breathing hard, but in the firelight his face was red.

Sadie took the bucket and carefully upended it near the base of the flames on the southern side of the fire. The sizzling was encouraging, but when the bucket was empty, there was still a lot of fire in the pit.

"More," said Sadie, holding out the bucket to Alex, who took off with it.

"Hey!" said a Saltrock boy I didn't know. "What are you doing?"

"We're putting out this fire so you don't get eaten by a dragon, Nathan." I wondered how Sadie knew everyone's name. "I can't run as fast as Alex, but I can run faster than you, which means you'll have a better chance of getting eaten if a dragon decides to come take a look at all this smoke."

Nathan was holding a plastic cup and seemed a bit unsteady on his feet already. I was pretty sure my chances were better than his too.

Alex came back with another bucket, and also with Jerry, who was very angry and kind of drunk. Jerry had the garden hose, though, and soon enough the fire was out. We stood there in the dark, all of us scanning the skies, looking for the airborne flame that would tell us we hadn't been fast enough to quench the fire.

Nathan wandered into the cornfield. I didn't pay much attention to him. I'd seen enough movies to know that what high school boys did in cornfields at parties was absolutely nothing I wanted to get involved in. Instead, we stood in the near dark of the Taggerts' yard. Someone gave me a cup, but I didn't drink out of it. I watched Sadie, since she was my driver, and she didn't drink anything either.

"So Siobhan," Alex said once we'd decided that there wasn't a dragon nearby. "What's it like?"

"What's what like?" I asked. I was starting to find the rhythm of the party, after the rocky start, but I still wasn't sure what my part was.

"Owen," Sadie said. "What's Owen like."

"You guys spend just as much time with him as I do," I pointed out. "I mean, you're in his classes and you eat with him in the cafeteria. All we ever do is homework."

"He spends half of lunch with you," Alex said.

"He watches me compose," I said. "It's not exactly thrilling."

"He must really like you," said a voice I didn't recognize. I turned toward the speaker, though I had no idea what I was going to say, but Sadie beat me to it.

"You know as well as I do that there are probably dragon slayer rules about that sort of thing," she said. I wasn't sure that there were, but if it made people stop asking, I might be willing to pretend. "And anyway, that's not the cool part. Lottie is teaching Siobhan how to use a sword."

That got a response. There were rapid-fire questions: everything from how one learned to use a sword to what Lottie looked like up close to whether or not that made me a dragon slayer. I was hard-pressed to keep up with the answers, since each one I gave seemed to spawn a new question. Sadie threw her arm around my shoulder and squeezed, somehow deducing, even in the dark, that I was starting to panic.

"Guys, guys!" she said. "One at a freaking time."

"Have you been inside Hannah's smithy?" asked a girl I was almost positive was named Heidi.

"No," I said. "I looked in the window, but it's quite small, and full of smith things. I watched her sharpen a sword, though. You don't need fire for that, so she does it outside."

"Cool!" said probably Heidi.

"Where the hell is Nathan?" another Saltrock boy asked.

There was no consensus, though several people besides me had seen him wander into the cornfield. It was quickly determined that no one else was missing, which meant that whatever mischief Nathan was getting up to in the field was of a solitary nature. They shouted for him, but there was no answer, and it was decided that he had probably succumbed to his alcohol.

"We should go," Sadie said.

"It's been less than an hour," I pointed out, even though I didn't particularly want to stay.

"The whole point of a field party is to get dressed, show up for a little while, and then leave before the boys start doing stupid things," Sadie said. "Apparently we missed the un-stupid part of the evening. If we leave now, we can still watch a movie before you have to be home for curfew."

I looked around. Probably-Heidi and a few other kids were getting into a car, and a couple of the trucks were already gone. Suddenly, getting out of here seemed like a very good idea.

"Let's go," I said.

We headed back to the car, and I rolled down my window

in the hope that the air would get the smell of smoke out of my clothes. If my parents smelled bonfire on me, they might never let me out of the house again. As we drove off, Sadie looked in the rearview mirror with a startled expression on her face.

"What?" I said, looking back over my shoulder.

"It's probably nothing," Sadie said. "I mean, it's probably just us, but I thought I smelled smoke."

She rolled down the other windows, the better to air us out, and the smell decreased as we drove. The rest of the evening was quiet. Sadie's parents seemed thrilled that we had smartly decided to forgo the field party, and offered up the entertainment center without protest, retreating upstairs and leaving us with enough chips and pop to stun a regiment.

"That's a big part of it," Sadie said in a conspiratorial tone after they had departed. "You show some good judgement, which happens to be what you wanted to do anyway, and all of a sudden they trust you to the ends of the earth."

I considered that as we watched a Jane Austen thing I can't remember the name of, and Sadie insisted on showing me how to use a curling iron. I'd never given my parents a reason not to trust me, but I'd never gone out of my way to show them that my judgment was sound either. And then I'd just announced that I was taking up with a dragon slayer and let Hannah do all the bargaining on my behalf. Maybe Sadie was right, and it was time for some judicious coloring outside the lines, the better to make me look good when I went back inside them. Maybe this whole hanging out thing was going to have unexpected fringe benefits. Sadie hadn't answered my question earlier about using me, but she hadn't denied it either. Turnabout was fair play, as long as neither of us deliberately hurt the other, I decided.

When she dropped me off at home, Sadie passed me the extra boots. I hadn't even seen her get them, and I wondered if she carried a pair around in the backseat of her car for emergency situations. She was that kind of person, I was starting to learn, and it wouldn't have surprised me.

"You should wear these on Monday," she said.

"Thanks," I said, and I found that I meant it, even though I had no idea what I should wear them with and had visions of myself falling down the stairs thanks to the not-unsubstantial heel.

It had been an odd night on all fronts, but I finally thought I was starting to get the hang of the whole high school thing, even if I was about three years later than most people. I clung to that good feeling until Sunday morning, when I went downstairs for breakfast and Dad told me that Nathan Brash had wandered into a cornfield at a party, lost his sense of direction thanks to the height of the late-season corn and the amount of beer he'd had to drink, and walked right into the squat of a corn dragon.

THE STORY OF MICHIGAN

Once upon a time, there was a little girl named Victoria who grew up to change the shape of the world. She loved twice and deeply: once a prince, whom she married, and once a Scottish dragon slayer, which was a bit of a secret because she was a widowed queen when she loved him. She worked hard to confine the dragons of England, and since she had the resources of an empire on which the sun never set to do so, she was largely successful. She lived a very long time and led her country through the bitter outcome of the Industrial Revolution, when the dragons on the island increased and the people had to learn to evade them or die in fire. Her story is the exception.

More common is the story of what befell the state of Michigan.

Like Mark Antony at Actium and Napoleon on his way to Russia, the settlers of Michigan started out well enough. The land was good for farming, and the weather wasn't terrible all the time, though for most of recorded history the blackfly population was something of an issue. Michigan joined the Union, and development proceeded apace through the turn of the century.

There had always been dragons in Michigan. It was said that a person in that state couldn't be more than six miles from water, and most of that water was small lakes and ponds, which are prime breeding grounds for dragons. There were several different species native to the area before the European settlers arrived, and they managed to bring three new breeds with them, trailing the burnt corpses of fallen livestock as they made their way west. The upside was that the newer dragons were bigger and quickly drove the older dragons out. The downside, of course, was that the new dragons were bigger.

The dragon slayers, both Native and European, adapted, and at last a balance was struck. Across the sea, Queen Victoria worked to contain the British dragons, and in Michigan, it seemed that it would be easy enough to follow her example. For a brief time, it looked like success would be had, but then came further expansion, and more and more industrialized use for coal, leading to more carbon emissions than ever before. In 1903, with the advent of gasoline and the internal-combustion engine, the Ford Motor Company was incorporated, and Michigan's economy turned into an automobile-producing giant.

The effects were immediate and disastrous. The dragon population increased as Ford built factories and pumped more and more carbon smoke into the air. New species appeared, and the dragon slayers were hard pressed to fight them off. There was no loyalty to Queen and Country here, and that forced Ford to do something that had never been done before. Rather than go back to the relatively safer steam, he sent out a call all across the USA, asking for dragon slayers of any skill to come and defend his plants, and he promised them unheard-of sums of money to do it.

And the dragon slayers came. They left their small towns to the fire and went to Michigan for a paycheck. By 1920, there were more dragon slayers concentrated in one area than there had been since the Romans burned Masada, and still the dragons multiplied. Ford hadn't stopped making cars, and now that more people were driving them and burning gasoline to do it, there was even more carbon for the dragons to hunt. Michigan became a series of fortified towns and cities, as close to the factories as they could get, because that's where the dragon slayers were paid to do their work. There has never been an accurate accounting of fatalities, but modern scholars guess that between 1903 and the start of the Great Depression, at least a hundred thousand people were killed by dragons or dragon fire.

The Depression bought Michigan some time. When the market collapsed, production was greatly diminished. More important, fewer people could afford to drive. Ford struggled to pay his dragon slayers, but he understood that they had to stay, or he would lose his factories entirely. By some miracle of finance, he managed to hold out, and when the war contracts began to make his factories viable again, Ford went back to work.

This time, Ford could only hire dragon slayers who had already completed their military service, and with the government's attention firmly overseas, the situation in Michigan quickly became untenable. By the end of the war, there was nothing that could be done, though Ford tried by offering more money to any dragon slayer who would come and work for him. Michigan went on for a few more years, desperately holding off an ever-increasing number of dragons while producing more and more of the very substance that drew them in.

In 1947, while the Detroit Red Wings were losing the Stanley Cup to the Maple Leafs in Toronto, Henry Ford was eaten by a dragon. He was old and his mental state was questionable, but he at least had the wherewithal to call for the army and the evacuation of the state before he died. Over the next few years, and at great cost, Michigan was abandoned. The Red Wings never returned and became the un-home team of the National Hockey League. Their logo served as a warning everywhere they went: the wheel, for the car that had brought Michigan up, and the wing, for the dragons that had brought it down.

This is the legacy of the once-great State of Michigan: a burned and ruined stretch of land that had once been green and free of poison. The lakes survived, only to serve as hatching grounds for generations of dragons to come. The Upper Peninsula, mostly unscathed but still perilous, fell nominally to the control of Wisconsin, but no one ventured there. Canada lost access to Manitoulin Island, due to its proximity to the fallen state, and was forced to strengthen its watch along the borders as well. Ford's factories stood only as husks, monuments to greed and lack of government oversight, and the brave souls who looked upon them from the questionable safety of Windsor quailed at the sight.

NATHAN'S NON-MEMORIAL

On Monday, Owen joined me for lunch as soon as the bell rang instead of going to the cafeteria. He sat in the corner, elbows on his knees, eating a sandwich and looking at his shoes. I let him stew for about two minutes before I couldn't take it anymore.

"What's wrong?" I asked.

"Everyone knows why I wasn't at that party," he said. "Everyone knows that I was home because my father was home, which means he wasn't patrolling."

"Owen, that's ridiculous," I said. "Your dad is usually in Exeter on Saturdays, so even if he'd been out, he still wouldn't have been in the right place, and you're sixteen! You don't have to slay anything yet."

"I know that," Owen said. "But that's not how it will look."

"It was a stupid thing to do, lighting that fire," I said. "They'll probably never figure out who did it, and I feel awful about that boy, but if you had been there, what would you have done?"

"Nathan," Owen said. "His name was Nathan, and he's in my gym class."

I quieted down and turned back to the piano. Clearly there was no making him feel better, even though I maintained that there was nothing he could have done.

"Were your parents mad?" he asked after another long moment passed.

"No," I said. "I mean, they were shocked, because they realized I had been at that farm when they read it in the paper, but they weren't mad at me. I told them I was the one who insisted the fire get put out, and that Sadie and Alex helped, and then I told them that Sadie and I left right after."

"I'm glad you did," Owen said.

"Well, look at it this way," I said. "It's at least as much my fault as it is yours. I was actually there, for starters, and even though I knew there had been a fire, I didn't call anyone to report it. I just left and let Sadie braid my hair for the rest of the night."

"Did you really?" Owen asked. He looked a bit startled.

"Well, not exactly," I said. "There was a thing with the curling iron."

"Did you paint your toenails and talk about boys too?" He had perked up a little bit, so I almost let him get away with teasing me like that.

"Well, we mostly talked about you, to be honest," I said. "At least at first. When she came to pick me up she had a bunch of questions, and then at the party, all the kids wanted to know all about you."

"What did you tell them?" he asked.

"That you sleep with a giant teddy bear," I said.

"You did not," he said, "because if you did, then you'd have to tell them that you saw me in bed, and that would lead to other questions that you don't want to answer."

"Dammit!" I said. "I knew I should have led with something else."

He laughed again, and I felt I had done my job as dragon slayer morale improver as well as was required. I turned back to the keys again and started to play. It was a new song, one that had been pulling at me since Sunday morning when Dad had read the news article about Nathan's death over breakfast. The bass didn't translate particularly well to the piano, but you could accomplish a similar effect by playing intentionally discordant tones. Now that I was feeling better, I didn't want to remind myself how the sound had felt.

"Dad and Aunt Hannah went out on Sunday afternoon and got it," Owen said, when it became apparent that I wasn't actually going to play anything. "The dragon, I mean."

"Was it still at the Taggerts'?" I asked.

"No," he said. "But it left a trail. It flew so low that it left broken corn stalks all the way into the trees, and then they just tracked it down until they had it pinned."

"Why did Hannah go out at all?" I asked. "I mean, no offense to her, but corn dragons aren't something your dad should need help with, especially not one that's just, um, eaten."

"Dad's been taking Hannah out on short trips lately," Owen said. "For practice."

"For practice?" I asked. Then I put the pieces together. "So that she can help Lottie slay dragons."

"Exactly," Owen said. "And me too, should it come to that."

I thought about Lottie facing a dragon on her own, and

my blood ran cold. When she had been at full power, that unrestrained trumpet soaring into the sky, she hadn't needed help from anyone. Except, she'd always had help. Hannah had made her swords since they were eighteen and sixteen, and Aodhan had always been her backup. Presumably, Lottie's mother had also helped her, if only while she was in training. Lottie and Aodhan had been born after their mother's days as an active dragon slayer. She had died of natural causes while they were on tour with the Oil Watch in the Gulf, but that didn't mean that Lottie had been tragically deprived of a mother. Living to old age was something of an accomplishment for a dragon slayer, and sixty-five wasn't fantastic, but it was nothing to sneeze at. It was entirely likely that, if I kept up my association with the Thorskards, the story would end with just Hannah and me.

"Will there be a memorial?" Owen asked.

I was so lost in my thoughts of his, his father's, and his aunt's mortality that it took me a moment to figure out what he was talking about.

"For Nathan," he clarified, just as I caught up. "In Hamilton, if a kid got eaten by a dragon, there was usually a memorial."

"Yeah, there'll be something," I said. "I'm not on the Assembly Committee, and they're the ones who usually plan that sort of thing. It'll be later in the week."

"How do they usually go?" Owen asked.

I abandoned the piano completely, turning all the way around on the bench to look at him. He had relaxed a bit but still sat hunched over his knees. If I couldn't convince him not to feel guilty, and it was clear I couldn't, I guess telling him all the gruesome details was the next best thing.

"Ms. Ngembi will make an announcement that we're to go to the gym instead of to class. Probably on Wednesday, but maybe tomorrow," I said. We hadn't done this so far this year, but it was a familiar ritual. "Everyone sits on the floor. It's a short assembly, so they don't bother with the chairs. The teachers will stand at the back, and some of the older kids will pull out the bleachers, even though they're not supposed to.

"When everyone's settled, Ms. Ngembi will make us all stand up for 'O Canada,' and when that's done and everyone's seated again, she'll tell us the school-safe version of what happened. Because it was such a dumb thing to do, she might have some strong reminders about fire safety, but she'll mostly stick to telling us about Nathan." I paused for a moment. "You know, she might not have known him that well. She might have one of the teachers who transferred in from Saltrock do that part. But anyway, once she's done she'll remind us that we stand for St. George, and that we must all be careful, and as dragonsafe as possible. Then she'll send us off to class, and it will be quiet all morning, but by lunch time everyone will be back to themselves."

"That's how it went in Hamilton," Owen said. "Sometimes there were candles, and we had a different mascot, so there was nothing about St. George, but it was basically the same."

"What makes me angry is that everyone will act like it was this terribly sad thing," I said.

"It is sad," Owen said. "Someone died."

"It's not sad, it's *stupid*," I said. "I was at that party. If Jerry hadn't come with the hose, if Alex hadn't been willing to run back and forth with the bucket, if Sadie hadn't agreed with me when I made a fuss about it, I could have been eaten instead!"

Owen looked taken aback. I was a bit surprised myself. I hadn't been aware I'd felt this strongly about it until the words came out of my mouth. But once I started, I couldn't stop.

"Everyone knows not to light fires, to stay inside if it's too dark to see incoming soot-streakers," I said. The jangling notes I hadn't wanted to play before rattled in my veins, and I wove my fingers together to keep them from playing notes that weren't there. "We were right next to a cornfield, and the stalks were more than six feet high! And they lit a fire, and someone died, and tomorrow morning we're going to have to pretend it was a terrible accident."

Owen waited a moment, to be sure I was done, I guess, and then leaned forward.

"Do you know why Lottie jumped that morning, the last morning on the Skyway?" he asked.

"To get to the dragon," I said. Everyone knew that.

Owen shook his head. "You never chase a dragon," he said. "You track it, maybe, if it can't see you, but as soon as you're its target, it only looks away if something makes it."

I thought about that morning on the Skyway, the fight I hadn't seen until long after it was over. I had been so polite, had never asked. I had relied on the news, on little Amelia, all those miles away at the top of the Escarpment. I had no idea why Lottie jumped that morning, but now that I was pressed to think about it, I had a guess.

"There was someone on the bridge ... with a camera phone, standing next to their idling car, and the dragon went for them instead," I said.

"And Lottie jumped without thinking about it," Owen said. "And it's this great tragedy, a career cut short by heroism, and no one knows how stupid it really was."

"No wonder your dad didn't want to deal with all that stuff," I said. "At least cows and chickens are smart enough to run away."

"Write the song," Owen said. "Write a song for Nathan that no one is ever going to hear, the song about what actually happened. Maybe if we do this right, someday it'll mean something."

I turned again, and he came and sat beside me on the bench. I put my hands on the keys, and the music was there. I didn't stop to write any of it down. There wasn't any reason to. No one would ever care that Nathan had died for someone else's mistake, because they were too drunk to go into the drive shed to warm up.

"Do your best to die of old age," I told him.

"I'll try," he said.

When the bell rang, I got up to get my backpack and caught him looking at my feet.

"Where did you get those?" he asked.

"Sadie loaned them to me," I said. "She thinks they look good, but I've been tripping over everything all morning."

"They aren't that bad," Owen said. "I mean, they're nearly practical. If you could walk in them."

"Thanks," I said.

"You know what I meant," he said.

"Yes, thankfully, or I'd probably be insulted," I said.

"What did you tell them, at the party?" he asked again. "About me?"

"I told them you were a dragon slayer."

Because it was the truth.

FIRE INSURANCE AND
MATERNAL INSTINCT

When my parents accepted that I was going to be spending a good portion of my time driving a dragon slayer around the county, they insisted I get better fire insurance. It was a pretty good idea, even though I couldn't really afford it. Until I started tutoring Owen, my primary source of income had been playing the organ on Sunday mornings and the small honorarium the hospital paid me to play piano for patients on Wednesday evenings. When Hannah found out, she insisted that I start keeping track of my mileage and expenses. I thought this was probably a good idea, until my dad found the spreadsheets I'd made up and started to obsess over them as only an accountant could.

I spent a couple of days trying to convince him that I didn't need to incorporate as a small business, though Lottie pointed out that it might be useful to keep in mind for tax purposes later. Eventually we decided that the Thorskards would pay for the additional insurance, whatever gas I used driving Owen, and my tutoring fee. For the first time in my life, I had more money than I could spend in a single trip to the music store.

That's an outright lie, of course, but it sounds good. The truth was that I could start saving money for university now, whether I planned to attend or not, and I could also treat myself to the odd extra piece of sheet music from time to time. This was a new luxury for me. Now, not only did I have a car with which to take myself to the music store, located an hour away in the opposite direction of Saltrock, and someone to share the gas with, but I could also purchase things instead of looking at them longingly, and, should we be attacked by a dragon on the road, my new insurance would help me replace my car. I even got snow tires and put them on the car in the first week of November to be extra prepared. The weather was unseasonably warm, but between dragon fire and regular run-of-the-mill climate change, that sort of thing was becoming more and more difficult to predict.

I had finally managed to make the horn sound like something besides a duck that had just realized it was going to be Christmas dinner, and I was celebrating by playing "Venezuela" as loudly as I could in the practice room. Owen walked in, like he did every day, and then his face fell when he recognized the song. I was surprised he knew it, as it wasn't all that common a folk song. He stayed to listen, but he didn't say anything to me for the rest of the day. I thought I was okay with waiting him out, but apparently there was only so much I was willing to take, and being in the car with him had put me at the end of my patience.

I checked the rearview mirror to make sure nothing was coming. Nothing was. Even though this was a main highway, it was still empty as often as not. Then I pulled over and put the car in park.

"What's wrong?" asked Owen. He was scanning the skies, looking for a dragon.

"That's what I was going to ask you," I said. "You haven't said a word to me since lunch, until just now, and I wanted to know what the problem was."

"It's nothing," he said shortly.

"You asked Alex for help in algebra instead of me," I pointed out. "It's definitely something."

He looked out the window for a long time. I was just about to give up and shift into first gear, my hand already on the gear-shift, when he turned back.

"Wait," he said, and put his hand over mine. "There's something I probably should have told you."

He balled his hands up and put them in his lap, looking back out the window, and I knew that whatever he was going to tell me was going to take some time. I didn't like to idle this close to Hannah's smithy, so I turned off the engine and settled in to wait him out, for real this time.

"You've never asked about my mother," he said after a moment.

"I haven't ever really thought about her," I said, which was the truth. I knew he had to have come from somewhere, but he had a family, and I'd never thought that there were any pieces missing from it. I had decided it wasn't my business.

"She's alive," Owen said. "If that's what you were worried about."

I'll admit, I had no earthly idea what I would have said if she'd been dead, but I didn't really have much to go on with her being alive either, so I just said, "Oh," and let him continue.

"She and my dad met in the Watch, in 1994, right near the end of their tours," he said. "Dad was assigned to the Middle East, but not Saudi Arabia like Hannah and Lottie. He was in Kuwait instead."

I winced. It had happened before I was born, but Kuwait was the one glaring failure in the Oil Watch's record. It hadn't been the fault of the dragon slayers, but of course they were the ones who had borne the blame.

"It got really bad, for a while. Bad enough that Hannah and Lottie and a bunch of others, including my mother, were eventually reassigned close by to help," Owen said. "And the dragon slayers were in the middle of the worst of it. It's why dad didn't go for a contract when he got home. He couldn't stop thinking about the fires. He still can't, not really."

A pickup truck drove past us, slowing down to make sure we were all right. I waved the driver on with a smile I didn't feel, and turned back to Owen. He was still looking out the window.

"They got really close," Owen said. "My mom and dad. Lottie says that's what happens in the Oil Watch. They put the dragon slayers together and hope they bond. Like Sparta, but without all the child sacrifice."

He laughed, but it wasn't because he thought his joke was funny.

"Anyway, I was one of those things that happen when people 'bond,'" Owen said. "Mom had to come off active duty, and the rest of the squad voted to give dad the safest tasks, not that there was much in the way of safety to be had. I was born in 1995, just before their time was up. Dad wanted to come home, train new dragon slayers and work with Lottie and Hannah. Mom, she just wanted to go home."

"And she wasn't Canadian," I said. I thought back to that history class, the one where Mr. Huffman had pointed out that despite the camaraderie the Oil Watch is supposed to inspire, very few dragon slayers actually stick with it.

"Venezuelan," he said.

And there it was.

"Do you ever see her?" I asked.

"Sometimes," he said. "About once a year. She wanted to come when Aunt Lottie was injured, but they couldn't spare her. It's different there, dragon slaying, because it's a smaller country, so they all live close to their oil fields. She didn't have time to train me properly. She takes her dragon slaying very seriously."

"And she didn't want to jeopardize her career by having a baby around?" I said, my tone as light as I could make it.

"It's more complicated than that," Owen said. "But she certainly wasn't looking to settle down with a family."

"But your dad was?" I asked.

"Hannah, actually." Owen smiled. "Theoretically, dragon slayers are supposed to provide their own replacements, and Hannah wanted to make sure that Lottie's replacement was the best."

"So no pressure then," I said.

"None at all," Owen said. He laughed, and this time it was real. "My mom is a national hero, just not from the same country. I can't be mad that she wanted to be the best at her job. And Lottie was already famous, even then, so when Hannah offered an alternative, everyone decided it was the best and most responsible thing to do."

"Hannah told me that the hardest times of her life were spent hiding in the dragon shelter after you were born," I told him.

"I know," he said. "She likes to trot that out whenever she wants something."

"It really does take a village to raise a dragon slayer," I said.

"If you say that too many more times, people are going to think it's my slogan and I'm going to end up with it embroidered on a pillow somewhere," Owen said.

Another car drove past us, and I waved to the driver. This time, my smile was real.

"Start the car, please," Owen said. He rubbed his hands together. "I'm starting to freeze."

"If I'd left the engine running, we might have been attacked," I said. It still wasn't cold, but if he wanted to change the subject, I was going to let him.

"At least I'd be warm," Owen pointed out.

"You have very strange priorities," I said. I started the car and shifted back into gear so I could pull out onto the road.

"Why did you pick that song, anyway?" Owen asked once I'd reached fifth and put the cruise control on.

"Because it has great range," I said. "It's up and down and sideways. And there are fast and slow parts, pauses and notes you barely play. If you have someone to play the bass, it's even better, but as a warmup song it's pretty much perfect. I don't mind finding something else, though. There are lots of songs."

"No, it's okay," Owen said. "I should have told you all of this weeks ago. And it sounded awesome on the horn."

"Thank you," I said. "I've been practicing."

"I noticed," he said, and then winced as I smacked him lightly on the shoulder. "Hey, I meant that in the good way!" he protested.

"Sure you did," I said.

"No, really," he said. "I've listened to it all, haven't I? And never once did I wear earplugs."

"My hero," I said. "They'll sing songs of your bravery in the face of bad horn playing for decades to come."

"They will if you write them," he said. "But I think we'd both be better off if we stick to dragons."

He was right.

PIPING DOWN THE SUN

Lottie didn't warn me that signing up to be Owen's bard would mean I got homework. It wasn't a lot, and it was mostly pretty fun, but it was still more work on top of my regular school stuff, the self-defense sword training, and my music. Mostly it was reading old stories, and some not-so-old stories, about dragons and dragon slayers. I would talk to Lottie or Hannah about what was true and what was fabricated, and then figure out if the fabrications were any good. It was way more interesting than *Heart of Darkness*, which, as promised, we had plunged into in English class. Not even the addition of stories about African dragons could make *that* book more appealing. Mr. Cooper said that Conrad had tried to keep the dragon lore in his book as true-to-life as possible, but I was under the impression that he just lacked imagination.

There are many things about dragons that are simply untrue, most of which will spice up nearly any story. They have no specific dietary prejudice when it comes to humans, for example. They don't really care if you're a girl or a boy, whether you're young or old, or if you've ever had sex. There was an antismoking ad campaign a few years ago that suggested dragons were more likely to go after people who smoked cigarettes or cigars, but the testing methods used in the research were fairly sketchy and nothing really conclusive was determined. It was still a fairly successful ad, though.

When I was still in elementary school, an animal psychologist had published a book about how dragons had come to associate humans with carbon emissions, thus accounting for the higher number of dragon attacks since the turn of the millennium. No one took him particularly seriously. This was a bit because his methodologies were faulty, but mostly because the psychologist was eaten trying to prove his point shortly after his book was released to the public. Those few copies he autographed beforehand are worth a ludicrous amount of money to collectors, but mostly the book is used as an example of how not to think about dragons. It did come in handy every time an animal rights group tried to have a certain species declared endangered or something stupid like that, though.

Each culture had its own myths and misconceptions about dragons and dragon slayers. As I read more of the chronicles Lottie gave me, the more I realized that misinformation could be a dragon slayer's greatest help and biggest challenge at the same time. My job as Owen's bard wasn't just to make him sound cool on the six o'clock news, though that was a big part of it. I also had to protect him from damaging rumors and false leads, like the ones from the summer about Aodhan's supposed incompetency. Lottie had dealt with those simply by being in a coma and then announcing the move, but I couldn't always rely on that sort of distraction. The most important thing was to make sure that the public stayed calm. There were several so-called preventative measures that didn't actually keep dragons away, but so long as no one was eaten while participating, they did no harm in keeping order and strengthening the trust between dragon slayers and the general public.

One such placebo was traditional Scottish bagpipes. (For whatever reason, Irish bagpipes were not considered effective dragon deterrents). As a response to the increasing number of dragon attacks on Saltrock, the mayor of the town had implemented a thoroughly ridiculous Saturday night ritual called "Piping Down the Sun," wherein local pipers would assemble on the beach and play their bagpipes at full volume from the time the sun touched the horizon until it disappeared completely. The noise didn't do much to actually keep the dragons away, but it certainly worked with the tourists, which seemed counterproductive for a town that was kind of off the beaten path when it came to tourism in the first place.

The piping happened every Saturday all summer long. When fall rolled around, the good weather encouraged them to continue, and it wasn't until the third week of November, when it snowed, that the pipers decided to stop. Owen and I didn't know that, though. In Trondheim, the consensus was that piping down the sun was a bit of a joke, and since Owen hadn't even been in town when it started, we had pretty much forgotten it was happening at all. This explained how we inadvertently attended the last piping of the season.

Our intent had been to get takeout and eat on the pier. It was a bit cold for it, but I liked the wind and Owen hadn't spent a lot of time by the lake yet, not being a swimmer, so he still considered it adventurous. I was halfway down the hill toward the beach before I figured out why there were so many cars parked along the side of the road.

"How do you feel about bagpipes?" I asked.

"I think they're noisy," Owen replied. "Why?"

"We're about to attend Piping Down the Sun," I told him.

"They're still doing that?" he asked.

"Apparently." I started looking for a parking spot. Or an escape route. I was still undecided.

"Can we turn around?" asked Owen, clearly having similar thoughts. "We could go eat at the lighthouse instead."

"We'll have to drive all the way to the end before I'll have space to turn around," I told him. I couldn't believe how many cars were here, considering it was November and only a few degrees above freezing. "We'll be okay as long as no one recognizes you."

The beach road ends in a giant traffic circle. It was lined with people who had come to hear the pipes. It took them about ten seconds to recognize Owen, and then the crowd started to cheer.

"So much for that," Owen said. He pointed at a man who was waving madly at us. "That's the mayor. It looks like he's got a parking spot for us."

"Fabulous," I said, but there was nothing for it. I followed the mayor's directions and parked.

"Game faces!" Owen said brightly, and I watched as he changed from a high school kid who couldn't get the hang of factoring equations to a dragon slayer in training. I did my best to follow suit, though I had no idea what a bard looked like.

"Owen Thorskard!" the mayor said in a loud voice. "I had no idea you were coming tonight!"

"It's been a busy few months," Owen said with an absolutely straight face. "I'm sorry it took me so long to attend one of these events."

"Oh, not a problem," the mayor said. "Your studies and training should come first." He looked at me for the first time, and a puzzled expression crossed his face. "Who are you?" he asked.

"This is Siobhan McQuaid," Owen said. I stepped up beside him and extended my hand to the mayor. He looked surprised, but shook it anyway. "She's my bard."

I wondered if I could get away with killing him later on this evening. Lottie had been saying things like "and we'll think of something to say when people ask you why you're spending so much time with Owen" for weeks now but hadn't come up with an actual pitch yet. And now Owen had just told the mayor of Saltrock that I was his bard, and I couldn't even glare at him because the mayor was looking at me with a mildly confused expression on his face. I suppressed a sigh and turned on what I hoped was my most charming, unthreatening high school girl face.

"I'm in training too," I said, my tone far more excited than any I usually used. I assumed bards were excited to meet important people, even when they found themselves unexpectedly at random town functions. "But not to slay dragons, I assure you! That's Owen's job."

My declaration did nothing to clear the mayor's confusion, but he nodded politely and told me that sounded very interesting and exciting. Then he excused himself to start the festivities.

While we watched, fifteen pipers lined up together, various tartans flapping gently in the breeze, and, at the mayor's signal, began to play "Scotland the Brave" at full volume. Saltrock was populated primarily by the descendants of Scottish settlers, unlike Trondheim, which was largely Norwegian, so many of the people in attendance knew the words to the song and were only too happy to add their voices to the din. I didn't know about the local dragon population, but I was certainly having second thoughts about ever coming back to Saltrock again. That feeling of discomfort was heightened when I looked away from the lake, up the bluffs to where the school board office stood, its windows still soot-stained from an attack earlier in the week.

It seemed to go on forever, but eventually the sun disappeared from the sky and the bagpipes were silenced. The mayor came over to introduce Owen to the pipers, and I tagged along for lack of anything else to do. Although of Norwegian descent themselves, Lottie and Aodhan both fought with Scottish-style broadswords on account of Hannah's ancestry, and since Owen did too, the pipers accepted Owen as one of their own immediately. When they found out my name was McQuaid, I was welcomed as well.

I recounted a couple of stories about Owen's training exercises, and once I had the crowd warmed up a little, I launched into a retelling of the dragon he'd help slay in the yard defending Hannah's smithy. Since no one present knew what happened to my backpack, I was able to get away with significantly more elaborate fictions than I had when I told my parents. By the time I got to the part where Lottie skewered the dragon, everyone in earshot was staring at Owen like he was the most amazing thing they'd ever seen, and I felt like there was a set of bagpipes inside me, singing in my blood.

When I finished recounting the tale, the pipers clapped and called for another, but I was cold, not to mention hungry since we'd never had the opportunity to eat the food that was now stone cold in the backseat of my car, so I held up my hands in front of me and affected my most overdramatic pose yet.

"I'm sorry, ladies and gentlemen," I said, "but we really do have to get going. As much as I'd love to tell you all more stories about our young dragon slayer, he has to get back to work. Those dragons aren't going to slay themselves!"

They laughed and clapped us both on the shoulders until I was sure I was going to have bruises the next day. Apparently playing the bagpipes is good for your arm strength. We made it back to the car, and I managed to drive all the way to the top of the hill and pull into the poorly lit parking lot near the lighthouse before I collapsed into giggles.

"It's not funny," Owen said. "They really think that bagpipes prevent dragon attacks."

"You heard the racket," I said. "For all we know, it actually works."

"It definitely does not work," Owen said. I did my best to swallow what was left of my laughter and reached behind me for the bag of food that was sitting on the seat. "Really?" said Owen.

"I'm hungry," I told him, unwrapping a cold burger. "I can't subsist on fame alone."

"Good point," he said, and took the bag. "You did a great job telling stories down there, by the way."

"Thanks," I said around a mouthful. "It was actually kind of fun."

"Let's never do it again," Owen said.

I laughed. "At least not until summer," I agreed.

Then there was a knock on the window of my car, and I screamed, jumping so abruptly that I spilled french fries all over the gearshift.

ARCHIE

Owen Thorskard walks around with a knife in each of his sneakers, though what good that will do him if he is attacked by a dragon he has never explained. He cannot hold both of them and a cheeseburger at the same time. These are things you learn in dark parking lots when a stranger knocks on the window of your car.

Once I had more or less recovered from my shock and Owen had more or less recovered from throwing his dinner into the front windshield, I looked out the window. The man who had knocked looked nearly as startled as we did—which I felt was distinctly unfair—and was holding his hands up in the universal sign for "I really, really promise that I am not a serial killer, please open your window." My car was still running, because of the outside temperature, so after making sure that Owen still had both knives, I cracked the window open about an inch.

"Hello?" I said, hoping that I sounded at least confident, if not outright dangerous.

"I didn't mean to scare you," the stranger said. "I'm sorry about that."

"Dinner was cold anyway," I said, still blustering. "Are you lost or something?"

"No," he said. "My name is Archie Carmichael. You go to school with my daughter, Emily, since the amalgamation."

I cast about in my memory looking for an Emily Carmichael. I could vaguely remember a flute player from tenth grade I was sure was at least called Emily.

"Okay, Mr. Carmichael," I said. "What do you want?"

"I saw you two at the piping," he said. He sounded vaguely scornful about the event, and my opinion of him increased slightly. "I wanted to talk."

"And you couldn't wait for daylight?" Owen said. "Or warn us first?"

"I'm sorry about that," Mr. Carmichael said again. "But I thought it was important that we speak as soon as possible."

The single streetlight that illuminated the parking lot provided a very thin orange glow in the darkness. It wasn't much, but it was enough for me to see Owen's shields go up. Archie might be harmless, but something about him sparked Owen's cautious side.

"About what?" he said.

"Dragons, of course," Mr. Carmichael said. "I think I know why they're attacking Saltrock more often."

Owen and I exchanged a look. If we were going to be partners long-term, I was going to have to get better at reading his mind, because I had no idea what he was thinking. Maybe I should ask Sadie to give me tips. She always seemed to know what everyone was thinking. Plus, it would give us something to talk about. She hadn't stopped initiating conversations with me, and I was running out of things to say. Owen sighed, bringing my attention back to the car, and put his knives back in his shoes.

"Do you have a car, Mr. Carmichael?" he asked.

"Yes," came the reply. "It's around the corner. I didn't want to startle you with the lights."

I managed not to say anything sarcastic to that, but only just.

"Great," Owen said. "Meet us at McDonald's. We need to buy dinner again."

"It's on me," Mr. Carmichael said. He turned and walked back to his car. I put the window up.

"Are we really going to McDonald's, or are we ditching him?" I asked. I was sort of hoping for the former. Whether Mr. Carmichael was nutty as a fruitcake or not, I was still hungry.

"We're really going to McDonald's," Owen said. "And when you drop me off at home, remind me to get you a knife for your shoe."

"I'm wearing ballet flats," I pointed out. "I don't think they can support a knife."

"Aunt Hannah will think of something," Owen said with absolute faith. I didn't disagree. "A dragon slayer should never be without a weapon."

"I'm not a dragon slayer," I reminded him. "And anyway, my sword's in the trunk."

"That's a start," he said. "Let's go."

I drove to the McDonald's and parked. Last time, we'd gone through the drive-thru to protect Owen's anonymity. This time we had no choice but to go inside. Owen got seats in the corner while I ordered with Mr. Carmichael, but by the time I sat down, there was a crescendo of whispers circulating through the restaurant.

"What did you want to tell us, Mr. Carmichael?" Owen asked. He was polite and formal, sitting up straight and looking directly across the table when he spoke.

"As you know, the number of dragon incidents up and down the shores of Lake Huron has increased in the past few years, and dramatically so since the spring," Mr. Carmichael said. "In particular, in the Saltrock area."

"That's because of the salt mine," I pointed out. It was one of those things that everyone knew: The mine was dangerous, but it was also one of our best local resources, so we lived with the threat it posed. "They have huge tankers in and out of the harbor all the time. It attracts more dragons."

"You're right, it does." He ceded the point by waving a french fry like he was conducting an orchestra. "But I think it's more than that."

It dawned on me that Mr. Carmichael was talking to us like we were adults and professionals. It made me feel a bit better about listening to him. Most adults, like those at Piping Down the Sun, talked to Owen like he was some kind of mascot, and they didn't usually talk to me at all.

"Please explain," Owen said. I wondered if he had noticed too, because he relaxed a little bit. We were definitely going to have to work on our telepathy.

"The mine wouldn't account for such a dramatic jump," Mr. Carmichael said. He stirred the fry around in his ketchup as he marshaled his thoughts. "Usually, dragons only attack in this sort of pattern when they have a hatching ground to defend."

"But there isn't a hatching ground anywhere near here," Owen pointed out. "Unless you think they're flying in from Michigan."

Michigan hadn't always been one big hatching ground. It was similar in climate to the Canadian side of Lake Huron, and before the invention of the car, the hatching ground was confined to the Upper Peninsula. Now, even northern Ohio was considered a dangerous place to live, and we held onto Windsor and Sarnia by the skin of our teeth to maintain the shipping lane in the St. Lawrence Seaway and guard the border.

"I think that the dragons have established a new hatching ground, just like they did in Michigan," Mr. Carmichael said. "Owen, until your father got here, the closest organized dragon slaying was an hour away. We know there's overpopulation in Michigan. It makes sense that some of the dragons would have had to go looking for other places to lay their eggs."

"But where?" I asked.

"We don't know," Mr. Carmichael admitted.

Dragons laid their eggs in the fall, in places where the soil was thin, where the trees were thick and where there was plenty of lakefront property. In Ontario, that meant the regions around Lake Muskoka and the Kawarthas. Both of those places were far enough from Trondheim that we didn't have to worry about the increased dragon presence. The Bruce Peninsula, which was directly north of us, and Eastern Ontario, where Queen Victoria had elected to hide our capital city in the hope that sticking it close to dragons would discourage American interest, were just different enough in terms of climate and geology not to attract a dragon population. This meant that it was possible to get from Southern Ontario to Northern

Ontario without having to go through the hatching grounds. It was a longer drive to go around, but it was certainly easier to drive in a car that wasn't on fire, so no one complained.

Owen looked at him, a polite expression on his face. "When you say 'we,'" he said, "you mean people on the Internet, don't you?"

"Of course I do," Mr. Carmichael said. "Who else would I talk to about dragons? Everyone in this town is convinced it's the mine, and people spend all their time squabbling over whether the economic gains outweigh the risks."

"Mr. Carmichael," Owen said at his most diplomatic, "while I am sure you and your colleagues have given your best efforts to your theories—"

"Please don't patronize me," Mr. Carmichael said. "I haven't patronized you."

"He has a point," I said quietly to Owen. "It might be worth talking about with your dad and your aunts."

"That's all I ask," Mr. Carmichael said. "I know what it sounds like, but I promise you that even though we are amateurs, we're at least smart enough to obsess about dragons from the safety of our basements and computer rooms instead of chasing after them in the field."

"Mr. Carmichael, that might be the smartest thing you've said all evening," Owen said, a genuine smile on his face.

"Please, call me Archie," Mr. Carmichael said. It made sense that his daughter played the flute. He was all scales, up and down again and never standing still. "And I'll leave you to your dinner. You can just let Emily know if you want to talk to me again."

"Thanks for dinner," I said as he stood up.

"Until next time," he said, and walked out the door.

Owen shifted into the chair across from me so we could face each other.

"Well?" I said.

"He may have a point," Owen said slowly. "Not much of a point, but a small one."

"Lottie is going to laugh at you when you tell her."

"I was going to let you do it," he said, grinning. He finished his hamburger and reached for his fries.

"Thanks," I said. I looked around the seating area. We were the center of attention, and now that Archie wasn't talking anymore, I could hear the hushed whispers again. I sighed.

"What?" Owen said.

"On Monday, there's probably going to be a rumor that we were on a date."

So far, the Trondheim SS rumor mill had mostly left us alone. Owen was forthright about his academic shortcomings, and it was easily accepted that I was tutoring him.

"Would that be so bad?" Owen asked. He was staring at the nutritional information on his tray liner as though it contained the secrets of the universe.

I had only just settled into my new, slightly more public life, my bizarre new friendship with Sadie and my added responsibilities. The melody finally made sense. I had no desire to move everything around again.

"Yes," I said.

"You're probably right," Owen said. He didn't look disappointed, and I let out a breath I didn't realize I'd been holding. He risked a look over his shoulder and the whispering intensified.

"At least they didn't see us sitting alone in my car in a dark parking lot overlooking Lake Huron from the scenic outcropping by the lighthouse," I said, grinning.

"If they had, I could have drawn a knife on them," Owen pointed out.

"I'm not sure that would do anything to lessen the rumors," I said.

"If it had been a journalist or something, we would have been in trouble," Owen said. "Aunt Lottie would kill me."

"And here I thought all you had to worry about was high school girls," I said. "Though, as a group, they are pretty determined."

"I've noticed," Owen said.

It wasn't until I'd dropped him off and got all the way home that I thought to wonder if it was actually Sadie he'd been talking about.

OWEN'S FIRST DRAGON

For two weeks, Lottie ignored us every time we tried to mention Archie Carmichael or his theories that there was a new dragon hatching ground close to Saltrock that no one knew about. I didn't really blame her. The government kept a fairly close watch on things like that, for obvious reasons, and there hadn't been any reports, official or not, from any of Lottie's old contacts, about that sort of migration. Hannah let us get all the way through it once, and then offered a few suggestions about what to do when some random person knocks on your car window in the dark, none of which involved McDonald's. I didn't see Aodhan, but Owen assured me he'd done his best to talk to his dad whenever he was at home.

At the end of the second week, Lottie changed her mind. It wasn't because Owen or I had had a sudden breakthrough of unassailable logic, and it wasn't because Lottie randomly decided to trust us. It was because in those two weeks, Aodhan fought dragons almost every day, and no fewer than four dragons attacked Hannah's smithy, drawn in by the same plume of smoke that had attracted the first one. I spent three of the battles in the shelter with Hannah, bouncing on the couch and making up songs about waiting. Owen was burned, seriously enough to warrant an examination from my mother, by the second one, and we both got out of our algebra midterm because of it, though he didn't have to spend the night in the hospital. The fourth one I witnessed with my own eyes.

I'll never forget what they looked like, Lottie and Owen, standing side by side with the slayed dragon all around them. Owen had landed the final blow this time. We'd been practicing again, and the dragon had been on us so quickly that Owen didn't have time to go for his real sword. The sword he used for training was longer than the one Lottie used to spar, and so it made sense for him to do it. It was the first time I saw Owen slay a dragon. It was the first time I had ever seen *anyone* slay a dragon, and the whole thing had happened right in front of me.

One moment, I'd been doing exercises under Lottie's supervision, and the next Hannah had been dragging me back toward the house. We were cut off from the shelter, so we just stood together under the eaves and watched while Owen and Lottie battled the dragon in the yard. Hannah held her hand tightly over my mouth, and I didn't even try to fight her. I had a chorus of screams in my throat and no wish to share them with the dragon. The exposed nature of the fight meant that Owen couldn't be the bait this time. He had to be moving, and he circled Lottie until the dragon went for her, headfirst and raining fire from the sky. I don't know how he stayed so calm, so patient. He waited until the dragon was so close to Lottie she could have tapped it on the nose with her sword, and then he slipped in next to it and drove his long practice sword into its chest.

The dragon reared up, flames shooting toward the sky before they went out suddenly, like water had been poured on a campfire. The tail slashed through the air, spines whistling a shrill counterpoint to the deep bass of the dragon's legs beating on the ground. It was a symphony of the dying, a moment of lasts. And then it was over, and Owen and Lottie stood in the wreckage, and for just a fraction of a second, the whole world seemed to still.

"Fine, then!" And the moment was broken. Lottie climbed laboriously over the dragon's tail, spitting out her words as she moved. The dragon had curled in on itself around Owen's sword, almost like it was hugging it, and they had to crawl over its tail or legs to get clear. Lottie had to maneuver her injured leg out first and then support her weight by leaning on the spines on the dragon's tale and using them to pull herself over. "Tell me again what this Archie Carmichael said about a new hatching ground."

"Inside," Hannah said. I think I might have been in shock, because I just stood there, staring at Owen with trumpets blaring in my head and not much else in the way of rational thought. "And congratulations, Owen," she added. "It was an excellent job."

He straightened and smiled, and then vaulted over the dragon's tail to stand beside his other aunt. Lottie turned to him as if seeing him for the first time in a while, as if she was surprised to see that he was as tall as she was. He was bleeding where the spines had caught his left shoulder. I don't think he'd noticed yet. More scars.

"It's been such a crazy week, I forgot!" she said. She hugged him, very nearly lifting him off the ground in spite of her leg. "Congratulations, Owen," she said. "We'll get the camera and take a picture."

Hannah still had me by the shoulders and was steering me toward the door. Lottie and Owen caught up with us, and by the time I was sitting at the kitchen table, they had the kettle boiling and Lottie was assembling the ingredients for crème brûlée.

"Have you been keeping that handy just in case?" Owen said. He was spooning powdered hot chocolate into mugs, as Hannah had declared that celebration was called for and tea was not appropriate.

"Of course," Lottie said. "Cakes take too long."

"Plus she can't burn them," Hannah pointed out. She looked at me, and I could tell she was sorry about having to restrain me earlier. I honestly didn't mind. "Siobhan, are you all right?"

The kettle whistled, and a few moments later, Owen pressed a warm cup into my hands. It made me feel slightly less weird.

"The first one is always the hardest," Hannah said. "Sitting through a hundred slayings in the shelter doesn't really prepare you for it."

"It was just so . . ." I paused, looking for a word. "Noisy."

"You get used to it," Owen said. He sat down beside me and we watched Lottie mixing things together at the counter. "Did it scare you?"

"It was a dragon!" I said. "Of course it scared me."

"That's not a bad thing," Hannah said encouragingly. She

took a sip of her hot chocolate and then decided it was too hot, so she set it back on the table. "Fear is a healthy thing when you're dealing with dragons. It keeps you from getting eaten or set on fire."

"I'll keep that in mind," I said.

"Seriously, though," Owen said. "You're okay?"

"Yes," I said. "I'm fine. I just hadn't expected to be that close so soon. It was just—I don't know. I don't know what I was expecting."

"Every dragon is different," Lottie said. She was cracking eggs against the counter and didn't look up. "It's important not to get complacent."

"No fear of that!" I said. I watched as Hannah set Lottie's hot chocolate down at her elbow and kissed her on the cheek.

"Do you think it will make a good song?" Hannah asked. My hands had been pressed against her side when she held me, so she must have felt them tapping out the beat.

"It's not that easy, exactly," I told her. "I mean, hearing it in snippets is one thing. Turning it into something that makes sense is another kettle of fish entirely."

"But you'll do it?" Owen asked.

This was it, I realized. This was what I had to make other people feel, even if they didn't get to see it like I had. I could already hear the first whispers, the line of brass and then the faltering drums of the dragon's dying hearts. This was something I could do.

"It's not going to be an opera or anything long and involved, but yeah. I can make it a song." I said. "If you want, I can sign up to play it for the Christmas assembly."

"I'm not sure a song commemorating my first dragon

slaying is thematically appropriate," Owen said. "Don't we have a pep rally or something you can use instead?"

Our school mascot was some senior dressed up in a very unrealistic-looking St. George caricature costume, a red dragon on a white surcoat and a foam lance in his hand as he stood at the front of the gym. I had a sudden vision of Owen standing up there too, the real dragon slayer and the simulacrum while the entire population of Trondheim Secondary yelled "GO, LANCERS!" at the top of their voices. It wasn't particularly inspiring.

"What's Christmas without a few dragons?" I said, and realized that maybe I hadn't kept my hysteria quite as at bay as I thought I had. "Give me some time, and I'll arrange for you to save some reindeer too."

"It may have been a mistake introducing you to my aunts," Owen said, but he closed his own hand over mine, to stop the shaking.

"Oh, don't be such a baby," Lottie said, obliviously spooning crème brûlée into the tiny white ramekins it cooked in. "You just slayed a dragon more or less on your own. I'm sure you can handle some musical accompaniment."

"Don't we have an English test tomorrow?" Owen said. He must have been desperate.

"Nope," I said. "We're in the clear until next week."

He looked at me like I had betrayed him, and Hannah, who had been watching me closely, laughed. Lottie put the ramekins in the oven and came over to sit at the table.

"You don't want to leave anyway," she said. "You're going to tell me about your Internet theorist friend before I change my mind."

I drank my hot chocolate while Owen outlined Archie's theory about a new hatching ground that we didn't know the location of. I was surprised that Lottie decided to pay attention to the idea at all. It was fairly farfetched. It wasn't like dragons were difficult to notice. And they couldn't have displaced a human population, or it would have made the news. There were very few places that a horde of dragons could just move into without attracting attention. When Owen finished, Lottie and Hannah looked at each other for a long moment.

"It would explain the increased number of attacks," Hannah said slowly. "And it's not just Saltrock. We shouldn't get four dragons in a month here at the house."

"Dad has been really busy lately, too," Owen added. "They used to have one sighting a week here, and maybe only two attacks in a month. Now there are sightings practically every day, and if there's a whole week without two attacks, it's a light week."

I should have known it was so bad. I'd been here for those dragon attacks. I'd brushed the death that landed on Nathan Brash. Whatever distractions I faced, at school or otherwise, I should have known. Trondheim was at the southern end of the region Aodhan patrolled, and if Owen was right, it meant that there were more dragons to the north of us than there had ever been before. We had to find where they were coming from. I thought about Michigan, what had been lost there when the dragon incursions couldn't be stopped.

"So what do we do?" I asked. Lottie and Hannah exchanged another glance.

"First of all, we make sure that Lottie doesn't burn the crème brûlée," Hannah said.

"And after that," Lottie took over, "after we celebrate Owen's first dragon slaying, we start looking for that hatching ground."

"You're not going to tell anyone?" I asked.

"Who would we tell?" Hannah replied. "We didn't have a lot of allies in Ottawa before we moved out here. Now we have fewer still."

"But," I started to protest, and then Lottie cut me off.

"We'll handle it, Siobhan," she said.

Owen didn't say anything, but he took a drink of his hot chocolate, and I saw the glimmer of resolve in his eyes.

"Just tell me what you need me to do," I said. "And I think your oven is on fire."

We ordered Chinese food instead.

OWEN'S SECOND DRAGON

Technically speaking, Owen was not supposed to slay dragons by himself just yet. It's not like this was a conversation we actually sat down with Lottie or Aodhan and had out loud. It was more of an implied directive. Owen had helped Lottie slay half a dozen dragons and had finished one off with her as the bait, but he was still in training and, theoretically, should not have started going on solo missions at least until he was in grade twelve. Most of the dragon slayers in the Oil Watch had only slayed dragons under carefully controlled circumstances before their enlistment. Once they joined up and were deployed to an oil field somewhere, they trained with veterans until they had mastered the solo battle. Apparently, fate decided that Owen was operating on a different schedule.

It was a sunny day near the beginning of December, as I have mentioned before, when I saw the Viking in Owen shine through. It was cold, but it hadn't snowed yet, and the grass was bent and brown. When he hung up the phone and asked me if I wanted to come with him, I didn't hesitate before saying yes. It was instinctive. "Siobhan, want to go to the movies?"; "Siobhan, did you want a tuna sandwich?"; "Siobhan, do you want to come and watch me slay a dragon?" I said yes without thinking, and we were in the car before I started to regret my decision.

Aodhan must have been desperate to call home, I thought as the car started. Hannah and Lottie were gone, off to Toronto for a week to talk to their few remaining (and frustratingly undisclosed) old friends about hunting for the hatching ground. Owen was the only backup his father had, and if he was busy fighting a larger dragon, there was really nothing for it but to ask for Owen's help. It was a sight better than the old days, I'll admit. If we'd had two dragons at the same time and had to send to Queen's Park for a dragon slayer, there might not have been anything left of Trondheim at all by the time he or she arrived. Still, Owen and I weren't exactly the cavalry.

"Are you sure this is a good idea?" I asked as I pulled the car out of Owen's driveway and turned onto the highway that would take us toward Trondheim and the dragon that waited for us there. "I mean, I know we're limited in terms of people in the field right now, but . . . really."

"I know," he said. For the first time, I noticed that he was very pale, and he was clutching the hilt of his broadsword very tightly. I hoped we didn't go over a bump, or he might poke the sharp end through the floor. "And I'm sorry, but there's no way I could have carried all this on my bike."

In spite of my nerves, I laughed. Owen smiled, and I wondered if that had been his intent all along. It was certainly easier to drive while laughing than it was to drive while I was on the edge of hysterics.

"So what's the plan?" I asked, switching to cruise control.

"I'm making it up as I go," Owen said.

"You're really not making me feel better."

"What if we leave the car running, wait for the dragon to attack it, and then I charge?" he offered.

"Are you kidding?" I said. "First, this is *my car* and I need it. Second, there's a bari sax in the trunk, and I think the school might have issues with their fire insurance if you willfully get it destroyed. Third, *it's my car* and you can't feed it to a dragon!"

"Pull over!" Owen said, and I slammed on the brakes. "And turn off the engine. I'll come up with something else."

I swerved to the side of the road and turned the engine off. There was a fairly good breeze, so the exhaust would clear quickly. I could only hope that the unappetizing color of my car would work in my favor and the dragon would ignore it. The same breeze that dispersed my exhaust was propelling a cloud of ash and soot toward us, and I knew that the dragon was on its way. Owen went for his seatbelt and I popped the trunk.

"You can't move fast enough with the sax!" he shouted, throwing his shield out of the car and pulling on his leather gauntlets. He didn't wear armor, but once he had unfolded himself and his array of weapons from the car, he pulled on a leather tunic that would protect him a bit from tooth, nail, and fire.

"I'm getting my sword," I shouted back, wishing I'd worn better shoes. "I'm not going face-to-face with a dragon without my sword."

"Good idea," he said and set his own sword in his hand. He tried to smile. "But stay back. If you get hurt, my aunts will kill me."

"They'd have to beat my parents to it," I said. I reached into the trunk and pulled out my sword. It so looked small out here in the open. In the training ring, it looked like a tool. Next to Owen's sword, it looked like a toy.

"It's just a small one," Owen said, more to himself than to me. "I can do this."

"Yes," I said, and he looked at me for as long a moment as he dared. "Yes, you can."

The air got thick with smoke then. None of the dragons that had attacked Hannah's smithy were soot producers, but I'd seen more than enough of them on Discovery Network specials. They were harder to fight, because they obscured the air, but every dragon had a weakness, and soot producers did not do well with sound. Owen was slamming his sword against his shield, careful to hit with the flat so he wouldn't dull the blade, and above us, the dragon roared its displeasure just as the wave of blackness engulfed us both.

"Siobhan!" Owen yelled.

"Just slay it!" I yelled back. "I'll be fine!"

I ran back to the car and pried the hubcap off the back tire with my sword tip. I plunged back into the soot, pulling the collar of my shirt over my mouth and nose, and started beating the hubcap with my sword. It didn't make quite as much noise as Owen's did, but it did free him up to think about things like hitting the dragon instead of hitting his shield, so I called it a win.

I heard a whistling noise and jumped back, seconds before the dragon's tail came hurtling out of the soot and whipped past my face. I flinched even farther away from it, trying not to think about the damage it could cause if it hit me, and tried to make more noise. I heard a thump as the dragon landed and hoped that it was only a matter of time before Owen would finish the job.

There were flashes of fire in the soot, which was a good sign. Dragons can't produce soot and fire simultaneously, so every time Owen provoked it into breathing fire at him, the air around us cleared. Before long, the grass in the ditch was burning, thankfully on the side of the highway opposite where I'd parked, and the air was much clearer. I got a good look at the dragon and decided that if this was a small one, I never wanted to be close to a big one.

Owen didn't seem to mind. He dodged spurts of flame like an expert, moving quickly and cleverly, luring the dragon onto the tarmac, which wasn't flammable. I heard a car pull up behind me and stop, and when I turned around, I saw that the driver already had his iPhone out to record what was going on. At least he was smart enough to stay in the car.

"Honk your horn!" I yelled at him, hoping he'd hear me through the glass. I waved my hands around to emphasize my point. He seemed to understand me, because he started to honk—loud, long noises that sounded like a duck was being murdered in the most horrible way imaginable.

Other cars were arriving on scene, and before long more car horns (and, presumably, smart phones) joined the chorus. I wasn't sure how I was going to represent them in the song I was already composing on autopilot, but I decided to focus on the problem at hand instead.

I turned back to Owen, who was taking advantage of the dragon's discomfited state and approaching it from the rear. The dragon's wings were flared, and Owen ran underneath them. His daring paid off, and he slid his sword into the dragon's chest before it had time to turn on him. The dragon screamed loudly, once, shattering the glass in Mr. iPhone's front windshield and making me drop my sword and the hubcap so I could cover my ears. Then it collapsed onto the road, wafting up a cloud of soot as it fell.

Owen pulled his sword out of the dragon's chest, and I held my breath until I saw the wound. He had managed to keep the damage minimal and deadly, and very little of the poisonous gas in the dragon's system escaped into the air. I blew out the breath I'd held and smiled as Owen turned to me. He was smiling too, and it was a moment before he realized that we'd accumulated an audience and switched back to his game face. Almost solemnly, he held his sword aloft, and the car horns sounded again, this time in celebration.

People got out of their cars to cheer and congratulate him, and Owen shook hands with all comers. I noticed that his hands were shaking, but no one else did. And then Aodhan was there, pushing through the crowds to get to his son. Aodhan caught Owen in a bear hug, lifting him—sword, shield and all—clear off his feet and swinging him around. The sound of cheering grew even louder, and then Aodhan set Owen down and reached into his pocket for his phone to call the disposal squad and an ambulance in case anyone had cuts from the glass.

Our audience returned to their cars, realizing that the show was over. Dead dragons don't smell very nice, even when they've been slayed properly, and there was the grass fire to consider. I could hear the sirens as the emergency crews approached. Aodhan hadn't been the only one to call them, which was nice to see, since, iPhone or no, coverage was still unreliable. I looked at my car and was relieved to find it was safe. I was making my way toward it when Owen caught my arm.

"Epic enough for you?" he asked. He was shouting, and I realized we should both get our ears checked. He looked absolutely elated, and I could hear the triumphal march that would end the song. I supposed he deserved it.

"Definitely worthy of song," I told him.

"Quick thinking about the hubcap and the car horns," he told me. "That was really helpful."

"Hey, we're a team," I said.

"Yes," he said. "We are."

That was the first time either of us had actually said it out loud, and when I tell Owen's story to strangers, it's usually how I begin.

THE STORY OF ST. GEORGE

Come, gather round, the poets say, and hear the words I sing. There are tales of kings and emperors, tales of queens and knights. But above them all is the story of St. George and the Dragon, and for my bread tonight, I will tell it to you.

The Romans were a cruel breed of men, who conquered all the world they could reach. If any dared rise against them, they would bring to bear the fire of the Empire, which they boasted was greater than any dragon could unleash. They burned across the world, from Britain and Gaul, to Egypt and Canaan, and everywhere they went, they stole dragon slayers for their legions.

The Romans were as clever as they were cruel, and they did not set their captive dragon slayers to slaying in the lands they had once called home. A dragon slayer stolen from Gaul could expect to be sent to Palmyra. A dragon slayer from Jerusalem might find herself in Hispania. There they would be set to their craft, unschooled in the subtleties of the native dragon population, and many of them died needlessly as a result. The Romans sent their scholars to learn all the ways of dragonkind, the better to train the transplanted dragon slayers, and by this price in blood we have our modern knowledge of Europe's dragons.

Some of these scholars were not Roman-born, but chosen on account of their intelligence and abilities. One of these was Georgios of Lod, who marched with the legions to see the world and had won honor on the battlefield, both for himself and for Rome. He was sent to Silene, in Libya, to study the dragons there, and when he drew close to the city, he beheld a terrible sight.

Silene's proud walls stood within a stone's throw of a great lake. The city founders had done this a-purpose, and used the water from the lake to provide for the people. Their plans had gone badly awry when a large dragon had also chosen to make its home in the water, and the people of Silene had sent their dragon slayer out to do battle.

The dragon slayer, it is widely said, was of Gaulish descent, used to fighting dragons amidst tree cover, with a sword. He was unfamiliar with the terrain, with the type of dragon he faced, and with his own lance. The result was the death of the dragon slayer, but not before he managed to wound the dragon, fouling the lake by means of the botched blow. The dragon retreated to the spring that fed the lake, leaving the people of Silene to sacrifice a sheep to distract it every day, in order to access the spring themselves and not perish from thirst.

The city soon expended its sheep, and then its goats. They went without fresh water for many days, but it was not the rainy season, and they knew they would have to attempt the spring again. A decision was made that young women from the city would be sent in place of the sheep (this was before it was determined that dragons had no preference when it came to what kind of people they ate), to distract the dragon and lure it from the spring. Georgios arrived just as the young woman in question, the daughter of the magistrate (who, by all accounts, was a lovely girl when not being sacrificed to a dragon), was being forced out of the city gates by a mob.

Now, Georgios of Lod was a scholar and a soldier, but he was no dragon slayer. The Roman Legions, under the orders of Emperor Diocletian himself, were sworn to give aid to dragon slayers, but never to join their ranks. Yet there before Georgios was the broken lance of the fallen dragon slayer and the hysterical girl who was about to become the dragon's next victim.

Georgios of Lod took up the lance and put heels to his horse's flank. He intercepted the dragon as it streaked toward the magistrate's daughter, and by some skill or the intervention of God (public opinion remains split between the two), he struck the broken end into the dragon, cutting through both its hearts, and it fell dead on the grass in front of the city gate.

In the city, there was much rejoicing. The lake would remain foul for many years, but the spring was now accessible and, with time, would clear the lake of the dragon's poison. The maidens of Silene had been spared, and the herds could be replenished. The magistrate hastened to write to Rome with thanks for sending the great dragon slayer, Georgios of Lod, to save them in their time of need.

Naturally, that's where the whole thing unraveled. There were those orders from Diocletian to consider, and when Georgios refused to make a public apology, he was taken to

Nicodemia and eventually beheaded for being a dragon slayer without the appropriate pedigree. When Lottie Thorskard started appearing on the news with St. George's iconography stylized on her shield in addition to her own family crest, no one guessed that she too would soon be at odds with the media and the status quo.

In any case, it's understandable that it was a few hundred years before anyone started thinking that Georgios was the type of man to emulate or admire, and by then, of course, the facts were difficult to assemble. He was eventually canonized, and several wildly conflicting accounts of his life, career, and death became the bread and butter of wandering bards throughout medieval Europe. The story was recounted at least once a year on St. George's Day if you went to the right kind of church, and even if you didn't, everyone in Trondheim knew him as the high school mascot.

Most of the later stories, though, focused on the dragon slaying part of the legend and not the resulting decapitation. The idea was promoted that St. George had done what was right, knowing the price he would pay. That he had made the leap from non-dragon slayer to dragon slayer without any thought for his own wellbeing. This was the kind of thing I had to live up to, the reason Lottie Thorskard was trying to so hard to make me step out of my comfort zone, so I think it is completely understandable that when Owen passed me the following note on Monday morning in English, I punched him in the shoulder.

My part was easy / I slayed it. You need a word / That rhymes with hubcap.

THE CHRISTMAS CONCERT

I didn't perform the song I wrote about Owen's first public dragon slaying at our school Christmas assembly. Well, not on my own, anyway. I'd written it by then, along with a shorter piece about the encounter at the house. I usually kept my own music to myself, but now that I was Owen's bard (in training), this was no longer an option. Luckily, my music teacher asked me to arrange the song for the band instead. Since I could fade into the back row and everyone's focus was on Owen anyway, I didn't feel as nervous as I thought I would. I did feel a bit like I'd thrown Owen under a bus, though. We did have to attend Trondheim Secondary for another year and a half, and neither of us really wanted to spend all that time living down embarrassing musical numbers.

The orchestration was accompanied by some of the smart phone videos that had been shot, cut with footage of Owen's training, as filmed by the local news. There were no lyrics, so technically it was not very bardly, but no one cared. Lottie,

Hannah and Aodhan couldn't attend. Aodhan was out on patrol, like always, and Lottie and Hannah were back in Toronto. They'd been driving back and forth so often that they'd barely been home long enough to switch to their snow tires.

The arrangement was theatrical and heroic, and the band was more or less competent at navigating the various parts. There was something not exactly right about the song itself. At the time, I assumed that it was the red streamers lining the stage and the Santa hats worn by the trombone section. It was hard to take the dragon's line seriously when fluffy white tassels were featured so prominently. I was the only person who noticed, and in the end I decided it wasn't too bad a first attempt. Everyone else thought it was perfect, and when the assembly was done, Owen practically had to fight his way out of the adoring crowds. No one paid any attention to me, except for the girl who held the back door of the gym open so I could maneuver the bari, my music folder, and my music stand through it.

"I liked the flute part," she said, smiling as I passed her.

"Any time," I said, returning her smile as I completed the awkward move that got me clear of the gym. "And thanks for holding the door."

"No problem," she said and fell into step beside me. "Thanks for not getting my dad arrested."

The notes fell into place.

"You're Emily Carmichael," I said. She seemed unthreatening.

"Yes," she said. "I've been meaning to introduce myself, but I was worried Dad might have made it a bit awkward. Sometimes he doesn't think things through."

"He seems to have thought about the hatching grounds a lot," I said. I didn't have a free hand for the rail on the side of the stairs, so I took the steps slowly.

"He has," Emily said. "I meant that he doesn't always think about practical things."

"What does he do when he's not looking up theories on the Internet?" I asked.

"He owns the used book store off the Hub," Emily said.

Saltrock didn't have a main street like a normal town would. Instead, their downtown was a large traffic circle that went around the town hall and courthouse. Calling it the Hub always gave the idea that it was an active sort of place, but the truth was that, unless it was beach season, the Hub was just as dead as the main street of Trondheim.

"I don't think I've ever been in," I said. Even though Trondheim and Saltrock were only fifteen minutes apart, most people in Trondheim only went there to go to the Walmart or to hit the beach.

"You should come by sometime," Emily said. "I can't promise he won't say something off the wall, but I got him an espresso machine for Christmas and he's already opened it because we both have a problem with leaving things wrapped, so at least the coffee will be good."

Emily opened the door to the music room and took my music stand to put it with the others. I unclipped the bari with some relief and started putting it back in its case. It was nearly lunchtime. We still had to get through the second half of the day before Christmas Break was upon us. The other band members in the room were excited, chattering loudly about the coming holiday, but I mostly ignored them as I cleaned up.

We usually went on vacation over Christmas, since it was the last time my father had any free moments until May, but this year we were staying at home. One of the new doctors in town had young children, and Mum had agreed to work his Christmas shifts for him at the hospital so he could have the time at home. I didn't mind. I was old enough now that the idea of spending two weeks mini-golfing with my dad in North Carolina no longer appealed.

Owen wasn't going anywhere either. The cold weather had brought about an increased number of attacks as people turned up the heat, lit wood fires to warm their houses, and otherwise bundled up against the snow. Owen hadn't had any more solo fights since the first one, but he was on high alert.

I fastened the bari case and wrinkled my nose in distaste. Mr. Huffman, ever eager to politicize our education, had given us all essays on the Oil Watch to write over the break. He had suggested very strongly that we look into sugar production, and it didn't take me long to figure out why. In Canada, the States, and Europe, dragon slayers were hired by wealthy corporations. The Oil Watch had expanded and now monitored forestry projects and large mines in addition to oil fields around the world. They claimed they did the best they could to allocate their "resources," but there was a decided gap when it came to protecting sugar production in developing countries.

I sat back on my heels and considered my options for the afternoon. I was pretty sure that nothing was going to happen in music, and in math we were probably going to do some sort of holiday-related pointlessness. I wasn't by nature truant, but sometimes it was worth it to consider one's options. I waved Emily over, and we headed for the door together. Owen had somehow managed to get free of the adoring crowd and was waiting for me there. He looked surprised that I had company, but I had already decided that, in addition to Emily being useful, she also had the potential to be kind of fun.

"Owen Thorskard, Emily Carmichael," I said, waving my hand back and forth between them.

"Please tell me we're not eating in the cafeteria," Owen said, and I decided that meant he had accepted Emily too.

"You're not very good at being famous," Emily observed.

"Don't remind him," I said. "Let's skip school this afternoon."

Owen looked at me like he suspected I'd been replaced by an alien of some kind. Emily beamed.

"I'm serious," I said. "What are we going to learn this afternoon that we can't learn at a bookstore owned by a conspiracy theorist with a brand new espresso machine? No offense, Emily."

"None taken," she said. "That's the life we chose."

I'd never skipped school before, and I wasn't entirely sure where the impulse was coming from. I was just, quite suddenly, very opposed to spending the afternoon doing anything that required me to sit still. I had never felt like this after a concert before, but I'd also never played a piece I wrote in front of such a crowd. I was restless and more than a little bit antsy. Espresso and wild theories were probably exactly what I needed.

Owen didn't need further convincing, and our ad hoc trio was headed for the parking lot in short order.

As we passed, Sadie slammed her locker shut. The noise drew my attention away from Owen, and when I locked eyes with her, she looked angry with me for the first time. I tried to think if I'd done anything in the last few days that would have set her off, but couldn't think of anything.

"Come on. Before Siobhan changes her mind," Owen said, and pushed through the door.

Neither he nor Emily saw Sadie. I thought I should say something, though, so as we walked past her, I reached out and tapped her arm.

"Merry Christmas," I managed. Not my best work.

"You too," Sadie replied. Her tone was completely flat. "See you in January."

I had too many thoughts. I had no idea what was up with Sadie, and I really wanted to get out of the school. I hovered for a moment in the door, undecided, until Owen turned around, still oblivious.

"You lost?" he asked.

I shook myself, and Sadie turned away toward the cafeteria.

"For that," I said, even though I didn't feel like joking, "Emily gets the front seat."

SKIPPING SCHOOL

Owen does not do well in the backseat of the car. He doesn't get carsick or vertigo or anything like that. It's like he's not getting places fast enough, so he spends the whole ride leaning forward between the driver and passenger's seats, like it would help if he got out and pushed. When I got around to asking him about it, he made up some excuse about sight lines and vantage points, but really I think he just can't deal with not being on the front line of something, even something as basic as a car ride. It's probably a good quality in a dragon slayer. I've never asked what happens when he, Aodhan, and Lottie are all in the car together. Hannah probably locks them in the trunk.

It didn't bother Emily in the slightest, even though he was hovering over her to avoid getting hit in the face by my shoulder when I shifted gears. She just turned in her seat, leaning back against the seatbelt clip so she could look straight at both of us. I was looking at the road, on account of all the black ice that had formed thanks to the recent cold snap, so I wasn't concerned by her gaze, but as soon as I put the car in cruise, Owen moved closer to me.

"So, what exactly are we going to do?" Owen asked her. He wasn't rude about it, just uncharacteristically direct. "I mean, once we get to the bookstore and assuming Mr. Carmichael doesn't yell at us and make us go back to school."

"There's no way my dad is letting you out of his store without showing you everything he has ever collected about dragon slayers," Emily said. "I'll understand if you want to back out, but at the same time, we might learn something."

"And here I thought the whole point of skipping school was to not learn anything," Owen said.

"Not learn anything we don't want to," I specified.

"Exactly," Emily said. "Except with better coffee."

"Well, I certainly have no problem missing one math class," Owen said.

Mrs. Postma had given us back our last round of algebra tests, and Owen's marks had been much better, but his general feelings on the subject were still predictably un-merry.

"Good," said Emily, completely unaware of Owen's scholastic shortcomings. "Then you and my father should get on just swimmingly."

Emily smiled, the same smile as her father, but where I saw the skittering flute counterpoint in his expression, her face was much more subtle, the humor less straightforward and more personal. She might play the flute in concert band, but out from behind the music stand, she looked quite different. There was depth and breadth to Emily Carmichael, and enough warmth to carry the weight of the world without being crushed by it. She was a tuba to the core.

"Tell me everything about hatching grounds," Emily said, leaning back in her seat, though she still faced a bit sideways.

"Don't you know some things already?" Owen asked. If the question caught him off guard, he didn't show it.

"Of course," she said. "But if we start at the beginning, we won't leave anything out."

Owen considered it for a moment, meeting my eyes in the rearview mirror. I shrugged. It wasn't like I had a better idea.

"Okay," he said. "Hatching grounds have to be really specific. The right temperature and all that."

"And there has to be carbon," I said.

"Not necessarily," Emily said. "I mean, they're attracted to carbon, but they don't need it to live."

"So a food source, then," I said. "Do dragons eat fish?"

"No," Owen said. "Well, not really. They tend to eat everything. That's why the bear population in Sudbury has declined so dramatically since the number of dragon attacks increased. There aren't enough moose or cows for the dragons to eat, so they're branching out."

"A dragon eating a bear?" Emily said. "Why are there no Internet videos of that?"

"Presumably because anyone who gets close enough to get it on video gets eaten for dessert," I suggested. "Bears can't possibly taste that great if you eat them hide and all. Human probably makes a nice palette cleanser."

Emily looked a little peaky at that. I pressed the clutch and dropped the car out of gear as we passed the "Welcome to Saltrock, Prettiest Town in Canada" sign and the speed limit changed to 50 kph. I hit Owen in the face as I shifted, gently of course, but he still grimaced.

"Where are your aunts, anyway?" Emily asked.

"Toronto, I think," Owen said.

"You think?" I asked. I really didn't want to get caught skipping school and hanging out with Archie Carmichael by Lottie Thorskard if I could possible help it.

"It's not like looking for a hatching ground is something you can schedule," Owen pointed out. "They track down leads and then they come home."

"There were three more sightings up around Southampton yesterday," Emily said. "Maybe they went up there to help your dad."

"It's possible," Owen said. "But I don't think they'd do that without calling."

We pulled onto the Hub and began the slow drive around the circle. There weren't a lot of cars around; almost no one did their Christmas shopping in Saltrock anymore—or if they did, they did it at the very last minute. There was snow on all the trees, and covering the bare ground, so the shops and the courthouse looked a lot prettier than they usually did. There were Christmas lights strung everywhere, though under the afternoon sky, they just looked like small teeth emerging from under the eaves and biting the edges of the trees. The outdoor skating rink had finally frozen, and a couple of toddlers were stumbling around on tiny hockey skates while their mother huddled behind the boards, clutching her coffee like it was all that stood between her and hypothermia.

"I've never understood that," Owen said, looking at them through the window with a vaguely wistful expression on his face. "I mean, I had a toy sword when I was little, but so did everyone else. Does skating before you can talk get you into the NHL someday?"

"They're probably just seeing if the kids can survive the cold," I said.

"I doubt they're cold," Emily pointed out. "They're both wearing more material than I am, and even their helmets are insulated."

We were so busy staring at the future hockey stars that I drove right past the turn to the Carmichaels' bookstore and had to go around again. This was not uncommon, but it always made me feel ridiculously like a tourist. On my second pass, I made the turn, and fortunately there was a spot close to the shop. It still wasn't super cold out, but it was cold enough that I didn't want to be outside for too long. Owen was still generally not prepared for the cold. Hamilton wasn't that far away, geographically, but it was well out of the snow belt and often less cold than Trondheim was. Furthermore, the Thorskard house was always very warm because the cold made Lottie's injuries worse. I hoped it was better when she was moving around on it. Hannah did as much as she could to make Lottie's life easier, but there was only so much help Lottie would take.

Since the rate of dragon attacks increased, Hannah and Lottie had become even more of a team than ever. Hannah was a capable swordswoman, which was quite natural since she'd grown up in a house full of swords and had spent the better part of her life making them for Lottie, but now she practiced a lot more in the ring. At first, it had been part of Owen's training, but as the attacks grew in number and severity, it became apparent that Lottie's retirement wasn't as ironclad as she had thought. She still couldn't move quickly enough to work by herself, but with Hannah's help, they had managed to bring down four more dragons when Aodhan was out of contact and Owen was stuck in algebra. (The accumulation of snow in the windows of the old stone part of Trondheim Secondary made cell phone reception even more sporadic than in the rest of town.)

It's counterintuitive, really, because you'd think that dragons, being coldblooded and otherwise reptilian, would hibernate or migrate or have the decency to die off in the winter. But we're not that lucky. For whatever reason, dragons are immune to the cold, and some species actually seem to prefer it. Immunity or not, the cold makes dragons waspish and easily annoyed. Or maybe they just want to warm up, and the carbon from furnace emissions does that for them. There is entirely too much pseudoscience when it comes to dragonlore, which is why it took literal fire from on high to get Lottie to pay attention to Archie Carmichael in the first place.

I parked and turned off the car. I pulled my heavy mittens on over my fingerless gloves. I couldn't drive with the mittens on, and in cold temperatures I wore the fingerless gloves almost all the time anyway, because they kept my fingers warm enough to play piano properly. Owen finally leaned back and passed Emily her backpack. He pulled his phone out of his pocket and checked it for messages out of habit. It sometimes seemed like Owen only ever got to talk to his dad on voicemail.

"Well," I said, "here we are."

Emily grinned and opened her door. I got out a bit more slowly, and Owen was even less enthusiastic. I could tell he was having second, perhaps even third or fourth, thoughts about this.

The sign above the door just said "Carmichael's" in a flowery black script on a white background. There was no indication of what Emily's dad actually did. I guess I had expected something in wrought iron, maybe words bracketed by the artistic representation of a dragon. Or even no sign at all, but a vacant-looking shop front you could only access with a secret knock and a series of passwords.

It's possible that I had given this entirely too much thought.

Under the sign, the whole front of the store was mostly glass. There were two large windows on either side of the door, both festooned with hand-painted Christmas decorations. If Emily had done them, my opinion of her was suddenly even higher: Painting letters backwards is no mean feat. In addition to the window trimmings, there were also two large Christmas trees, one on each side of the door. Both of them were covered in gold and red balls and had stars on top. It was easily the most decorated shop on the street (except for the bakery, which obviously had an amazing window display), but it was still entirely tasteful. It was certainly better than the unfortunate Santa hats from our Christmas concert.

We were the only people on the street. It was so quiet that I could hear the kids on the ice rink laughing at one another. The streets weren't deserted because of dragon attacks but simply because it was the middle of the day in a small town. It was a sad fact of life, but shopping was safer (and cheaper) in cities. The local economy suffered, but there wasn't a lot businesses could do. Or at least there hadn't been, until the Thorskards moved to town. Already my father had told me that the local economy was up, as people stopped going to the covered parking garages in London or Stratford and started shopping close to home. It was another unexpected benefit of having a dragon slayer on speed dial who would actually arrive in a speedy manner.

"Ladies first," said Owen, hovering on the curb.

"This was your idea!" Emily pointed out.

"It's your dad's bookstore," Owen protested.

"Oh, you're both impossible," I said, rolling my eyes. I pushed past them and walked through the door.

THE HATCHING MAPS

There was a bell above the door. I wasn't at all surprised by that, but I was a little startled by the fact that the bell was connected to a series of other bells, strung out across the ceiling like a row of sentries, all ringing at pitches just different enough to put my teeth on edge.

"Really?" I said over my shoulder to Emily, who was still beaming.

"I'm sure the people in the apartment above are thrilled," Owen said.

"There is no apartment above," Emily said. "It's the old Masonic Lodge, so it's just a meeting room and Dad's office. He hangs out there, and this way he hears everyone who comes in. He'll be down in a minute, unless he's into something," she said. "Or we could go up?"

"Maybe next time," said Owen, and I could tell that I probably shouldn't push him any further out of his comfort zone than he already was.

I looked around the store. On the inside, it was exactly what I had expected: hardwood floors covered haphazardly by a collection of incredibly uncoordinated rugs; shelving units, all so close to one another that the aisles were only wide enough for one person to walk down at a time. I looked more closely and thought that the shelves were unusually big. If Mr. Carmichael had had smaller shelves, he might have been able to fit more of them in. I looked on the floor, where the rugs stopped, and saw tracks on the boards where heavy wheels could pass.

"Oh!" I said, not having meant to speak out loud.

"Neat, eh?" Emily said, having followed my train of thought. She reached up to the shelf in front of us, braced herself, and pushed. It slid toward the back of the store, revealing another equally crowded shelf behind it. "This way dad can have way more stock."

The back of the store was dominated by a large old-fashioned electric stove, a hideously orange shag rug, a low coffee table, and several overstuffed armchairs. Off to the side were the counter and till.

The counter and the coffee table were both buried in papers. Newspaper clippings about dragon attacks in the area, Internet articles about the geography and geomorphology of the areas Aodhan patrolled, and maps. The maps drew my attention. I wanted to see the story in pictures before I read it in words.

At the bottom of the pile, right on top of the old-fashioned blotter, was a large map of Canada, filled in around the corners by the states that shared lakefront property. Archie, or someone, had marked it up with sticky notes and a red Sharpie. It wasn't difficult to determine the pattern. Michigan was covered in notes, areas marked off as known locations for egg depositories and the few carefully guarded enclaves where dragon corpses were disposed of after they were slayed. No one actually stayed in those enclaves longer than was necessary to drop off a body, but the machinery used to lift the dragons off the tankers and the piers themselves had to be maintained—and occasionally defended as well.

There was a red circle around Saltrock and a question mark on the school board office, along with a matching circle around the mine. Other places were marked as well. Tobermory and Wiarton were close to old border crossings to Michigan and had RCMD outposts. Similarly, Sault Ste. Marie and Thunder Bay fell under federal protection because they were ports, while Sudbury's nickel mines were wealthy enough to afford the best in corporate dragon slaying. Leamington stuck out into Lake Erie and was generally considered too warm to support dragon eggs, which were laid in the fall for a reason, but it had been marked anyway. Rounding out Ontario were, of course, Barrie, Penetanguishene, and Peterborough, the southernmost edges of our two hatching grounds. I looked for a pattern.

I couldn't see what Archie was looking for. I could only see what he had found. There were more dragons in places where there had always been large numbers, and there were more dragons in places where attacks had always been comparatively light. I knew that Hannah and Lottie had been spending a lot of time looking into areas with small lakes, like Muskoka or the Kawarthas, but so far they hadn't found anything that would explain the increase. It wasn't like dragons could hide where they were laying their eggs. They had to be somewhere. Something had to have changed.

"It has to be lakeshore, right?" Emily said. "Erosion or global warming or something. Something that would make the dragons shift away from small lakes."

She was holding one of the geological articles and standing on her tiptoes to look over my shoulder at the map. Owen was sitting in the desk chair, spinning around and holding onto the most recent edition of the Saltrock newspaper that told the story, yet again, of the dragon he slayed on the side of the road. There was a picture of him, sword aloft, with me hammering on the hubcap in the background.

"What do little lakes have that big lakes don't?" I asked. "I mean, Barrie and Orillia are less than an hour apart. And it's only a bit farther around Georgian Bay to Collingwood or Penetanguishene. Why does Orillia get eggs and they don't?"

"Current?" Emily said. "Water temperature? Moisture levels in the air?"

"But the eggs aren't actually in the water," Owen pointed out. "They're in or on the ground *near* the water."

I squinted at the map, staring north of Orillia to Huntsville, the most concentrated area of the hatching ground.

"Bays," I said.

"What?" said Owen. He sat up and stopped spinning. Emily gave up trying to be polite and elbowed me over so that she could see the map too.

"Little lakes have lots of bays, sheltered areas on shore where dragon eggs aren't overly exposed to the elements," I said. "That's why there are no eggs on the Great Lakes or along the St. Lawrence. That's why there isn't a hatching ground closer to Trondheim. There isn't enough protection. The Great Lakes spawn bigger storms, and the bays don't give enough shelter."

"Okay," said Emily. She was speaking slowly, and I could tell she was still putting pieces together. "That fits with what my dad thinks. But it still doesn't explain why the dragons are moving to a new hatching ground, or where that hatching ground is."

"Oh!" Owen said. He got up and came over to look at the map.

"What?" I said. Apparently it was my turn now.

"Michigan wasn't always a hatching ground," he said. "There used to be cities there, places like Ann Arbor and Lansing. The dragons only came when the factories starting producing enough carbon to attract them. Before that, they were just like us."

"But Michigan has little lakes," Emily said.

"Exactly," said Owen. "Right now, the fact that we don't is the only thing that's saving us. The dragons want to come here to lay their eggs, but they can't, so they made a hatching ground as close to the mine as they could, and they come here for snacks."

"You say that like they do it deliberately," I said, supressing a shudder. "Dragons can't think."

"Instincts are a good reason for doing something too," Owen said. It sounded like the voice of experience.

I looked back down at the map, and my eyes widened. I saw the pattern, red notes across the map, composing a song in fire and warning bells. It was so clear, now that I knew what I was looking for.

"Manitoulin," I said. "The northern side. Gore Bay and all the inlets there."

Owen drew a red circle around the island. "It's the closest they can get."

"They've come for the mine," Emily said. She sat down heavily in the chair Owen had just vacated. "They've come for Saltrock, and they're going to keep attacking it until it burns to the ground."

"We'll stop them," Owen said. "It's why we came here."

"How?" Emily said. "Your father runs all over two counties trying to hold everything together, and as soon as you graduate, you have to join the Oil Watch. Lottie can't do it on her own."

"No," came a voice from the door to the upstairs, and we all jumped. "I can't."

We spun around, all looking guilty. It was still the middle of the afternoon, and we were clearly supposed to be elsewhere.

"I'll spare you the obvious questions until later," Archie said, appearing behind Lottie and Hannah. "Why don't you all sit down, and we'll talk about what you've just figured out?"

We filed toward the chesterfield and took our seats while Archie pulled the papers back into what order he had arranged them. Hannah was smiling indulgently as she took her seat.

"When did you get back?" Owen asked.

"Don't change the subject," Hannah said. "But we got here just before you did. I'm sorry we missed the concert. I'm sure it was lovely."

"Now who's changing the subject?" I muttered.

"Manitoulin Island, eh?" Lottie said, slumping into an armchair next her wife and bringing us back on track. She propped her leg up on the coffee table. Car rides always left her stiff.

"It makes sense," I said. "Well, it makes enough sense to investigate further, don't you think?"

"I do," Hannah said.

"Um, I'm Emily Carmichael, by the way," Emily said, a bit awkwardly. "It's nice to meet you."

"Likewise," Lottie said. I knew she must have recognized the name. She winced as she shifted in her chair.

"Manitoulin does explain a lot," Hannah said. She took Lottie's hand and leaned over to kiss her lightly on the forehead, and Lottie stopped shifting.

"Emily's right about the problems, though," Lottie said. "There's no way to get Owen out of his Oil Watch tour without undoing all the work we've put into making rural dragon slaying attractive, and Aodhan is already stretched thin enough."

"You could recruit," Archie said.

"Who?" Lottie said.

In this moment I got another brief glimpse of how much of Lottie's plan was dependent on force of personality and intuition—the same personality that allowed her to rise to the top of a bridge in Hamilton and the same intuition that let her jump off it without a moment's hesitation. At the time, I resolved to follow a different course.

"Half the senior class thinks that Owen has a good thing going," I said. "I know dragon slaying is hereditary, but where is that written? There's got to be someone who thinks your life is glamorous enough to give it a try."

"Those kids would still have to join the Oil Watch," Owen pointed out. "But it might be worth considering long-term."

"As a resident of Saltrock, I'd prefer a more immediate solution," Emily said.

"Well, there's no point in closing the mine," Archie said. "The damage is done. There haven't been emissions in

Michigan in more than half a century, and the dragon foothold there is still strong."

"What about the hatching ground itself?" I asked. "What if we destroyed it?"

Lottie and Hannah looked at me like I was insane, and both Emily and her father looked startled, but Owen looked thoughtful.

"Siobhan," Hannah started, but then words failed her.

"It's never been done," Lottie said.

"That we know of," Emily said. "My father has all sorts of contacts with bizarre claims."

"They're not bizarre," Archie said defensively, looking quite betrayed. "They're unorthodox."

"We'll look into it," Lottie promised. The she reached across the table and grabbed Owen's hand, squeezing hard. "No field trips."

"I don't think this was his idea," Hannah said, looking at me with a knowing expression.

"Then that goes for you too, Siobhan," Lottie said.

"Okay," I said. They didn't make us promise. In hindsight, that was probably a good thing.

JANUARY SLUMP

Draconic reconnaissance is a necessarily covert activity. It is important not to cause civil panic. It would never do for unsubstantiated rumors of a new dragon hatching ground to leak to the public before there was a good defensive plan in place. In the end, though, we needn't have worried.

For the whole month after Christmas Break, which I had taken off from tutoring and from thinking about dragons in general, we came up with nothing incredibly productive—never mind panic-inducing. My first idea had been to move Owen's tutoring to the Trondheim public library, so we could research without supervision, but Hannah was no slouch, and she quickly figured out that my motivations were not related to a sudden fear of being attacked by a dragon while driving. I had not expected her to play dirty, but she called my parents.

"Hannah called me this afternoon," Mum said at dinner the night before my first exam. "She's worried that all the driving might be getting to you, and she suggested that you could tutor Owen here, and they could pick him up after you're done."

"I—I hadn't thought of that," I stammered. It was a terrible idea. At least if we were at Owen's house, one of the grown-ups might let something slip. All my parents ever talked about was work, the price of various household commodities and the fact that I had yet to begin seriously working on any of my applications for university. "I think it's just the exam pressure getting to me. I'm seeing dragons in every bush. Once things calm down again, I'll be fine to drive to Owen's house."

That was the end of that, and Owen and I continued to do our homework under Lottie and Hannah's watchful gaze. Soon enough, the end of the month rolled around, and after we recovered from our exams, it was February and we were no further along than we'd been in December.

A new semester meant new classes. Owen celebrated passing algebra by starting finite and rounded out his schedule with French, world issues, and a study period. I had French, drama, and the afternoons off to work on composition. I couldn't help him in finite, but it turned out that Owen's fluency in Spanish was just enough to mess up his French vocabulary, so I still had a job.

We discovered on the first day of the new semester that Emily was linguistically precocious: she had signed up for grade eleven French immediately after finishing the grade ten course, and when we arrived in the classroom, she waved us over to where she was already sitting with a smile.

"I need to apologize to you both," she said, as soon as we were seated. Everyone else was still milling around, so she probably didn't have to whisper, but she did anyway and we both leaned in a bit to hear her.

"You're sorry you saved us seats by the window?" Owen guessed.

"No, I meant something occurred to me yesterday and I'm sorry I didn't think about it earlier," she said.

"Well, it's not like we're doing so well either," I pointed out. "What did you think of?"

"Remember how my dad is a member of all those fringe Internet theory chat pages?" she asked. Owen snorted.

"Like I could forget," he said. "My aunts complain about that all the time."

"Hey, it's not like he goes out hunting dragons with an iPhone," Emily said defensively. Owen looked immediately contrite.

"Yes," I said, "We know he's one of the good ones."

"Thanks," she said. Her sarcasm was a thing of beauty. "Anyway, everyone on the boards uses pseudonyms, but sometimes it's really obvious who they are in real life."

"And you want to blackmail one of them?" I said, having no idea where this was going.

"No, that would be silly," she said. "One of them is Mr. Huffman, and I think I can manoeuver him into assigning Owen homework for world issues that will require him to research hatching grounds. In the Saltrock archives."

"Man, your small-town 'have the same teacher for multiple classes' thing is paying off!" Owen said.

"It's your town too," I pointed out.

"Fair enough," he said. "But seriously, I like this idea. It will seem so reasonable."

"We just need to decide what the homework should be," Emily said, just as the bell rang.

—ᵗ— —ᵗ—

I spent most of drama lying on the carpet pretending to meditate, which my drama teacher insisted would help me get in touch with my inner stage persona. Since I was taking the class in case I ever ended up directing music for a stage production, I was less than concerned about my persona, but I did take advantage of the time to think.

We needed something that Owen could research that would be useful, but subtle enough not to pique the interest of any of our parents. This included Lottie and Hannah, as Owen generally liked to refer to all the adults in his house collectively as such. (I don't know if he ever noticed, but every time he said something like "I'll have to ask my parents" and gestured in her general direction, Hannah smiled at him like the sun was coming up.) So it had to be under the radar, but it also had to lead us to the answers we were looking for.

The ceiling of the drama room is not the most inspiring of views, and even that was technically cheating, as I was supposed to be meditating with my eyes closed. Still, I risked a glance at the walls and saw the old posters for plays Trondheim Secondary had done in years gone by. The words "The Scottish Play" caught my attention.

"Miss McQuaid," said the drama teacher, having caught sight of my raised head. "You are not appreciating the exercise properly."

The senior beside me was snoring, which I thought was worse than looking around, but I obediently lay back and shut my eyes. I wasn't meditating, though, and I continued to not meditate until the bell rang, startling the snorer awake with a rather ungentlemanly grunt, and I finally got to leave the room.

I met Owen by my locker, and we waited for Emily to join us before heading to the music room. Even though I was no longer taking a class, my arrangement with the music teacher still stood. This was important because it guaranteed us the privacy to talk, and because I really did need to work on pieces for those applications my parents kept bothering me about, just in case I decided on university after all.

"I thought of something," I said. I sat down on the piano bench while Owen slumped to the floor and Emily took the chair. She leaned forward with her elbows on the music stand. "It has to involve a hatching ground," I went on, "and preferably someone moving a hatching ground."

"You can't move a hatching ground," Owen said. "All you can do is shift it around a little bit."

"Semantics," I said. "Or possibly lack of something we haven't figured out yet."

"And you think we can figure it out?" Emily said. "People have been trying to do this for centuries."

"Weren't you the one going on about how we would think of crazy things and then try them because we were relatively new at this?" I said.

"Well, yes, but I think this is different," Emily said.

"This hatching ground is different," I said. "Maybe we'll find something that the professionals overlooked for all the reasons you said."

"Okay, so we figure out how to move—shift—a hatching ground," Emily said. "What's your idea?"

"Scotland," I said. "Queen Victoria compressed a relatively large hatching ground in order to access Scotland. We just need to figure out how her dragon slayers did it and see if there's anything we can use."

"We know how they did it," Owen said.

"We know it took a lot of them," I corrected. "We don't know exactly what it was they actually did. If we can figure it out, it might help us. Besides, the real point is that you'll have to research hatching grounds to write the paper."

"That actually makes a lot of sense," Emily said. "Well done."

"Thank you," I said. "But I also think we should add a second component, one that will require Owen to look at old maps in the archive."

"Offense/Defense Friday!" Owen said. Our telepathy had improved a lot, I noticed, because that was exactly what I had thought of.

"Yes," I said, for Emily's benefit. "The second part of the assignment will be to design a defensive plan for the Saltrock and Trondheim area, at specific points in history."

"Now comes the hard part," said Owen, drawing up his knees so he could lean forward and rest his chin on them. He seemed thicker, somehow, but I couldn't tell if that was because of his pose or because he'd grown a bit while I was distracted by exams.

"Doing the research?" I asked.

"No," he said. "Getting Mr. Huffman to assign the project as homework."

Emily smiled, and I immediately got the impression that we had somehow created a monster. Perhaps turning her loose on the Internet wasn't the best idea, but it was the only one we had, and we'd come too far to turn back now.

"I've had a name on the board dad uses for two years now," she said. "I lied about my age and where I'm from, and Dad hasn't worked out the whole IP thing yet, so I'm pretty sure he doesn't know it's me. I have a modest reputation on the message board, so if I make a suggestion, it'll get picked up and repeated by the right people. I'll just suggest that there simply isn't enough focus in schools given to the pre-World War I history of dragon slaying, and that if I were a teacher and had the power to do so, I'd make my kids research it independently and write papers on their findings."

Emily folded her hands against the music stand and looked at us, the picture of innocence.

"I'm a bit scared of you," Owen said. "But I like it."

It occurred to me later that Emily wouldn't even be lying. Pre-Oil Watch dragon slaying was hardly curricular these days. Lottie was by no means the only adult content to face oncoming dragons largely unburdened by the lessons of history.

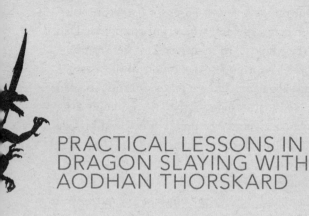

PRACTICAL LESSONS IN
DRAGON SLAYING WITH
AODHAN THORSKARD

It was very nearly that easy. I mean, Owen still had to write the essay, which can't be anyone's idea of a good time, but the topic passed muster without raising any eyebrows. We spent several hours in the library learning more about Queen Victoria than any of us ever thought we'd learn. Fortunately, she was quite an interesting person, beginning with the part where she was the shortest person ever inducted into—and the only non-dragon slayer member of—the Order of St. George.

More relevant to our concerns, we learned that her shifting of the British mainland hatching ground (there were smaller subsidiaries on the unfortunately-named Isle of Man, amongst others) had been accomplished thanks to an incredibly large number of dragon slayers, employing tactics that the Redcoats had developed in India to deal with jungle infestations. There had followed a period of strict border enforcement, resulting in dozens of dragon slayer deaths. Clearly, we were going to have to come up with a better plan, but at least we had the beginnings of some precedent to reference when we started strategizing.

We'd had much less luck with the Saltrock archive, since Mr. Huffman had made Owen's class draw their historical time periods out of a hat, and Owen's ended up being during the late '90s. All that information was readily available on the Internet. Emily was undeterred, though. She seemed to be intent on getting into the archive herself, since her father encouraged all forms of independent research, which meant, she told us, that he didn't really ask her where she had been. It was worth the risk.

Hannah and Lottie, along with a couple of their friends from the Oil Watch days, had planned a trip to Tobermory and a second to Sudbury, to see if they could find out any more about the goings-on around Manitoulin. Owen had originally thought that their absence would give us the opportunity to assist Emily with her more direct research, but once again, Hannah played dirty and my parents intervened.

"We're going to what?" I said, nearly choking on the mouthful of lasagna I'd eaten just before my mother made the announcement.

"You're going to start going around with Aodhan on weekends," Mum repeated, rather calm in the face of my reaction. "Hannah suggested it. It will let Owen learn how to track dragons properly, and it will keep you out of the library, where you might get into something you're not supposed to."

"Let me get this straight," I said, having swallowed. "You are sending me out in a minivan whose date of manufacture predates the year of my birth, so that I can watch two dragon slayers track down enormous fire-breathing animals, in an effort to prevent me from spending time in the *library*?"

"There's no supervision in the library," Dad said. I wasn't entirely convinced that I hadn't somehow ended up in bizarro world. Also, I couldn't tell if he was worried that Owen and I might get up to something inappropriate, which was unlikely, or if we'd stumble into some political firestorm, which was kind of our plan. "Hannah says it will be much safer in the long run, and we agree."

"Plus it will give you more exposure to dragon slaying," Mom said. "Which will help you with your compositions."

Supportive parents, I tell you. I never thought they would get me killed *before* I graduated from high school.

And that was more or less how I found myself packed into a Volkswagen minivan immediately after school on the third Friday in February, with an all-weather tent, a brand new pair of long johns, and more homemade chocolate chip cookies than I had ever seen in one place in my life. As far as punishments go, it was fairly unconventional. I had never been camping before, and while Owen assured me that most of the time Aodhan stayed over at the houses of various generous locals, I was decidedly less than enthusiastic about the whole idea.

There are all kinds of stories about heroic quests, where dragon slayers traverse the countryside saving villages and preventing small-scale ecological meltdowns. They are typically very loud and very dramatic, all brass over strings with appropriately placed cymbals. What they don't tell you is that dragon hunting is, on a perfect day, *really boring*. We drove for hours down plowed side roads and past endless snow-covered fields without seeing so much as a scorch mark.

I had thought that the Friday section of our expedition would be short, due to the fact that the sun still set relatively early. It turned out that Aodhan often patrolled after dark as well, because fire was visible a bit sooner than it was in full daylight. Since I was sitting in the backseat and didn't even have the headlights to illuminate my view, I spent the last few hours of the night trying not to fall asleep.

Finally, at about midnight, we pulled down the lane at a farm outside of Hanover where Aodhan was apparently well known. They were clearly expecting us, all of us, despite the lateness of the hour, because there was hot food on the table, and a fresh pecan pie for dessert. The family that owned the farm was very excited to meet Owen, about whom Aodhan had told them a great deal, and if they were initially confused by my presence, they made me feel no less welcome. Owen was on his second piece of pie and I was nodding over a hot chocolate when Aodhan finally declared it time for bed.

In days of old, dragon slayers had slept in haylofts, camped by the roadside, or in rooms donated by local innkeepers. We slept in the den on pullouts, or at least Owen and I did. Aodhan said he was too tall to fit, even once the chesterfield was converted to a bed, so he slept on the floor. I was asleep before Owen turned out the light, and not even Aodhan's rumored snoring was enough to wake me up before sunrise the following morning.

We had breakfast with our hosts before piling back into the van for another day of driving.

"Does that happen a lot?" I asked once we were on the road and the farm had faded into the rearview mirror. "People just letting you stay overnight, I mean?"

"Yes," Aodhan said. "I saved that barn from a dragon in July, and the family told me that I was welcome to stay with them whenever I needed to. I don't always stay with them when I am patrolling, but I stop in every couple weeks or so, and there are plenty of other places where I can stay if I need to."

"So that part of Lottie's plan is working out then," I said.

"Yes," said Owen. "People are so relieved to have a dragon slayer in the area, even an area as big as this one, that they are generous."

"Well, we still aren't paying you," I pointed out. "It seems fair."

"Yes," Aodhan said. "It's what we were hoping would happen."

"And you're okay with it too?" I asked Owen.

He shrugged. I knew that as much as I tried to put off thinking about life after high school, whether it would be university or something else, Owen tried even harder. He wasn't afraid of his required service in the Oil Watch, but given the uncertainty of where he might end up, it was understandable that he put off thinking about the future as much as possible. This included thoughts of what to do *after* his time was up and he was free to pursue dragon slaying on his own terms.

"It has its upsides" was all he said.

"I don't miss the city one bit," Aodhan said. He turned onto a paved road and I looked out the window to see the sign. I'd gotten turned around in the dark last night and wasn't exactly sure where we were.

"What's the biggest difference?" I asked.

"Onlookers," he said, without a moment's hesitation. "In Hamilton, there were always people standing around gaping. Out here, if a farm gets attacked, the family has the good sense to hide until it's over. Usually."

I could see how that would be preferable, and I said as much.

"Also, it's nice not to have a corporation breathing down your neck all the time," Aodhan said. "Lottie didn't mind as much, but I like not having to worry about sponsorship and motivational speaking tours and shooting commercials."

"Aunt Hannah says we were meant for a quiet life," Owen added. "And Aunt Lottie agrees—even if she misses the rush."

"Well, this whole thing was her idea in the first place," I said. "Did she plan to do it before her injury?"

"As much as Lottie plans anything," Aodhan said. "Though in this case, I think she might have. She would have made an excellent figurehead. Better than me, for sure. But we make do."

"I think you're doing very well," I said. It was true. Lottie might have been a legend before her arrival, but Aodhan was slowly carving out a place of some stature in local folklore.

"Thank you, Siobhan," Aodhan said.

We drove on in silence, but not an uncomfortable one. I took advantage of the daylight to get a good look around the inside of the minivan. Aodhan had cleared it out when Lottie announced that Owen and I would be joining him on weekend patrol, but there were still all sorts of interesting things left behind. Aodhan had modified the back of the van so that the middle bench was gone and only the rear one remained. This meant that the bulk of our gear, aside from the two broadswords which were strapped in oiled cases to the roof rack, was packed into that space. I sat on the bench in the back, only slightly cramped on account of the luggage.

What drew my attention the most, though, was a picture taped on to the window behind Aodhan's seat. I had to lean forward to get a good look at it, so there was no way to disguise what I was doing. It was an oil rig in the desert, and the Aodhan in the picture was young and sunburnt almost beyond recognition. A woman with dark hair and a bright sword stood beside him. At first I thought she was very tanned, but then I realized that it was her natural skin color. His arm was around her shoulder and they were both smiling. I sat back with a guilty expression on my face and looked up at the rearview mirror. Aodhan looked at me in the glass and smiled, but the smile had more sadness in it than the smile in the picture did.

"That's Catalina," he said. Owen sat up straight in the passenger seat. "Owen's mother."

"You look very happy," I said, because it was the first thing I thought of.

"We were," he said. "It wasn't a happy time, particularly, but we found moments in it."

I was saved from having to make a reply to that by Aodhan's phone ringing. He pulled over so he could answer it. It was the ringtone that indicated Hannah was calling, which could mean anything from a request to bring home milk to a dragon sighting. I could tell by Aodhan's voice as he spoke that it was the latter.

"Sighting," he said after he hung up. "Owen, get the map and navigate. Siobhan, keep your eyes peeled. It's a soot-streaker, so you should be able to get eyes on it early."

I glued my face to the window as Owen rustled the map open and began giving directions. Aodhan drove carefully, but with good speed, and the siren on the top of the van told other vehicles to get out of our way. Before long, I saw soot-stained snow in the fields we passed. We weren't going to have to track this dragon very long.

THE SECOND LIE

This is the story I told the *Hanover Post*.

When Aodhan got the call that the dragon had been spotted just south of Chesley, he drove full-tilt into the face of danger to protect those as-yet-unknown people who were in peril. With the siren blaring, the highway before him was emptied, as though he had been a dragon slayer on horseback with a trumpeting herald to clear his way. When we arrived at the small hobby farm the dragon was attacking, the scene that greeted us was terrifying to behold. The barn was already in flames, and the roof of the drive shed looked like it was going to be next. Only the direction of the wind, and the fact that the ground was covered with snow, was keeping the house unlit.

The family was already in the dragon shelter when we arrived, the small red flag waving bravely against the white snow and orange flame to let us know they were safely inside and out of harm's way. Aodhan leapt from the driver's seat almost before he turned the ignition off, with Owen just behind. I stayed in the backseat and the relative safety that cover would provide once the dragon was engaged. I watched as they untied their broadswords from the roof rack and then moved to flank the dragon.

And what a beast it was! Nearly the size of the barn itself, and streaking soot everywhere between fire-laden breaths. The dragon didn't even notice the dragon slayers at first, so intent it was upon the unfortunate miniature ponies who called the benighted barn home. Their tiny screams filled the frosty air as the dragon picked them, one by one, out of their burning stalls.

Before the dragon could finish its horrible breakfast, Owen set upon its tail. Soot-streakers have spines there with nerves in them, and if you can break them you can distract the dragon without releasing any of the toxins contained in its gullet. When dragon slayers are fighting together, this is the preferred tactic. It certainly got the beast's attention, and it roared in pain, shattering the front windows of the tractor parked next to the garage with the force of its voice. It tried to turn on Owen, to defend itself against his sword, but by the time it turned, Owen had already danced out of its way.

Too late, the dragon realized the trap it had fallen into. By turning its head and extending its neck to protect its tail, it had exposed quite a bit of the opposite flank, leaving itself wide open for Aodhan's attack. The older dragon slayer rushed in, his heavy sword held aloft and glinting in the bright morning sunlight, and before the dragon knew what was happening, Aodhan's sword slid between its ribs, piercing its soft under-belly and slicing through both of its hearts at once.

Aodhan jumped back as the dragon flailed in the throes of death, its legs and tail slashing through the air beyond its control. At last, the great beast lay still, and the two dragon slayers stood on opposite sides of its massive body, victorious, while the fire raged around them, until the local firefighters, who had arrived at about the same time, realized that it was finally safe to go put the fire out.

It fell to Owen to go to the dragon shelter and tell the family their house was safe, along with most of their garage and all but the windows of their tractor. They were relieved to be out of danger, surveying the wreckage of the barn with some sadness, but also with hope for the future.

"Thank you so much!" said the good farmer once Owen had delivered the news.

"You're welcome," said Owen, polite even in the aftermath of a dragon slaying. "It is our job, after all."

"I'm sorry about the barn and the ponies," Aodhan said. "But you did the right thing by hiding in the dragon shelter as soon as you spotted the creature. And I think the house escaped without even getting singed."

"All's well that ends well," said the farmer's wife.

They all stood together and watched while the firefighters put out the fire in the barn, leaving a smoking hulk of blackened wood sticking out in contrast to the snowy background. There was soot everywhere, thanks to the fire and the dragon, but it would be cleaned away when this snow melted and probably covered by new snow before tomorrow. When the firefighters were done with the fire, they turned their attention to the dragon, though due to the size of carcass, it was quickly evident that a helicopter would probably be required to remove the body. It wasn't pretty, but the work was done efficiently, a sign of the practice and good effort on the part of everyone who was involved.

That is pretty much entirely not exactly what happened.

To start with, when we arrived on the scene, the entire family was standing on the front lawn in their pajamas, watching as their barn burned. Admittedly, the dragon was fairly well focussed on the ponies by that point, but those things were really small. I had a suspicion that the dragon would not be feeling full after eating them, at which point it would turn on the humans. Aodhan was really trying to encourage the locals to go straight to their dragon shelter and put up the signal flag as soon as they spotted a dragon, since he felt that it would increase safety for everyone involved, so I altered that detail when the friendly man with the tape recorder asked me what had gone on.

I also edited the length of the battle quite a bit. While Owen found it useful to be told every single detail of his encounters with dragons so that he could improve and catch any mistakes before they became potentially fatal habits, most people were not interested in the minutia. They wanted to hear that the fight was over quickly and with as little damage as possible, so that's the story I told. In truth, Owen had been required to harry the dragon's tail three times before Aodhan had a clear enough opening to get a shot at the dragon's chest, and in that time, the beast managed to eat three more ponies and irreparably damage the aboveground swimming pool in the backyard.

Aodhan hadn't been able to slay the dragon cleanly either. As was often the case, the dragon's soft underbelly was covered in harder callouses, which were strong enough to deflect

Aodhan's broadsword. His first blow had merely opened a wound on the dragon's chest, destroying any potential for a family vegetable garden in that part of the yard for at least two generations. It wasn't until the fourth time Owen harried the dragon's tail that Aodhan had been able to land his sword in the dragon's hearts.

Dragons also take a long time to die, even once the death blow has been landed, and even if the blow is clean. Owen and Aodhan did manage to jump clear of the dying dragon, but the playhouse that had once stood next to the similarly destroyed aboveground pool didn't have that option, and it was reduced to kindling underneath the dragon's flailing tail.

After the dragon died, the real chaos started. The firefighters went to extinguish what was left of the barn and see if they could save the drive shed, and the family ran out of the dragon shelter and started screaming about their miniature ponies, some of which were still alive in spite of the attack. It's against firefighter policy to risk the life of a person to save an animal that cannot be carried, so they refused to enter the barn. At that point the farmer tried to go in and had to be forcibly restrained by Aodhan, who didn't even put down his sword before grabbing him around the waist. Fortunately, no one was around to photograph that, or to record the very impolite things the farmer said about Aodhan's ancestry.

I was thinking that this would probably be one place where Aodhan would never be invited back for pie when the fire was finally extinguished and the farmer went to look at the extent of the damage.

"Pleasant types," I said to Owen under my breath as he wiped his sword down with snow, dried it with a towel and lifted it back on to the roof rack.

"They'll calm down," he said. "They've had a scary morning. You take these things for granted, but this is their home."

"Miniature ponies, though?" I said.

"Hey, people get attached to their animals," Owen said.

My dad owned fish. I would leave them behind in a heartbeat if a dragon was closing in on the house. "I suppose," I said.

"Just wait," Owen said. "By the time the press shows up, they'll be over the worst of it and singing Dad's praises."

"Yours too," I reminded him. He turned a bit pink at that, but it might have just been the exertion.

"Make sure you talk to the reporter first, Siobhan," Aodhan said, coming to join us by the van and cleaning his own sword. "Everyone else will follow your lead, and you can shape the story however you want."

"Do you want me to make the dragon bigger so you look cooler?" I asked, only half kidding. It was a pretty big dragon. Making it bigger wouldn't be that hard.

"I think I'm cool enough, thanks," he said with a smile. It wasn't quite the smile from the picture in the window of the van, but it was the most open expression I'd ever seen on his face. "Just make sure that everyone looks like they did the right thing. We can use the publicity to control what the public does in the face of a dragon attack."

And that's why I altered the details of what I told the *Hanover Post*. I made everyone look like they had done exactly what they were supposed to do, and since I spoke first and with great authority, everyone else who was interviewed afterward matched their details to the story I'd told.

Once the cleanup was done and the helicopter arrived as hoped, making for some truly spectacular pictures, the reporter went back into town with the firefighters behind him. We saw the family off to their relatives for the time being and got back in the van. It was well after lunch by now, and we had nothing to eat except the chocolate chip cookies and some bottled water I found in the back, but we made do.

"So," said Aodhan, as he put the van in gear and we headed back out onto the road. "Better than spending time in the library?"

Neither Owen nor I answered that, but then again, we didn't really have to.

THE STORY OF ELOISE
AND ABELARD

One of the most important things about history is that it loves to place the blame, to pin an entire shift in thought and behavior upon one single larger-than-life man (or woman), and hold that person up as an example to the ages. Alexander the Great. Julius Caesar. Thomas Edison. Adolf Hitler. Pol Pot. Vlad the Impaler. Narrowing the focus makes it easier to remember, easier to teach, and it definitely makes for a better story. The only cost is the truth, and so our history is stripped down to its simplest form and passed down through the generations until you forget about the Phillips and Nikolas altogether.

(It didn't take long for me to realize that part of Lottie's vision for me included keeping Owen on the right side of the Edison/Tesla divide.)

There are generations of dragon slayers who were happily married, to one another or to non-slayers both. They managed to balance the dangers of their livelihood and the safety of their lives at home, without causing hurt or damage to anyone. And they had families, or not, as it suited their natures. So it is, of course, quite natural that the only case most people can cite is that of Eloise and Abelard.

Eloise was a twelfth-century dragon slayer and a member of one of the most prominent French bloodlines. As was the custom in France at the time, she was trained, not by her family, but by a dragon slayer who was hired specifically for that purpose. His name was Pierre Abelard, and by all accounts he was rather magnificent at pretty much everything, and also very handsome, though since it was the twelfth century and bathing was still considered unhealthy, it is important to remember that the modern definition of beauty can't really be applied. Eloise was no mean talent herself, and also somewhat renowned locally for her appearance, and before long the two of them were absolutely inseparable.

They married in secret shortly after Eloise's sixteenth birthday, intending to go on a quest together in order to conceal their marriage from Eloise's family.. Unfortunately, Eloise rather shortly became pregnant, and her condition became apparent before they had mustered themselves to leave. Eloise's family was quite put out and attacked Abelard, leaving him alive and capable of slaying dragons, but castrated.

In a bout of depression, Abelard joined a monastic order of dragon slayers and encouraged Eloise to do the same. Her convent forced a vow of silence on her and fostered her child with her parents, leaving her separated from everyone she loved. She wrote letters, none of which ever made it past the abbess, and eventually her story was made famous by Alexander Pope in 1717, who wrote the story as a verse tragedy where Eloise prays for forgetfulness, so that her pain will end.

Much like *Dracula*, written much later, the story of Eloise and Abelard missed one very important fact: Neither of them had actually done anything *wrong*. They were of similar station, married in the eyes of God, and, theoretically, would have raised their children to be dragon slayers, thus fulfilling the unwritten but universally acknowledged requirement that all dragon slayers produce a replacement. All of their misery was forced on them by outside sources, and over the centuries, the story started to treat them like they deserved it, and the entire history of dragon slayer relationships changed course on this one point.

By the time the Oil Watch was codified in the 1950s, it had become customary for dragon slayers to marry and have children only after their active careers were over. This usually meant that female dragon slayers, at least those who retired in their early forties, could only have one child, depending on how long they chose to extend their careers, though male ones could usually manage a few more. It also became very rare for dragon slayers to form any sort of bond with one another, particularly across gender, as this would lead to rumors and speculation. There was no official code in the Oil Watch Charter, but it's probable that the writers thought that the traditional rules about fraternization that came with the military would cover it.

This was a large part of the reason why, as the numbers of dragons increased dramatically after World War II, the number of dragon slayers did not. In addition to the obvious limitations in terms of procreation, dragon slayers who worked by themselves were much more likely to get killed. Separating dragon slayers from one another, and then, as previously discussed, from their bards, made the stories juicer. There was much more heroism and desperate tragedy, but the actual tradition of dragon slaying suffered a great deal.

And then, as seems to be the case in many of these tales, came Lottie Thorskard. She married young, and though the child she was helping to raise was not biologically hers (or her wife's), they were still related. The heights of Lottie's fame made her nearly untouchable, and instead of being the victim of storytelling, Lottie began to rewrite perceptions, one at a time, of what it meant to be a modern Canadian dragon slayer. Not even her historic fall and injury could derail Lottie's plans. It was said that her decision to relocate and to focus on her nephew's training made her few friends, but once again, that was not the truth. It made her no friends in Ottawa or in the corporate world. It made her a hero to everyone who lived in rural southwestern Ontario.

Lottie was not the only person pushing for change. Like Alexander the Great or Caesar, her voice was simply singing in the right place at the right time. Those before her had paved the way, and those who followed would pay for what changes she fought to make. Lottie had learned how to make the story do what she wanted it to, and she was determined that her legacy would be of her own choosing. She would not be punished, as Eloise was. She would love where she willed and train whom she wished, and she was popular enough that no one could stop her.

What they could do, of course, was set up obstacles for those of us who came after. I escaped the worst of it, but the same cannot be said of Owen and Sadie.

HOT CHOCOLATE AND TAI CHI

We saw neither tooth nor claw of a dragon for the rest of the weekend. We didn't even see any smoke. We did camp on Saturday night, which was very cold, and by the time Aodhan stopped the van at the foot of my driveway on Sunday afternoon, I was very happy to be home. If nothing else, I wanted a proper shower and a real toilet. I stayed in the bathroom until the steam was so thick I pretty much had to swim from the shower to the door, and I was completely prepared to crawl under the covers and not come out until school on Monday when I remembered that I had homework.

I had a perfectly good desk in my bedroom, but I nearly always did non-musical schoolwork in the kitchen. It was brighter there, for starters, and when I was taking math, my dad was available to help if I got stuck. Plus it was a good way to keep up with what my parents were planning. I never understood teenagers who escaped to their rooms and hid all the time. If they didn't know what their parents were up to, how did they hope to properly evade them?

Anyway, tonight I had to write five hundred words on the meditation technique of my choice for drama, and then write a couple of paragraphs in French about what I'd done over the weekend. Owen and I had done the French in the car, at least out loud, and it was a matter of a few minutes for me to commit it to paper, but the drama homework took actual research. I used Mum and Dad's desktop, which Mum had put in the kitchen so she could use it for recipes before tablets were invented. She hadn't gotten around to moving it since she bought her iPad.

Searching "meditation" brought up about 144 million results. Apparently people took this very seriously. I skimmed page after page until I saw an entry for "Tai Chi." What caught my eye was the use of the words *dragon* and *army* in the blurb, and I clicked through to the page with more enthusiasm than I had expected to feel as a result of this assignment. As I read, I started to smile.

"What's that?" Dad asked, stepping into the kitchen. Both of my parents had eaten before I got home since Mum was working nights, but they had saved a plate for me, and when I got out of the shower, Dad had said he'd come down to sit with me while I ate.

"Drama homework," I said.

"There's homework in drama?" he asked. He put my plate in the microwave and pressed START.

"It's a serious subject," I said. "And you forgot the cover."

"Shoot," he said, and pressed pause on the panel. There was already sauce spattered on the roof of the microwave, but he put the cover on anyway. "Don't change the subject, what are you doing?"

"Researching meditation techniques," I said. "There's this cool one called tai chi that's actually about dragon slayers."

The microwave beeped and Dad took my plate out. He set it on the table, and I turned away from the computer as he sat down. I could tell by his face that we were about to have one of his trademark Very Serious Conversations, but that didn't stop me from taking a large bite of meatloaf.

"Siobhan," he said. "You know your mum and I are proud of you, right?"

I nodded, hoping that my expression looked more "thoughtful on account of chewing" than "desperately trying to find an exit." Apparently it was going to be one of *those* conversations.

"We used to worry that you spent too much time with your music," he said. "But it made you so happy, and your teachers always told us how gifted you were at it, so we encouraged you to go as far as you could."

I swallowed. "Is this the 'we worry that you don't have a peer group at school' conversation again?" I asked. That was an old favorite. It didn't matter how many times I explained that I didn't particularly feel I was missing anything. They still worried. You'd think I was antisocial or acted like I'd been raised by wolves. I tried to act like Sadie hadn't been completely ignoring me since Christmas. Mum had to have noticed that she'd stopped calling.

"No," he said, smiling. "This is the 'you don't have to follow the dragon slayers around and camp in the winter if you don't want to' conversation."

I laughed. "Thanks," I said. "But it wasn't so bad. Well, once I mastered going to the bathroom in a snow bank, anyway."

"Too much information!" Dad said, throwing up his hands

in mock defense. "But we're serious. Dragon slaying is an old and noble tradition, but it's not part of our family's heritage. Owen was raised for dragon slaying to take over his life, but you don't have any such obligation."

"Dad," I said, speaking slowly as I put voice to an idea I'd been turning over in my mind for a while, "please don't take this the wrong way, but that's kind of the point."

"I'm not sure I understand," Dad said.

"Someday, even though I'm not born to it, maybe even *because* I'm not born to it, I'm going to choose to follow a dragon slayer," I said. It was the first time I'd ever said it out loud, and all at once the world seemed both smaller and distressingly big. "And Owen is going to very publically turn down a contract in order to come back here and defend farm animals and a salt mine that can't pay him a third of what he'd make in a big city. The whole idea is to get people to stop thinking of dragon slaying as a family obligation, as something only a select few can do. I'm a really good musician and I am not going to try to make it big. Neither is Owen. We're going to do a job, and do our best to make it seem like other people can and should join us."

"You know, I figured you'd at least wait until university before you got all radical on me," Dad said. He was still smiling, though, and I knew that he was at least half-convinced. "Is that why the two of you have been trying to research hatching grounds? Because you want to make a difference as soon as possible?"

"There are three of us, actually," I said. "You haven't met Emily yet. She's from Saltrock. And yes. We are trying to think outside the box, because sometimes adults aren't really good at that." It sounded absolutely ridiculous as soon as I said it out loud, but by then it was too late. I gave Dad the opening, and he jumped on it.

"Neither are dragons," he said. "While you were gone, the sign at my office got scorched again. Some stupid dragon, creature of habit, went for it even though there aren't any pictures of treasure on it anymore. Sometimes, people will just do the same thing over and over again, hoping for better results."

"Does that mean we can go back to the library?" I asked.

"No," he said. I slumped. "But only because it's not just up to me. I'll have to talk to your mother and to the Thorskards as well."

"I'm glad you understand we're not just being deliberately obstinate," I said.

"Isn't that teenager default?" Dad asked.

"Very funny," I said.

"I thought so," he said. "Ice cream?"

"No, thank you," I said. "I never want anything cold ever again. Until summer."

"Hot chocolate it is, then," he said, and moved to the kettle. He filled it and plugged it in, then turned around and leaned back against the counter. "You know, Owen is a nice kid and I know he's got friends and all, but it really is too bad he can't fit in any sports."

"Tell me about it," I said. "If I have to hear any more cleverly worded suggestions from Ms. Ngembi, I might lock myself in the music room and never come out."

"I mean it, Siobhan," Dad said. "Think about it. You want people to think they can do what Owen does, you should make it so that they see more of him."

I hadn't thought of it that way. Dad didn't offer any suggestions, though, so I put it out of my mind while I finished my dinner and hot chocolate, which, I should mention, was about 75 percent marshmallows, and therefore quite adequate as a stand-in for dessert. When I was done, I went back to the computer and printed out the page on tai chi I'd found so I could make notes at the table. Most kids typed their written assignments, but years of writing on staff paper had given me decent penmanship, and I liked to show it off every now and then.

As I read the pages I'd printed out, my brain split focus. While I picked out bits of information that would make it easy to write five hundred words about the idea of tai chi as it was used today, I filed away the much more interesting facts about why the discipline had been invented in the first place. As I wrote the homework assignment, I planned what I was going to say to Lottie and Hannah (and my own mother, for that matter) to get them to accept my idea. If it worked out, Owen would get to play soccer and Trondheim, not to mention the other small towns in the area, wouldn't be left high and dry while Aodhan was out on patrol and Owen was otherwise engaged.

By the time I crawled under my covers, with a hot water bottle for good measure, I considered this weekend's work very well done.

THE GUARD

Lottie went for the whole idea way too easily. In hindsight, that should have made me realize how bad things were about to get, but at the time I was just relieved that she didn't make me back up my assertions with actual research instead of the fifteen minutes I'd spent on the Internet and the car ride's worth of talking it took me to get Owen on board. Apparently he really wanted to play soccer.

"Why tai chi?" was all Lottie said, once I finished outlining my plan.

"Well, nowadays it's used for active meditation," I said.

"I know," she said. "We did it in the Oil Watch. It's supposed to be relaxing while at the same time keeping a warrior's instincts sharp."

"It's based on an old Chinese style of dragon slaying," I said. "It means *great pole* or *lance*. The idea was that the dragon slayers could practice their forms without weapons in their hands and build up muscle memory."

"You know, if someone had just explained that, we probably would have taken the exercise seriously," Lottie said.

"Oh, please," Hannah said. "Like you dragon slayers ever took anything seriously."

"We were all young once," Lottie said, smirking. Owen did his very best to disappear. I decided I didn't want to know.

"Anyway," I continued. "I think the kids at school could do it too. It's supposed to foster teamwork as well, so it would play well with the sports teams."

"You did say you wanted me to be a part of this town," Owen said, right on cue. His acting needed work, though. He was ridiculously earnest. "And playing sports isn't the only way, but it is pretty easy. I'll spend more time with my classmates and they'll get to know a bit of what a dragon slayer really goes through. While I'm gone, you and Dad will have some backup and when I get back from the Oil Watch, I'll have a support group that won't be tied to a contract or a corporation."

It's possible that Lottie believed him, but it's more likely that she just decided to show mercy and get him to stop talking before she laughed in his face.

Anyway, that's how I ended up skipping one of my spare periods that Friday to spend it in Owen's world issues class, drafting what would become the Trondheim Dragon Guard Charter. Mr. Huffman was thrilled to death, which I suspected was because he hadn't yet found a way to incorporate Offense/Defense Fridays into a class about current events and missed the activity. And the shouting. For posterity, we won't talk about the fact that the first draft was written on unicorn stationery, as I got all the way to the front of the classroom before realizing that my backpack was full of staff paper, and Sadie Fletcher was the first person to offer a substitute, smiling at me for the first time since Christmas. She didn't say it, but I knew I was forgiven for whatever I'd done.

It was written by committee, by which I mean I spoke out loud as I wrote, and everyone yelled suggestions at me, the bulk of which I ignored. I won't include the whole document here, as it is readily accessible in the Trondheim Public Library archive (not to mention on the Internet), but I'm quite proud of parts of it.

"We, the students of Trondheim Secondary School, being the amalgamation of said school and also of the former Saltrock Collegiate Institute, do hereby enter into agreement with Owen Thorskard," I dictated to myself. "In return for his participation in school sports, specifically the soccer team . . ."

"And cross country!" added Alex.

"I was getting to that," I said. "I can only write so fast."

"Sorry," he said.

"Specifically the soccer team," I continued, "but also in likelihood the cross country team in the fall, we will, with due permission from our parents and guardians, join in portions of his training regimen, the better to defend our homes."

"We will become Lancers in truth," Mr. Huffman said, and I scrambled to write down his words. "Fully realizing our mascot, St. George."

"Our mascot, comma, St. George," I repeated slowly.

"And become proficient in the tools, trade, and strategies of dragon slaying," Owen said. "Even if it turns out I really suck at soccer."

"Very poetic," Sadie said, her tone more amused than mean. She was a shoe-in to be captain of the senior girls' soccer team this year, even though she was only in grade eleven, so she took this as seriously as the boys did.

"Siobhan will fix it," Owen said.

"What are we going to call ourselves?" Alex asked as I finished Owen's line.

"The Guardsmen?" asked one of the seniors.

"I don't think so," said Sadie, beating me by a breath. "At least half the girls' team is going to sign up, if our parents let us."

There were nods from girls I hadn't even been aware played soccer. Apparently this was going to be a banner year for tryouts, for the girls' and boys' teams both.

"Good point," Owen said diplomatically.

"How about just the Guard?" Mr. Huffman said. "That way, there can be smaller subunits for Saltrock and Trondheim, as well as any farms that are close together."

"I like it," Sadie said.

"And no one gets cut," I added. "From the Guard, I mean. You don't have to be on any of the soccer teams to be part of it."

"Agreed," said Owen. "Though if you aren't very good with a sword, you might be repurposed into some sort of support role."

"That sounds good to me," Mr. Huffman said. "I also think you should add that any member of the Guard must be at least sixteen and in good academic standing. That will help sell it to the school board."

I added the subclauses and agreements to the bottom of the charter, writing over the top of the unicorn's sparkly horn. I was going to be covered in glitter for the rest of the afternoon, and we were definitely going to have to find something more appropriate to write the finished version on.

"Okay, then!" I said after adding the final touches. "We'll have Lottie and Ms. Ngembi read it over this weekend, and hopefully we'll have the completed draft on Monday. Then it will be a matter of writing up permission forms, answering questions, and having everyone who wants to be a member of the Guard sign the charter."

"Can we have some sort of official signing?" Sadie asked. "Like we're a secret society or something?"

"A secret society would never have a public ceremony to declare itself," Mr. Huffman pointed out. "But I think it's a good idea."

"This is going to be the best season for soccer ever," Sadie said. "Assuming no one gets lit on fire. Does that happen a lot?"

For the first time, there were some concerned faces in the crowd. If nothing else, the idea of potentially being set on fire would probably make it difficult to obtain the necessary parental permission.

"Well, I've been to several dragon slayings now," I said. "Including front-row seats to a soot-streaker's final moments last Saturday, and I have yet to even get singed."

"That's encouraging," Alex said.

"What about the Oil Watch?" That question came from Robert, a friend of Alex's who didn't play soccer but did run cross country and would probably be coming out for the Guard. "Will we have to join it?"

"I don't think so," I said. I looked at Mr. Huffman.

"No," he said. "The Oil Watch is for registered dragon slayers and volunteers only. This would be along the lines of a local militia. There used to be plenty of those before Vlad the

Impaler gave it such a bad rap. The government would have no legal recourse to make you join the Oil Watch."

"Now we just have to get our parents to sign off," Sadie said. "I think mine might have a few issues with it."

There had been so many attacks since exams that the school board was considering banning outdoor sports altogether, which annoyed pretty much everyone except the badminton coaches. A few parents had pulled their children out and started homeschooling, even though TSS had an excellent dragon shelter, but most of the grown-ups in Trondheim and Saltrock were determined not to give any more ground. It made sense that the kids felt the same way.

"Well, you've got all weekend to try it," I said. "Plus, once we get it approved by the school, it should be an easier sell. And our parents all really want Owen to come back once he's finished his tour. If they think this will make him do it, so much the better."

"Why are you going to come back here?" Alex asked. "You could make a pile of money in the city, just by virtue of being related to Lottie. Most of us aren't planning to stay here after we graduate high school, much less come back after university. Why are you?"

Mr. Huffman leaned forward, and I had a sneaking suspicion that everything Owen was about to say would be showing up on the Internet this afternoon as soon as school got out. Owen shifted uncomfortably in his seat and looked at me. I shrugged in what I hoped was an encouraging manner. This was one question I couldn't step in for. Every time it was asked of him, Owen was going to have to answer it himself.

"In Europe, back in the day, every town had a dragon

slayer," Owen said. "Imagine: Trondheim, Saltrock, Kincardine, Hanover, Southampton, even smaller places like Vanastra and Chesley, each with its own dragon slayer. And they didn't get paid. Or at least they didn't get paid very much. They protected their homes, and the homes of their friends, in return for food and other simple things like that. I don't need commercial endorsements or more money than I can spend in my lifetime. I need a home, and friends I can count on to help me put out the fires."

"Isn't that socialism?" Robert asked. He was already eighteen and had voted in our last election. Our riding was typically bellwether and had gone Conservative again this round, even though it was blatantly obvious that the government had no intention of actually carrying through with its promise of making dragons slayers more accessible to the rural public.

"Probably," Owen said. "But you'd have a dragon slayer on speed dial instead of two and a half hours away. Or more, depending on traffic on the 401."

"Sounds like a no-brainer to me," said Sadie. She looked oddly content, and there was a fire in her eyes that hadn't been there before.

The bell rang, but no one moved, not even to pack up their stuff. They waited until Owen did it first. I walked beside him out of the classroom, with everyone else behind us.

At that exact moment, somewhere inside Owen, a leader, a dragon slayer, a grown-up Viking was born. I was going to have to learn how to play soccer.

SADIE'S FIRST DRAGON

Ms. Ngembi was thrilled. She had Owen try out for defense, on the basis that he could run forever, and it turned out that he was pretty good at tracking the ball across the field. It probably worked in his favor that no one on the soccer field could light him on fire for getting in their way. The senior boys' soccer team had a record turnout. Ms. Ngembi was able to field an entire practice squad who were so excited by the prospect of playing on the same team as Owen that they showed up for practice in the snow even after being told they'd probably never play during a real game. The senior girls' team had a lot of people sign up too, though more of the girls bypassed the soccer team and just signed up for the Guard instead. The junior teams, made up of players too young for the Guard, had good turnouts as well, as students hoped to join the Guard when they were old enough.

Lottie came and did a share of the training herself. This was her own idea, and I know for a fact that it helped seal the deal for some of the more reluctant parents. Whatever concerns they had about the flammable nature of their children were assuaged by the promised involvement of Lottie Thorskard.

For about a week, we were beset by news cameras at every practice. This forced us to evolve a system a bit more quickly than we'd planned. We decided it made sense to warm up on the track, which was big enough to accommodate all the soccer players as they trickled out from the change rooms, and then everyone lined up on the field for whatever exercise Lottie was demonstrating today. Somehow, I found myself promoted to assistant coach for that portion, even though I'd only signed on as team manager for the senior girls. For two weeks, we did mostly tai chi exercises, conditioning everyone in the movements of sword usage before we added actual weight of a sword. I thought there would be complaints, or at least insinuations of impatience, about that, but the students weathered the whole thing. In hindsight, this may have been because with school, Guard training, and soccer practice, they were all exhausted. After two weeks, we added wooden practice swords, which Hannah and Lottie had made out of old and broken hockey sticks donated by the Trondheim rec center. They weren't perfect, but they'd do.

After the training with Lottie and Owen, the four teams split off for the soccer portion of the afternoon. TSS was so small that we only had one field. General practice was to have the senior teams use either end of it. The juniors were consigned to the smaller flat area by the tennis court, which meant missed balls tended to end up in the pond. This year, however, there were simply too many kids on the teams. The elementary school down the block volunteered its soccer fields, which were

221

small but lacked water hazards. Every day after Guard training, the boys split off and headed down the road, while the girls used the fields on campus. This stymied the news cameras, because they were forbidden from entering the elementary school grounds (it's a long story, concerning a dragon, an idling news van, and an unfortunately abbreviated Junior Farmers presentation on how to raise goats) and they didn't really care about watching the girls practice since Owen wasn't there.

The reporters gave up on us at that point, but we had received enough coverage by then that word started to circulate outside of the county. Hanover and Kincardine both petitioned Lottie to help them train their own Guards, with charters based on the one we'd written on unicorn paper in Mr. Huffman's classroom. Hannah took over the training at Trondheim so that Lottie could travel to other high schools in the area. Aodhan did his part too, adding one high school stop per day to his patrol schedule whenever he was in an area that was training a Guard. And it went further than that, too. Rural schools all over the province started requesting the help of a government dragon slayer to help them train their own students, and even city schools started to approach their local corporation-backed dragon slayers on the subject.

Even though we had driven off most of the local news coverage, we generated a flurry of media activity on a national scale. The idea of training teenagers to help with the dragon problem was debated on talk shows and radio programs from Victoria to St. John's, with opinions ranging from those who believed in the Dracula myth strongly enough to declare it child abuse, to those who thought the Guard was a magnificent idea and something worth fostering across the country. The political split did not go unnoticed by any of the commentators, but as we got closer to actually starting our official season, more than a few Conservative MPs were starting to change their minds on whether or not it was a good idea.

Things came to a head the week before our first official game. We'd been playing preseason games against other schools, those training a Guard and those that weren't, for almost a month by then, starting pretty much as soon as the snow melted and playing through some fairly horrific mud. The game in question took place in Wingham. Unlike in years past, where the girls' teams had traveled together, this game featured both the senior squads against Wingham's two senior teams. The girls played first, Trondheim winning handily (footishly? I was still working on my vocabulary that early on), mostly thanks to Sadie's complete inability to stop moving once she decided she would like to take the ball somewhere. Seriously, I'm pretty sure she could have taken down a brick wall, so something as inconsequential as the other team proved no barrier to her.

Anyway, by the time the boys' game started, we were all in high spirits, and even though they'd lost, the Wingham girls' team stayed behind to cheer as well. Since school was out for the afternoon by then, the audience had increased, and since Owen was playing, the news cameras were on scene too, rolling film. Lottie and Hannah were sitting away from the crowd and had brought a blanket to sit on. They waved me over once the game started, and I dragged Sadie, who was so excited I thought she might explode, with me to sit with them. Aodhan was in the area, Hannah told me, so he might show up after halftime to watch Owen play.

We were about ten minutes into the game when Lottie's cell phone rang. She looked down at the screen, and I knew immediately that it was Aodhan, and that it was bad news. She got up and walked farther away from the crowd (there were no bleachers since, before now, no one ever actually came to soccer games), and Hannah followed her. I watched, waiting for some indication of what I should do. Sadie grabbed my hand, and I knew that she had figured it out too.

It didn't take long. Lottie ended the call and headed straight for the announcer's bench while Hannah made her way back to us.

"Dragon incoming," she said as quietly as she could, confirming my suspicion. No one but Sadie and me heard her above the roar of the crowd.

Instinctively I braced myself. Dragon attacks in congested areas are the worst, I knew, because it's hard for people not to panic. At least with the ground this wet, chances of a grass fire were slim. And then I remembered whom I was standing with. Not just Hannah, but the Trondheim Secondary School senior girls' soccer team, more than half of whom had been in training for two months for a situation just like this one. This would be our test.

At the announcer's booth, Lottie got control of the mike.

"Attention, everyone," she said. The Trondheim players, accustomed to following her orders, froze in place on the field or straightened where they stood in the crowd. The Wingham players followed suit. I saw Lottie's face and wondered how she was going to do this without causing a melee. She smiled slightly and held the microphone out from her face so she could yell without causing feedback. "Dragon drill!" she shouted.

The effect was immediate, as the forty-odd members of the Trondheim and Wingham Guard immediately took charge. With Lottie, Hannah, and Owen present, everyone knew to be in evacuation mode, and the Trondheim students knew to defer to Wingham, as the host school. I followed along, even though I knew that this was no drill, and kept the pace up, as some would have straggled behind on their way to the enormous dragon shelter underneath the Wingham gymnasium.

Gradually, all of the students, parents, coaches, players and news reporters were corralled into the shelter. Sadie, Alex, and Owen had all gone to Lottie's car to retrieve the swords, Sadie carrying Lottie's like it was some kind of holy relic. I could tell by the looks on their faces that Sadie had told them it was no drill.

"Get inside," Hannah said to Sadie and Alex as the swords were handed over. "You too, Siobhan. Keep everyone calm. The important thing is that everyone got in before the dragon got here."

I heard the screech of tires and knew that Aodan had just pulled into the parking lot. The dragon must be nearly over-head. I smelled smoke and turned, and there it was, perched on top of the Trondheim bus. It was just a corn dragon, small enough that the bus wasn't broken under its weight, but it was big enough, and we had successfully evaded it. Now it was up to our dragon slayers to finish the job.

I pulled the shocked Sadie and Alex, neither of whom had ever been that close to a dragon, into the shelter. I pulled the door shut behind me and latched it. "Okay, everybody!" I shouted. "Move all the way to the back!"

"Aren't we done?" asked one of the Wingham players.

"Not quite," I said. I noticed the new cameras were still rolling and decided to take advantage of it. "Congratulations on our first successful dragon evasion," I said, loud enough that everyone heard me. "Our dragon slayers are outside finishing off a corn dragon, but you should all be proud of yourselves. No one panicked and everyone is safe."

"You mean the dragon is *real*?" demanded one of the parents.

"Yes," I said. "Aren't you glad you gave your kids permission to learn how to deal with such events in a helpful manner?"

Sadie grabbed my hand again and held on like I'd held on to Hannah all those months ago, but she never stopped smiling. I thought for a moment she must be crazy, but then I realized she was still on pure adrenaline. I looked straight at her and realized that she, like Lottie, was trumpet-shaped in spirit, and bold. Until now, until the Guard, she hadn't had a place to work. That's why she was jealous of my relationship with Owen, not because of romance, but because I had effectively shut her out. I was in-the-know and she was not, but she wasn't out of the loop any more. Her piccolo trumpet soared above the worried murmurs of the crowd in the dragon shelter, and I mentally kicked myself for having missed it all this time. When Hannah finally came to let everyone out, the pair of us were still holding hands and grinning like lunatics.

The rest of the game was cancelled because the soccer field had been set on fire, but there were no hard feelings. We were delayed getting back to Trondheim because the bus had been caught in the fight after we'd gone underground and was no longer road-safe, to say the least. Aodhan offered me a ride home with Owen, but I didn't want to break my newfound solidarity with Sadie, so I declined.

"I'm sorry I'm so dense," I told her, once the Thorskards had gone. They'd left us their blanket, and we were sitting on some grass that wasn't burned, away from the rest of the waiting team.

"It's okay," Sadie said. "It's not like I was straight with you either."

"Still, next time I will talk more," I promised impulsively. "Though I'm not sure what about."

"Deal," she said.

I got home just in time to record the news that night. The Prime Minister was forced to reverse his party's standing on the issue of training students in basic dragon defense, and then he had to publicly commend every single member of the Trondheim and Wingham Guard. It's the little things in life, I tell you, that make it all worthwhile.

SADIE'S DREAM

Sadie called on Thursday evening, just before dinner, and asked if I was free. Mum was on nights, and Dad was starting to get into tax crunch season, so I had an exciting evening of leftovers and homework planned.

"Oh, good," said Sadie. "My mom and dad are out too. I'll order something. Bring your workout clothes!"

"Okay," I said, even though she had already hung up.

Just last week, we were cautious acquaintances, and now, thanks to a dragon attack, we were friends. I was starting to realize we had been friends for a while, and I just hadn't noticed. To be honest, it was kind of exciting. I put the casserole back in the fridge and then went upstairs to grab my gear. The Guard mostly practiced in yoga pants and gym shorts, but Hannah had modified the leather arm guards once used by the now-defunct Saltrock archery club into gauntlets for sword fighting. I had a pair of real ones, of course, and a spare. I threw both into my bag. Sadie would probably appreciate a real pair as well.

Sadie lived close enough to my house that I could have walked over, but I was hungry so I drove instead. I got there just as the pizza delivery guy (who also delivered for the Chinese restaurant and doubled as the only taxi driver in Trondheim) was pulling out of the driveway. Sadie waved, the box balanced precariously in her other hand, and I waved back before turning off the engine.

We ate quickly, but I was still worried that it would be too dark to go outside and swing swords at one another. When I said as much, Sadie only smiled and finished her last slice with a flourish. She reached over her shoulder toward the back door and flipped a light switch, and the backyard was flooded with more than enough light to practice by.

Dragon slaying, even for pretend, is not really something I'd recommend doing after one has eaten three or six slices of pizza, so we started off slowly. We moved through the tai chi forms together, not requiring the count that Lottie still had to give to keep some of the students on track. I had worked for months, back before the Guard was even a thought, to perfect these movements, but Sadie had taken to them as naturally as if she'd been doing them her whole life. After about half an hour, by which time we'd done the whole routine twice, Sadie cracked her neck and headed for the practice swords.

"I really wish you wouldn't do that," I told her. "It gives me the heebie-jeebies."

"You stood by during a dragon slaying, but bone cracking makes you nervous?" Sadie asked. She picked up the swords and threw one at me. I managed to catch it, but only just.

"It's important to know your limits," I said, and she grinned at me.

I dropped into *guard* and she mirrored me. Lottie had taught us forms for this too, numbered hits in sequence that had been passed down through the generations and had altered only slightly from the days when people used swords to fight one another instead of dragons.

"Do you ever wonder why we learn sword fighting this way?" Sadie asked as we moved through the first sequence.

I was still slightly better at this than she was, by virtue of having a few months' experience on her, but I had trouble talking while fighting.

"What do you mean?" I ground out, hoping my fingers wouldn't get snapped as a result of my inattentiveness.

"We learn sword fighting against a person," Sadie said. "Dragons don't exactly have swords and follow the rules of chivalry."

I actually knew the answer to this, having come across it in all the background reading Hannah had made me do, but I waited until the pause between the second and third form to start explaining.

"It's about muscle development," I told her. "Muscles work based on memory, just like your brain does when it's doing math or driving home from school. By learning the forms, we train our muscles to keep moving from thrust to parry without having to think about it. That way, when you're fighting a dragon, you don't panic."

"You didn't panic?" she asked, sliding into fourth form with a grace that made me profoundly jealous.

"Oh, I panicked like there was no tomorrow," I told her. "But I didn't stop moving."

Sadie thought about that as we went through fifth and sixth, and then went back to the beginning to start again with her as the aggressor and me on defense. I braced myself. Sadie hit hard.

"But dragons are so much bigger," she pointed out. She did this a lot faster than I did, and I tightened my stance to compensate.

"True," I said, "but the important thing is to get a foundation. Mum tells me I made up my own songs when I was little, but it wasn't until I learned the notes and how to write them down that I was able to really make music. I think it's the same for dragon slayers. You have to learn the basics before you try it with fire."

Sadie finished sixth in a flurry that left me too busy to talk, and then held her sword up in salute. I mirrored back.

"Do you really think I'll ever try it with fire?" she asked.

"I think you could," I said. "I mean, eventually. With more practice. I'm no expert, but I've been watching a lot of swordsmanship since the fall, and you're a natural."

"Has Lottie noticed?" she asked.

"I don't know," I told her. "We don't get much time to talk anymore. They're all really busy."

"Has Owen noticed?" Her voice was so quiet I nearly didn't hear her.

Her question flustered me, and therefore I said the first thing that popped into my head.

"He might if you invited him over instead of calling me."

"I didn't want to put him on the spot," Sadie admitted. "I could call you both next time, if you think that would help."

"It might," I said. "But trust me when I tell you that you're probably going to want to tell Owen in very precise terms what you're trying to do."

"I don't really know what I'm trying to do," Sadie said. "I mean, at first I thought I just wanted to date him, but then I realized that I wanted more than that."

"How much more?" I asked. "Because there are rules about that sort of thing, and Owen has his own code I can't really tell you about, because it's not common knowledge."

"You mean the fact that his mother lives in Venezuela?" Sadie asked.

"Um, yeah," I said.

"Because you can find that out on the Internet in about ten seconds, if you know where to look," Sadie said.

"Oh," I said. "Well, you should still talk to him. Because I'm sure the Internet isn't really comprehensive."

"I know," Sadie said. "But that's not even what I meant by *more*. I look at Hannah and Lottie, and see everything they've accomplished together, as a team, and I want to be part of something like that, something more than the Guard, even though that's a really good start."

It hit me like a ton of bricks. Sadie wasn't looking for a boyfriend or a meaningful charity or an easy way to quell the voice inside her that called for civic pride. She wanted to be a dragon slayer in her own right, working with others like Owen and Lottie and even me, but she wanted to hold the sword herself, and face the fire so that others didn't have to. I had no idea if this was part of what Lottie had planned on, but I was almost positive she wouldn't be averse to the idea.

Sadie was watching me with a nervous expression on her face, like she was worried I was about to shut her out of the world she wanted into so desperately. Instead, I smiled at her.

"You know," I said with exaggerated lightness, "Hannah

makes me carry my sword with me all the time. My real sword. The sword that used to be Lottie's. It's in the trunk right now. If you wanted, I could maybe go and get it for you."

Sadie didn't have to answer, and before long, I was watching her swing through all the forms by herself, because my sword would have killed any of the wooden practice ones. I took advantage of the time to watch her without worrying about my own form. She was much better than I was. I could mirror all the movements, thanks to months of practice and hard work, but Sadie made them her own, and moved through them with a sense of the natural that I couldn't achieve. She might not have been born to a dragon slayer family, but she was born to be a dragon slayer.

"It's a lot heavier," she said. "But I like it!"

"I'll come over after Guard practice every day, if you like," I told her. "And when you work up the courage to talk to Owen, and then to Lottie, about it, maybe Hannah will make you a sword of your own."

"You really think they'll be okay with it?" she asked. "My wanting to be a dragon slayer?"

"Lottie is the most open-minded person I've ever come across," I told her. "And Hannah loves people who make their own decisions."

"What about Owen?" she said.

"He might be jealous that you're better than he is," I said with a smile.

"That's not what I meant," she said.

"I know," I told her. "I don't think he's ever given much thought to having a girlfriend. He hasn't told me straight-up, but I get the impression he doesn't want to put a kid through what he's gone through, and he also doesn't want to mess with some girl's feelings."

"And they say chivalry is dead," Sadie said, rolling her eyes.

"Well, I don't think you'd be 'some girl,'" I told her. "I think if you're both honest, it would be okay."

"And you wouldn't mind?" she asked.

"Don't take this the wrong way," I said slowly, "but I'm still half convinced that dragon slayers are crazy. I'm good with my music and my friends and family. I'm not really looking for anything else."

Sadie looked at me for a long moment, as though trying to determine if I was telling the truth or just humoring her. Whatever she saw must have answered her questions, because she smiled and raised the sword again.

"Do you mind if I keep going?" she asked. "I've got a lot of catching up to do."

"Go ahead," I told her, and went over to the picnic table to sit down and watch.

She started with the forms again, but when she reached the end, she kept going into free form, shifting her aim from the imaginary person across from her to up where a dragon's hearts would be. I could hear the first notes of her symphony in the wind, and see the rhythm in the floodlights that reflected off of her sword.

SPORTS METAPHORS

One of the challenges in describing the weekends that Owen and I spent traipsing around the countryside with Aodhan is that it's difficult to pass along what Aodhan taught us without making it sound like I am reciting some kind of textbook. No one wants to put up with that in their spare time. While we were busy practicing for soccer and the Guard during the week, the two of us continued to travel around with Aodhan, cramming our homework into Sunday evenings and stretching our spares as far as they would go in order to keep up with the workload. Busy as we were, and as much as we learned, none of it was particularly story-worthy.

Emily was busy too. Since she didn't have quite the same parental supervision problem we did, she was actually able to keep researching the hatching ground, using both the Saltrock archive and the Internet boards as her primary media. Most of the time, she didn't even have to do the research herself. She would just ask a question or put forth some kind of theory, and the other members of the chat room would fall all over themselves to answer her (or "him," depending on the ID she was using at the time). She didn't join the Guard, but she did keep track of the news surrounding it, and using her reports we made various changes in the Charter leading up to the Wingham game, after which we were pretty much set.

Like we had in the fall when I had started my sword fighting lessons, we fell into a pattern. School, Guard, and soccer during the week, and random tours of the area on the weekend, with as much conspiracy stuffed in around the edges as we could fit. If it was a symphony, then it was the part in the middle when most of the audience fell asleep, except it was getting harder and harder to get anything like decent sleep in Trondheim and Saltrock, because the dragon sirens sounded nearly every night. Dragons were spotted, trailing fire through the dark, and Aodhan almost never came home at all because he was so busy on patrol. The news out of Northern Ontario was grim, with more RCMD slayers called to duty than ever recorded, and Emily reported that there were a growing number of survivalist websites, as well as theories about a possible evacuation. Owen's grades started to slip again, but no one really cared this time. The teachers were giving him participation marks for the classes he was missing, and I didn't tutor him anymore. All we ever did was train, or hide.

Lottie came to school in late March, after the Wingham game, to give a talk about what to do when a dragon attacked. It was all things we already knew, but with the formation of the Guard, it was worth repeating. She organized the younger students into teams, making sure that a member of the Guard was responsible for each team and knew how to lead them to safety.

"What if we're at home?" Robert's younger brother Adam called out. "We don't have a dragon shelter."

"Then find out which of your neighbors has one," Lottie said. "Now is not the time to keep that kind of thing secret. We need to work together."

"Are you going to be able to stop it?" Alex asked.

It wouldn't have shown up to many people in the room. Hannah knew, and so did Owen, and I could see the edges of it around Lottie's face, but no one else could tell. They couldn't see the stress and the worry—the fear, even—that with her injury she wouldn't be able to do enough to help. The mute was out, Lottie was in full dragon slayer mode, and almost no one noticed that it was an act.

"We will," Lottie said, clear trumpet ringing. "My brother and my nephew will, and we have friends we can call if the government is moving too slowly. We will not let the dragons run us out of here."

There was a rumble in the crowd, but Lottie was already moving forward. She put up photos of dragons, species after species, and made sure to remind the students what their weaknesses were. It was a trifle macabre, but the entire student body listened to her every word.

"And if you see an *ornus*," Lottie concluded. "Run. Run as fast as you can and hide. Don't stop for your phone or your purse or your dog. Get to a shelter immediately, and once you're safe inside, use the landline in the shelter to call for help. You can see a soot-streaker coming from a goodly distance, so take advantage of that."

The kids in the audience were dead quiet when she finished, and it took her a moment to realize that she had probably scared them. She walked forward to the edge of the stage, leaning on her cane, and even though I knew it was a difficult manoeuver for her, she sat down on the skirt with her legs dangling over the side. All of a sudden, the mute was in the trumpet, and she was just Lottie again. A dragon slayer still, but a person too, and a person who could help.

"I know it's hard," she said. She sounded like everyone's mother, and every kid in the room relaxed, even if the teachers didn't. "We've lost property and stock and, yes, people, but you guys are doing everything right. I'm just here today to remind you of that, and to encourage you to keep going."

"What's the most important thing to remember?" Sadie called out from near the back of the gym. She was wearing short sleeves, and I could see the new muscles in her arms.

"Don't panic," Lottie said. "We have brains that we can use to think and reason and form logical plans. Dragons are just mindless creatures. If you use your brain, you can outwit them, but to do that, you can't panic."

Ms. Ngembi decided that would be a good note to end on and stepped out onto the stage to thank Lottie for coming. Lottie couldn't get back to her feet without sliding down onto the floor, so they shook hands somewhat awkwardly, and Lottie made a face so that everyone laughed. Then she and Hannah headed home while the rest of us went for lunch.

"She talks a good game," Owen said quietly in my ear as I stood at the back of the gym and waited for the crowd to subside. Emily squeezed in beside me, and Owen nodded at her. "But she's afraid."

"There aren't any other dragon slayers who can come," Emily said. "Even if she asks for help and plays every card she can and calls in every favor."

"Why not?" I asked.

"Because all the government dragon slayers are being sent to Sudbury and Thunder Bay as soon as they're sure the snow is melted for the hatching season up there," Emily said. "And everyone else is tied to their contracts. If we didn't have Aodhan already, we'd get no one."

"It must be Manitoulin," Owen said. "Saltrock isn't the dragons' only target. They're going north as well."

"And the federal government likes the paper mills and the nickel mines more than they like the salt," I said. "We need a plan."

"Tell me about it," Owen said. "The Guard was a good start. It makes me feel better about leaving town all the time, knowing that at least people are organized and can hide properly, but it's not enough."

"We need to do something on the offense," I agreed. "There's no point in putting all our best players in to play defense and guard the keeper. We need someone to attack midfield."

Emily stared at me. Owen laughed.

"I think you've been watching too much soccer," he said.

"Sometimes you need a good sports metaphor," I told him airily. "Music won't always do. If I told you we needed more bass and countermelody and less canon round, you wouldn't know what I was talking about."

"That is true," Owen said. The gym had finally cleared, and we headed for the door. "But we still need to think of something."

"Tonight after practice," I said. "I'll drive all three of us to your house and we can come up with something."

"Hannah and Lottie will be there," Owen reminded me.

"It's time we start working together," I said, quoting Lottie deliberately. Emily nodded. "You'll be seventeen in three weeks, and I'll be seventeen in May. I don't think we can wait for it to be official."

"Okay," he said. "I'll see you after classes."

I spent the afternoon in the practice room. There was a song at the tips of my fingers, but the melody just wouldn't make it onto the keys.

THE STORY OF MAPS

History will tell you that mapmaking started with the Egyptians. Maybe, if it is feeling inclusive, in India, or with the Chinese. As usual, History is lying through its teeth.

The truth is that ever since the first Australopithecine looked up at a flaming sky and thought "Dear God, what is that thing?" people have been drawing maps of the places that dragons live, the better to avoid them altogether. We have very little evidence from those early days—cave walls and volcanic happenstance for the most part—but we know that maps were made: lines of demarcation, whether on the edge of an uncharted sea or deep in the heart of Africa, yet unseen.

In some places, those lines were reinforced in stone, and later in steel. There is a wall in China, and another on the edge of the English moors. The Government of Canada destroyed the Ambassador Bridge, and halted construction on the Bluewater before the piers had set. Do not enter. Here there be dragons. For most places, the smoke on the horizon was warning enough, and people stayed close to home.

There were, of course, the very foolish and the very brave. They went out from the safe places and found new ones—or didn't. Once they were secured, more maps were made to guide the cautious to the new havens, pushing back against the blank edges of the world. Thus was mapped the globe, and Canada was no different.

Our mapmakers were French, to start, because the French were the first to arrive. These *coureurs de bois* ventured out from the shelter of the city wall at Quebec and found trails to the homes and havens of the local First Nations. What followed was ugly and shameful, and not at all improved by the subsequent arrival of the British. The First Nations were promised European-style maps, and those maps were delivered, but the cost was high. Corralled into too-small villages on the fringes of the Upper Canada hatching grounds, the population plummeted.

That's the other thing History likes to forget about maps. Their cost is not just in the blood of people killed by dragons, but in the blood of people killed by other people.

The mapmakers pressed on, north and ever-west, and the First Nation groups they encountered were more cautious, slower to bargain and treat. But the maps were made, shaping Canada as much as war or our constant struggle not to be annexed by the United States did. Those were the maps I learned in school: those thirteen provinces and three territories. I could recite their capitals and spell them. I knew which parts of them were safe and which parts were not. I didn't know what they had cost, because they don't tend to tell you that sort of thing in elementary school, but I learned that too, in time.

In school, they give you a blank sheet and you try to squish "Saskatchewan" into a box that's always too narrow while you fill in the familiar words and shapes. Those maps are copies and cost nothing. Their price has already been paid. The map I saw in my head was different. It wasn't some faceless prairie far away. It was my home. It was towns I recognized, places I had been. Names that were a mix of English holdovers and Algonquin prayers to Manitou confused people who weren't born there, but they were second nature to those who were.

Even if we succeeded, there would be fire. And if we failed, there would be so much more, and blood besides. My home would be gone, swallowed up like Michigan while progress marched on around me. And there would be another line— another boundary—that only the foolish and the brave would dare to cross.

SPARKS

I hadn't thought of anything by the time we made it to Owen's house that night, but Emily looked decidedly optimistic. I wasn't sure when she'd had time to do any research, since she didn't have a spare, but she did spend the whole car ride typing something on her phone, so I guessed that one of her Internet sources had come through with something she liked. Owen didn't say anything in the car either. He spent the whole drive scanning the horizon. It was a habit Aodhan had instilled in us, and while I couldn't do it very well while I was driving and also watching the road, Owen took his copiloting duties very seriously.

Hannah and Lottie weren't in the house when we got there, but there was smoke over Hannah's smithy, so we knew they were home. We set up on the kitchen table, notebooks and maps and sticky notes, and by the time we were settling in, Lottie came back inside.

"Homework?" she said, kicking off her shoes a bit laboriously. "And are you all staying for dinner?"

"Sort of," I said. "And yes, please."

"I'm not sure I like the sound of that," Lottie said. "But the second part is just fine. Hannah's making pizza."

"In the smithy?" Emily asked skeptically. "Isn't that a bit, you know, hot?"

"Probably," said Lottie. "But she's more or less mastered it. I don't ask questions."

"It's really good," Owen said. "Plus it means she can make dinner and swords at the same time, and that's just cool."

"Fair point," Emily said.

"Don't distract me," Lottie said. "What are you doing?"

"You said we should work together," I started to say, but Emily pulled out a folded piece of paper and leaned forward to unfold it on the table.

"Sorry, Siobhan," she said. "I figured we should start with this."

I turned to get a view of what I thought was the top of the paper.

"It's a map of the salt mine," Lottie said. "Where did you get that?"

"The Saltrock archive," Emily said. "Did you know that back before it was common for people to have their own dragon shelters, the main plan for evacuation in case of a major dragon attack was to funnel everyone into the mine?"

"Really?" Owen said. "How big is that place?"

"It goes out for miles under the lake," Emily said. "You could fit everyone from the whole county down there with room to spare. Well, until the oxygen ran out, but still."

"I had no idea it was that big," I said.

"Technically, the size and structure of the mine are

classified," Emily said. "But this plan was made and filed before the government classified the information, and I guess everyone forgot about it."

"How did you find it?" Lottie asked, somewhat suspiciously, even though she was poring over the map as intensely as we were.

"One of my online contacts told me it existed and where it was, and then I went and got it," Emily said.

Lottie looked at her for a long moment and then sighed. "What else have you got?" she asked.

"Does that mean you've given up trying to shut us out?" Owen asked.

"It doesn't look like I've got much of a choice," Lottie said. "I can't do as much as I used to, and getting more people involved was the whole point of moving here. I guess I just thought it would take longer to come to this."

Owen reached across and took her hand. She looked down, as through realizing for the first time that his hands were bigger than hers were.

"Well, the mine plan gives us a kind of backup if something really big should go down," Emily said. "We can plan for a large-scale dragon encounter and not have to worry about the populace getting in the way."

"We don't have anyone to fight the dragons with," Lottie said. "It's just us."

"We know," Owen said. "Everyone else is going north."

"It's a numbers game," Lottie said. She didn't look down at her leg, but she did tighten her hand on her knee, and I saw her wince. "It's exactly the sort of thing I wanted to stop by coming here, that kind of cold government decision that punches everything into a spreadsheet and decides who is worth saving.

But there were more dragons than I could have ever expected, and I don't know what to do."

"Pizza's here!" said Hannah loudly from the doorway, and we all jumped. She set the trays down on the counter and looked at our serious faces, her levity vanishing. "What's going on?"

"Just put them on the table, love," Lottie said. "And we'll serve ourselves."

Hannah shuffled the trays and a stack of plates onto the table and sat down. Owen passed the plates around so we could take our own slices.

"They've figured out that we're not getting any backup," Lottie told her wife.

"That doesn't mean we're outmatched," I said. "It just means we have to stop playing defense."

"What do you mean?" Lottie said.

I took a bite of pizza before answering and immediately burned the roof of my mouth on the sauce. Smithy pizzas were definitely hot.

"She means that we shouldn't wait around for the dragons to come to us," Owen said. "That we should go to the hatching ground and end it."

"You can't just *end* a hatching ground," Hannah pointed out. "If you could, the Americans would have been back in Michigan two decades ago."

"Queen Victoria did it," Owen said. "Sort of."

"She had countless dragon slayers at her beck and call," Lottie pointed out. "We have two and a half."

"Three and a half," Emily said. Everyone looked sharply at her. "Hannah's not registered, but everyone knows she's at least as good as Owen."

"It's true," Owen said to his aunt. "If I count, so do you."

"Thank you," she said, and squeezed his hand.

"There's also the Guard," I said. "Which means we can leave any actual evacuation or crowd management to other people and focus on the dragons themselves."

"You think people will listen to teenagers?" Hannah said.

"They did in Wingham," I pointed out.

"And you've had very good press since then," Emily added, speaking with her mouth full.

"I'm glad we have you to help us manage that," Hannah told her. "I thought the Internet was going to make our jobs more difficult, and for a while it did, but I have to admit that with control and practice, it's been as useful a tool as Siobhan's songs or Owen's sword."

"It's the timing," Lottie said, steering the conversation back on track with a fond look at Hannah. "That's what's been slowing us up."

"What do you mean?" I asked.

"The dragon eggs will hatch in three weeks, give or take," she said. She looked at Owen. "Just in time for your birthday."

"Great," he said.

"When that happens, the baby dragons will swarm down from Manitoulin, or up to the stacks in Sudbury, and we'll be overrun." She reached under the map of the mine and pulled out the map of Ontario so we could see what she was talking about.

"So we have to get to the eggs before then," I said.

"Yes, but the adults will be guarding them," Lottie said. "And we don't have enough dragon slayers for that kind of frontal assault."

"Is there a way to lure the dragons away from the island?" Emily asked.

"There's always a way to do that," Hannah said.

I knew exactly what she was talking about. I'd seen it in a classroom, the first time Mr. Huffman ran the Offense/Defense Friday exercise with us. There was always a way to lure a dragon, but it involved setting yourself on fire.

"We could blow up the mine," Emily said. "And hope for prevailing winds."

"No one is going to go for that," Owen said. "And even if they did, we'd be so busy defending Saltrock that no one could be spared to go to Manitoulin."

"Plus, your first plan was for everyone to hide in the salt mine," I told her.

"I didn't say it was a *good* idea," she said. "I just didn't want to leave anything out in case it sparked an idea in someone else."

"I think you're on the right track," Hannah said. She held a pizza crust in her hand and was using it to draw circles on her plate. "We can't blow up the mine, but there are other things. It just needs to be a big enough explosion."

"Big enough to make Saltrock a more appealing target than Sudbury," Lottie said. "Which won't be easy. But I think we can do it."

"Do it like the canal," Owen said. "Like the Suez Canal, but your version of it, Siobhan. The one where you lit yourself on fire."

I didn't say anything, even though I could hear the opening chords of the piece. The others looked confused, but they hadn't been in class that day. Owen grabbed the sticky notes and started to place them offshore of the mine. Hannah whistled, and Lottie's eyes widened.

"We'll use tankers," Owen said. "We'll push them out toward Michigan. When they're far enough offshore, we'll blow them up remotely."

"It's still not that easy," Emily said. "There will have to be the right wind conditions and a dragon attacking so it can call in others."

"That hasn't been a problem lately," I pointed out. "There have been sightings all the time."

"What about the environmental fallout from the tankers?" Emily asked.

"You can't make an omelet without breaking the eggs," Lottie said, and then grimaced at her inadvertent pun. "But we'll do our best to limit the damage."

"That still leaves us with the problem of who goes to Manitoulin," Owen pointed out.

"I might be able to help with that," said Aodhan from the doorway. I hadn't even heard him come in, but before I could turn around to say hello, I caught sight of Owen's face and froze.

I looked at Hannah and Lottie, and they both seemed surprised as well. Emily just looked as confused as I felt. Slowly, I turned around. There was Aodhan, sure enough, and behind him there stood a woman with dark hair. She looked vaguely familiar, but I couldn't place where I had seen her. She was well-muscled and she stood like a fighter, so I knew she must be a dragon slayer too. But there was no one we could call. All the Canadian dragon slayers were spoken for.

And that, of course, was it. She wasn't a Canadian dragon slayer. She was here for reasons that had nothing to do with patriotism or pragmatism, and had everything to do with family and personal loyalty, even though she looked like she wasn't sure how she would be received. I had sat next to her picture in the back of Aodhan's Volkswagen, and now she had traveled all this way to help. I looked back at Owen and waited to take my cues from him.

He found his voice at last and stood up from the table.

"Hi, Mom," he said, and the symphony flared to life, waking up every single person who sat in the audience.

THE STORY OF AODHAN

And now we come at last to the story of a dragon slayer who is not a hero, though if you live in a small town in southwestern Ontario, you might recall his name. Aodhan Thorskard was born to a fine dragon slayer line, descended from Vikings and famed in both Europe and North America for the fighters it had produced. He trained from when he was old enough to hold a sword, fighting side by side with his sister Lottie, who was two years his elder, under their mother's tutelage. Though he grew both taller and broader than his sister did, he could never match her speed or her skill.

There was no rivalry between them on this point, however. They worked in concert throughout their training, playing to one another's strengths. For where she was fast-thinking and impetuous, he was often a keener mind in strategy and by. far a better a tracker. Together, they made a nearly unstoppable team.

But *nearly* is *not quite.*

Both were sent to the Middle East when their tour time came. Lottie went two years before, and when she was finished her required four, she volunteered for another pair of summers in the desert, so that she could see her brother to the end of his time. They fought side by side, with the others in the Oil Watch and with the regular military, for three years.

While the Iraqis and the Kuwaitis fought bitterly in the desert for the ownership of the oil beneath the sand, the dragons gathered in the skies. "Thank your lucky stars the dragons don't realize they could light the oil fields aflame," the drill sergeants would say, risking a cigarette because there would be better targets elsewhere. "Or we'd be in real trouble." As though the trouble wasn't real enough.

Lottie wasn't on duty the day the fires started in earnest, but Aodhan was. He saw the Republican Guard strike team at the very last moment, right as they stood poised to shoot. He could not stop the shot; he could not stop the flames that engulfed the oil rig closest to the Oil Watch barracks. But he thought he might be able to stop the dragon that made straight for the smoke.

The Oil Watch is supposed to patrol in teams, but the fires were hotter than ever, and Aodhan's non-dragon slayer support crew hesitated when Aodhan made his charge. He ordered them to stay and call for reinforcement, and he sent one of them— the youngest, who could run the most swiftly—to bring Lottie as quickly as she could. Then Aodhan turned back to the fire and went in.

No account was made of his exploits when he passed beyond the sight of his support crew, and there was no bard to make guesses at his tale. The soldiers could see his dark shape, and the bigger shape of the dragon, through the flames, but they could see no detail. They could hear the dragon roar, and with each bellow it spit more fire into the air, and the flames spread from rig to rig, with nothing done to check their terrible march.

The screams of dragons filled the air, as more came scenting on the carbon fumes and they turned to fight with one another. And still Aodhan strove against them, though it seemed too hot to bear, and Lottie did not come.

The flames engulfed the barracks too, spreading to the infirmary and mess before anything could be done. Human screams joined the dragons' then, and Aodhan could not go to them, could not stop the flames. Finally, in the distance, there was the whine of helicopters that could, at the very least, evacuate the Oil Watch until the worst of the frenzy had passed.

In this moment of desperation, a Venezuelan dragon slayer, who had escaped the barracks with nothing but her sword, her shield, and the clothes on her back, came to fight by Aodhan's side. Her name was Catalina, and in her time with the Oil Watch, she and Aodhan had often trained together. Their friendship was great, and she would not let him fight alone. She leaped into the fire, and they stood back to back, with their swords before them while the dragons circled. He had slayed two of them already, too hurried to make it clean, and now they faced a third.

"We must get clear of them," they say she said, though how anyone could know is unclear. "We must not stay!"

Together they struck, each of their swords slicing through one of the dragon's hearts as it reared above them and then fell dead to the ground. They vaulted over the dragon's body, grasping at the spines along its back when they would have slid across its scales, and pulled themselves out of the fire. Then, though it went against both training and instinct, they ran. They ran until the dry air seared their lungs more caustically than the fire had, and when they could run no more, they lay down in the desert to die.

At last came Lottie Thorskard, with the helicopter that bore her brother and her compatriot to safety. They were both of them burned, but they were alive, which was more than could be said of those who had been trapped in the barracks and the infirmary when the flames took hold. Fully half the company had burned, and the oil rigs with them. It was the worst loss of life since the Oil Watch was begun. Also dead were the sentries who guarded the outer reaches of the camp; the Iraqi strike team had killed them when they breached the perimeter. It was some small solace that the strike team had not escaped either.

There are many ways for people to deal with trauma. Some drink to forget. Some pretend it never happened in the first place. Some commiserate and forge bonds in grief that might not otherwise come to be. Thus it was with Aodhan and Catalina. One month later, during a physical to check the progress of her healed burns, the Watch Doctor determined that Catalina was pregnant, and she was immediately retired from the Oil Watch—though not discharged, on account of her bravery on the day the rigs were burned.

The surviving members of the company voted unanimously to relegate Aodhan to safer duties, but in truth this was a formality. Though his body had healed well from the fight, his mind was slower to follow. None spoke against him, on account of Lottie, but everyone knew that he would never be the giant he had been. He took to his new duties with the same loyalty he had always shown, but with none of the vitality.

Owen Thorskard was born on the twenty-third day of April, 1995. On the first of May, his mother was sent back to Venezuela. Her time in the Oil Watch was done, and she longed for home. Two weeks later, Aodhan Thorskard landed in Trenton with his sister, his soon-to-be sister-in-law, and his son. Catalina would become a hero in her own country, and songs would be sung of her for long years after her death. Lottie's tale you know already, for she is the most famous of all the dragon slayers since St. George. Owen's story is still being written, but you have heard it whispered on the wind.

Of Aodhan Thorskard, I cannot sing. His mission failed. The oil fields he watched over burned. I cannot sing to you of him, for there are no songs to be sung.

MEETING CATALINA

There have been a few moments in my life when I have felt more awkward. Once, when I was playing at an outdoor concert, a sudden gust of wind had made off with my sheet music. I had to stop an entire jazz orchestra while I and helpful members of the audience chased the pages. Another time, I got turned around in the middle of "Für Elise" and skipped the entire fast part. But this, sitting at the table with my cooling pizza on my plate and Owen's mother behind me, was the worst.

For her part, Emily looked genuinely curious. I couldn't remember if Owen had ever mentioned his mother to her, but I figured she probably had the Internet to fill her in. Fortunately, she was way too smart to accept everything she read as fact, and she was way too gracious to ask questions. She usually reacted to things more quickly than I did, and I hoped that she would come up with a reason for the two of us to leave the room, but she didn't say a word.

"Aodhan, Cat, come on in," said Hannah, like this was a

weekly occurrence. "There's lots of pizza. Grab a plate."

"Still making it in the forge?" Owen's mother asked, sitting down and helping herself to a slice. "I hope so. I've missed it."

"There are other ways?" Hannah said, smiling. She elbowed Lottie in the stomach, subtly, but I still noticed.

"Perish the thought," Lottie said, having swallowed her surprise. "Owen, get your parents something to drink. There's more pop in the garage and it should be cold enough."

"I'll help," I said, and jumped up from the table. I felt extremely gauche, but Owen looked at me gratefully. "Anyone else want a refill?"

Once we had safely escaped to the garage, I watched Owen get cans out of the carton.

"You can call her Catalina, by the way," he said, as though that was my biggest concern. "She prefers it. She says North Americans always butcher her last name."

"Okay," I said. I took a few of the cans. "Are you all right with this?"

"I just wish Dad had told me, that's all," he said. I couldn't tell if he was telling the truth. "I don't like being surprised."

"He probably just didn't want you to be let down if she said no," I said.

"She never says no," Owen told me. His voice was flat. "Well, she said no twice: once to marrying him and once to moving to Canada, but Dad wasn't willing to move to Venezuela either, so . . ." He stacked the cans up in his arms as he trailed off.

"Are you sure you're okay?" I asked again.

"You know how in stories, there's always the hero and the heroine, and they can't live together for whatever reason, and

258

everyone always says how romantic and tragic it is?" he said. I nodded. "Well, it just sucks," he continued. "But you learn to live with what you've got, and appreciate the fact that people love you."

"Oh," I said, tremendously grateful for my excessively normal parents.

Owen took a deep breath, like he was getting ready to take a penalty kick or make a run at a dragon's hearts, and expelled it in a huff.

"Okay, I'm ready to go back in now," he said. "And thanks, Siobhan. For understanding."

"No problem," I told him. "But you realize that this just became the best night of Emily's life, right? Even without giving away any details, she's going to be famous on the Internet tomorrow when she says she met your mother."

"She can't say anything," Owen said. "It'll blow her anonymity."

"It might be worth it," I said, and he laughed as he held the door open for me.

When we got back to the kitchen, Catalina was telling a story about defending an oil well near Caracas, and Emily was hanging on her every word. Lottie was looking on indulgently, but Hannah and Aodhan both turned, concern on their faces. Owen smiled at them, and they relaxed. Owen passed his dad a can and poured a glass of ginger ale for his mother, and then tucked in to his pizza again.

"Emily tells me you have an ambitious plan," Catalina said, turning to Owen. "I am happy to help."

"We're still working on the details," Owen said. "By which I mean please suggest anything you can think of."

"What have I missed?" Aodhan asked, chewing while he talked. The cello in him was in full swing now, low and strong, and so, so sad. I did my best to focus on the part where he was so enormous it looked like he could break a tree in half with his bare hands.

I finished my pizza while Lottie brought him and Catalina up to speed.

"Do you think the town councils will go for that?" Aodhan asked. "Particularly Saltrock's?"

"They might if it comes from Lottie," Hannah said. "And it's not like we're strangers to property damage. I think Lottie can convince them. We'll just leave out the part where the bulk of the plan depends on two sixteen-year-olds."

"How quickly people forget that young dragon slayers were once commonplace," said Catalina. She wasn't wrong. In the years since the end of World War II and the rise of the Oil Watch, dragon slaying become something controlled by the age of the dragon slayer instead of by his or her capabilities. And even that much I only knew because of the research Emily had done. We were encouraged not to think about it.

"It's harder now," Hannah agreed. "Times have changed, and tying dragon slaying so tightly to the military only re-inforced the idea. No offense, you two."

"We're almost seventeen," said Owen at exactly the same time I said, "What?"

"You two will be the ones to go to Manitoulin," Hannah said. "I thought you suggested that in the first place."

"Not by ourselves," I said.

"There's no other choice, Siobhan," Owen said. "My parents and my aunts will have their hands full, the RCMD slayers in Tobermory will cover everything north of Kincardine by default, and that leaves us to actually go to Manitoulin."

"And do what, exactly?" I demanded. "Light the whole island on fire?"

"If we have to," Owen said.

"Great," I said. "Just give me a minute."

You might think it's hard to freak out when you are sitting at a table with three living legends, but I can tell you that it is not. The eighth notes that had skittered around in my head while Hannah and I hid in the shelter the first time split into sixteenths and became even more cacophonous as my thoughts tumbled over each other, close to panic. My parents were definitely going to kill me, or ground me, when I went home and told them what our plan entailed, but that was probably the least, not to mention the most unlikely, of my worries. Panic made for unlikely thoughts—thoughts I knew were inadequate for the moment but were all I had nonetheless. The extended Thorskard family, and Emily, watched while I sorted myself out, which was a blessing because I couldn't forget that I was not going to do this alone. I leaned forward and set my hands on the table.

"Okay," I said, taking a deep breath. "Okay, I'm good to go. Whenever we need to go. Just tell me when that is."

Catalina smiled at me, and I could tell she was thinking "Where did they find *this* one?" But the music in my blood was evening out, so I didn't really mind.

"It will probably take us at least a week to get the town councils on our side," Hannah said thoughtfully. "Not to mention get the tankers."

"We'll have time to run plenty of drills in the meantime,"

Lottie said. "Which is good. I don't want people to panic when they find out that they have to hide in the salt mine."

"Should we encourage people to leave town altogether?" Emily asked.

"Where are they going to go?" I said. "Toronto will be bracing for Muskoka hatch, and everywhere south of us will be getting ready for Michigan."

"Siobhan's right," Catalina said. "The important thing is to stay close to home and close to a shelter where we know that people can be protected."

"Aunt Lottie could go on the radio," Owen suggested. "Not the CBC, but the local channels."

Emily was taking notes.

"Owen and Siobhan are going to need a boat as well," Aodhan reminded us. "Siobhan can drive as far as Tobermory, but after that they'll need a boat."

"I don't really fancy swimming with my broadsword," Owen said. "So yes, a boat would be appreciated."

"Will the RCMD get in our way in Tobermory?" I asked. That could throw a rather large wrench into our plans.

"No," Aodhan said. "I was in Basra with the commanding officer there, and he owes me one."

"He owes you more than one," Catalina said quietly. Aodhan flinched, and she squeezed his hand.

"In any case," said Aodhan, pressing on as if nothing had happened, "they can't do much to help us, because they're going to be under attack themselves, but they can stay out of your way and that will be enough."

"Do you know how to drive a boat?" I asked, turning to Owen.

"No, but it can't be that hard," he said. "Plus, I figured you'd drive."

"You really need to get your license. You know that, right?" I said.

"When we're done, I promise I will take the test," he said.

"I can monitor the news for you," Emily said. "And plant suggestions, if you need them."

"You really think that'll help?" Aodhan asked.

"I got Mr. Huffman to assign that essay on the history of dragon slayer cooperation while pretending to be an Australian graduate student," she said, somehow managing to not look guilty. "I think with a bit of practice I can handle national media."

"You and your father are dangerous people," Lottie said. "I'm glad you're on our side."

"Always," Emily said. "I want my town to be safe as much as anyone does, but I can see the big picture better on account of not actually owning a house there."

"Wait a minute," I said. "When you were talking about burning the hatching ground, you were exaggerating, right? We can't actually use fire or we'll destroy Manitoulin."

"Before they hatch, dragons aren't really as toxic," Lottie said. "They haven't had time to ingest carbon yet. Physically smashing each egg would take forever, and if the dragons are close enough to hatching, you might just release them. Fire is the only way. Manitoulin is already abandoned because of how close it is to Michigan, so this will just be finishing it off."

"There really isn't a choice in the matter," Hannah said. "It's like the tankers. Some things are going to be sacrificed."

"Some people, too?" I asked.

The adults froze. And then Hannah took me by the shoulders and held on so tightly, I thought I might fold in half.

"We will do everything we can," she said. "You know that we will. But yes. Some people too."

I looked around the table. Lottie couldn't fight as hard as she wanted, but I knew she wouldn't flinch from whatever battle was thrust upon her. Hannah was a smith, not a dragon slayer by trade, but she wouldn't let anything get between her and Owen's safety. Aodhan couldn't look up from his hands, which I knew were twisted in his lap, caught in a fire only he could see, but he would face danger head-on. And Catalina, who'd come all this way just because Aodhan had asked. I looked at Owen, who was wider now than he had been at the start of soccer season and looked more like his father than ever before. When I met Emily's eyes, she was still smiling. This might be the last time we all sat together and had pizza made from the same forge that made our swords. If I had to, I couldn't have made any other choices than the ones that had brought me to the table with them.

"Okay," I said, and the orchestra swelled into the final act behind me as all the parts were finally assembled. "Okay."

THE LAST DAY ON EARTH

It took Lottie three hours on Monday morning to make her case to the town council in Trondheim, and another six to get Saltrock to agree. After that, the town and county councils to the north fell in line as well, as did the ones to the south, though they were mostly out of the line of fire. By Tuesday, the leaflets were made up and distributed. On Wednesday I skipped school for the second time to learn how to drive the boat that would carry me, Owen, and my car from Tobermory to Manitoulin.

There were three dragon attacks during the week, but none of them were in places where we could spring the trap we'd set in Saltrock. They were all too far inland, and the wind was blowing the wrong direction. By Friday night, Owen was nearly frantic with impatience, and Hannah made him turn over the vegetable garden by hand just to get him out of the house. Aodhan and Catalina patrolled together, both reacquainting with each other and introducing Catalina to the local color. Everyone seemed quite taken with her, even though it was made very clear that she would not be staying, and before long she had at least as many fans as Aodhan did. I have no idea what Lottie did to pass the time.

My mother made me stay pretty close to home that week. I still went to school, which, as I said, was sort of an exercise in futility, but at least it was something to do. If nothing else, the meditation portions of my drama class were handy. Soccer was cancelled until further notice, but Guard practice continued after school. That was the only time I saw Owen relax.

Emily, whose father might not have been quite as sanguine about her Internet activities as she had thought he would be, reported that the news was quiet. The whole country was holding its breath and waiting for the hatching season to begin. The only big piece of news came on Friday night, when it was officially announced that the government dragon slayers were being sent north to protect Sudbury and the shores of Lake Superior. This was the only official admission of the new hatching ground on Manitoulin, though the specifics were not given on the broadcast, and it was as close as we got to receiving any government help. As we had suspected, we were on our own.

I spent my time reading books about boats, writing songs about boats, and trying not to think about all the ways in which a dragon could sink a boat. I had gone down to the lake a few times to watch the tugs in the harbor as they moved the tankers into place. This was before Mum decided we needed to spend more quality time together. She even took a week off from work. I know she was trying to be supportive, but the way she complimented all of my musical endeavors and cooked my favorite foods all week only made me feel more and more like I was never coming home. It was kind of nice not to face questions about my future, though. ·

Saturday was probably the longest day of my life, Bolero over and over again, with its unchanging melody and its slow, slow build to an entirely anticlimactic finish. It was a beautiful day, bright sun and blue sky, like the trumpets in the song, but I couldn't shake the urgency of the ostinato snare drum under-neath. What few clouds dotted the sky all looked like dragons to me, and every time one shaded the sun, I couldn't help but flinch.

I had planned to go over to Owen's house and work off some tension by sword fighting, but Dad was home along with Mum, and they had the whole day mapped out, starting with Dad's mission to turn the garden over.

We worked side by side, hacking through the newly thawed ground to turn over the fresh brown earth that would grow vegetables and flowers. Dad had decided to plant more food this year, a sign of forethought that I at first took to be opti-mistic, but as I looked at the expression on his face, I started to wonder if maybe having his own food source was his way of coping with such an uncertain future. At least he was growing enough to feed three.

"Just after your third birthday," he said, carefully lining pea seeds along the furrow he'd just finished, "your mother read an article in one of those parenting magazines that said if kids only colored in coloring books, it would stunt their creativity."

I stopped shaking soil out of grass roots and looked over at him. He didn't stop working. He didn't even look up. But he did keep talking.

"I don't remember the details, exactly," he went on. "Something about how it limited imagination and how, with small children especially, there would be frustration because you wouldn't have the motor skills to stay inside the lines. So we took away your coloring books and replaced them with blank paper."

I don't remember any of this, but it's a very good story. Perhaps I come by storytelling more naturally than I'd thought.

"And then, it was the craziest thing," he said. "Because you drew nothing but lines. Lines and dots and lines and dots. And it didn't make sense."

He smiled, lost in this memory of me that I could not recall, and started covering the peas with dirt.

"We used to keep your grandmother's hymnal on the piano, do you remember?" he asked. "Before it was covered with your sheet music, back when the piano was more of a decoration than anything else."

"I remember that," I said.

"Well, it was always open," he said. "And somehow, somehow you knew it was music. So you drew it. You drew your own notes and staff, even before you knew any of the rules. You made music."

I was never one of those kids whose artwork decorated the fridge. Now I knew why. I also knew, without asking, that those childhood symphonies were packed away somewhere in the house, and that if I someday wanted to make sense of them, I would be able to.

"You're the daughter of an accountant and a doctor," he said. "We just assumed school was in your blood, and that you were hedging because you were starting to wonder if we'd appreciate it more if you went into something like biochemistry."

I made a face at that, and he laughed. I wanted to hear him laugh again. For years.

"I won't lie," he said. "We'd rather it was something safe. But I think I understand. Most people have a job. They find their community, their people, at school or in the workplace. But you have a vocation, same as Owen does. Same as your mother does, really. And I would never dream of discouraging either of you."

"I wish it was something safe too," I told him. "But it isn't, so I do what I can."

"I know," Dad said. He came to stand beside me. "Will you join the Oil Watch? See the world? Or maybe just Alberta?"

It was an old joke, but the old ones are always the best. The important thing was that he laughed again.

"I'll have to talk to Hannah about the civilian branch," I said. "And then hope I can pass the physical requirements, but yeah. That's what I've been thinking about."

"We didn't expect you to find your calling so young," Dad said. "But you did. And we'll do our best to make it happen."

I didn't say anything, because the tears were too close. They hadn't volunteered to send their child off to possible death; I had made them do it. And still, they were going to. And they were going to do their best to make sure I had a house and a garden and a future if I came back home. My hands were covered in dirt, and there wasn't any music in them at the moment, but I hugged my father anyway. And he hugged me back.

We finished the garden without talking, and then we went inside for lunch with Mum. She had rented a movie the night before, *Singing in the Rain*, and announced that we would watch it when we were done eating. Dad made popcorn in his old-style popcorn maker, which invariably burned everything so Mum always made sure to have some of the microwave stuff standing by, and I made root beer floats. By this point, even with Dad's earlier reassurances, I was discovering nerves I didn't even know I possessed. Sugar was probably the last thing I needed, but at least the root beer didn't have caffeine.

Just as the movie was ending, the phone rang, and for just one moment, I hoped it was the dragon attack we had been waiting for so I could finally put myself out of my misery. Dad answered it before I could, and I could tell from his expression that he was seriously debating whether or not to hand the receiver to me, before he finally did.

"Hello?" I said, a bit cautiously because Dad hadn't told me who it was.

"Hi, Siobhan." It was Catalina. Her accent was a bit thicker over the phone, but I still had no problem understanding her. I'd realized by now that her English grammar was probably better than mine was. "How are you?"

"Oh, you know," I said casually. "Keeping on."

"As are we," she replied. "Owen has finished in the garden if you would like to come over, but your father said it was some kind of family day?"

"We're watching my favorite movie and drinking root beer floats," I admitted.

"Siobhan," Catalina said, all business. "Are they acting like it's your last day on earth?"

"Kind of," I said. I knew my parents couldn't hear her, but the urge to whisper my responses was overwhelming.

"In that case, you must come," she said. "You do not need

any more nerves than you have."

"Thank you," I said effusively. I looked at Mum and saw the beginnings of a frown.

"Put your mother on," Catalina said. "I will straighten her out."

I handed the phone to Mum and listened to her half of the conversation with Owen's mother. Mum's face started off looking very determined, but as she listened to Catalina speak, her expression shifted, until finally she bid Catalina good night and hung up.

"Apparently Owen needs you," Mum said. She almost looked like she believed it. "Hannah has some updated charts of the area you'll be boating through, and she wants to the two of you to go over them together."

"Well," I said in my very best *man, I really wish I didn't have to leave* voice. "At least we got the gardening done."

"You are a terrible liar," she said, and pulled me in for a hug. The worst part was that I really wasn't. I just had better secrets to keep. I felt Dad's arms wrap around the pair of us. "We're just so worried."

"I know," I said. "And believe me, I'm worried too. I just can't think about it anymore unless I'm doing something active about it."

"Like looking at charts?" Dad asked.

"Yeah," I said, not fooling anyone.

"Drive carefully," Mum said, and of course I did, both there and back home again. I slept safe and sound in my own bed, where I could pretend that they didn't each get up three times in the middle of the night to come into my room and stare at me for a while.

On Sunday, the Anglican church held a special St. George's Day ceremony. I played the organ as usual and did my best to ignore all the stares I could feel boring into the back of my head. Traditionally, all the churches in Trondheim got together and put on a picnic (if it was warm enough), or something, for St. George's Day, but this year no one decided to force joviality on the day. The holiday was technically on Monday anyway, the same day as Owen's birthday, and the town seem stuck between bartering that coincidence for all it was worth and trying to ignore it in case they somehow jinxed us.

Catalina fell solidly into the celebration side. She baked a cake to celebrate Owen's seventeenth birthday, carefully recreating an iconic image of the saint slaying a dragon in candy and sugar on the top. It was delicious, which I know because she let me eat the cake scraps that were left over from transferring it from the pan to the plate after I had finally escaped my parents and made it to the Thorskard house on Saturday. But Owen never got to eat it.

Instead, in the early afternoon, there was a call from the weekend janitor at the school board office on the cliffs in Saltrock. A dragon had been sighted, weather conditions were perfect, and everything was in place.

EN ROUTE TO MANITOULIN

Owen Thorskard turned seventeen in the dark on Country Road 10, just north of Hanover. Neither one of us noticed until nearly a quarter past midnight. Our minds were elsewhere.

"Happy birthday," I said when I saw him staring at the clock. I didn't want to know what he was thinking.

"Thanks," he said. "I wish I'd thought to pack some cake."

"It'll be there when we get back," I told him. Assuming the house was there too, of course. I suspected that Hannah would have at least put the cake in the fridge, if not the freezer, both of which were typically unharmed in all but the most severe dragon attacks. "And we've got enough food for an army."

It was true. When the Thorskards planned, they planned inclusively. As soon as the dragon sighting in Saltrock was confirmed, Hannah had produced fully-stocked hampers for all of the groups, though the ones for Lottie and Aodhan were mostly packed with first aid equipment, since they would be in a place where food would be easy to find. Our hamper fit into the trunk of my car. It nestled between the extra gasoline we'd laid aside for when we were on the uninhabited Manitoulin, and the flamethrowers that Hannah had spent the week developing off of plans that Emily found on the Internet.

"I'm not sure I'm okay with this," Hannah had said when Emily had produced the blueprints.

"I don't know what your problem is," Lottie had said, one of her increasingly rare smiles on her face. "You're not the one who is going to have the Ministry of Defense wondering why you Googled 'how to make flamethrowers.'"

"I'm not worried either," Emily had said brightly. "I used a school computer."

Hannah had sighed and then proceeded to make several modifications to the plans that she absolutely forbade Emily from uploading to the web.

"I'm still not comfortable with the part of this plan that involves the trunk being full of flammable gas and a machine designed to create flames," Owen said.

"Well, we couldn't put the flamethrowers in the backseat, because if we hit a bump the swords might pierce the gas can," I reminded him. "And if the gas is in the backseat, it's too hard to secure."

"I know *why* we did it," he said. "I just don't like it."

Neither did I. But I wasn't going to say it out loud. We had enough to worry about.

Outside the car window, it was pitch dark. We saw the odd stop sign with a blinking red light on it, and on the rare occasion when we crossed what passed for a major intersection, there might be one streetlight to keep cars from T-boning each other, but aside from that, the countryside was dark. Even in the places where I knew there were farms, I saw only blackness. Anyone who was home had turned off all the lights and retreated into their dragon shelters, just as they were supposed to.

"I hope the evacuation went okay," I said, mostly because the silence was getting more and more terrifying for me.

"We've had lots of practice," Owen reminded me.

"I meant in Kincardine and Southampton," I said. We had just passed the turnoff for those towns. "I hope they've all battened down like they were supposed to."

It was some distance from Saltrock to Manitoulin, even with the wind and the attraction the mine held for the dragons. If our plan worked, and we got a full-blown aerial assault, I'd hate to be the one person in Kincardine who was dumb enough to be idling in the Tim Horton's drive-thru when the dragons flew overhead.

"Everyone will be fine, Siobhan," Owen said, and I knew to drop it.

"I don't suppose you could nap?" I told him. At least then I could talk quietly to myself.

"I really doubt it," he said. We were going to arrive in the dark as it was, and we'd have to wait for sunup before crossing the strait in the waiting boat, but I didn't think I'd be doing any sleeping either. "You could sing," he said.

"I am not going to sing," I said.

"You sing all the time!" he said.

"I do not!" I argued.

"You really do," he said. "You don't even know it, but you do. Half the time, I don't recognize the song, either, so I assume it's something you've made up, but you sing all the time."

"I'm not going to sing," I repeated.

"Fine," he said. "Then tell me a story."

"That I can do," I said. "What do you want to hear?"

"Tell me how perfectly everything is going to go tomorrow," he said. I could hear his hands tightening on his kneecaps, as he willed the car forward and the sun to rise and everything else he couldn't control. "Tell me how we win."

"Okay," I said. "But you have to close your eyes and pretend you're sleeping."

"Deal," he said and closed his eyes.

"Once upon a time," I started. I went with a traditional opening because I was stalling for time. "Once upon a time, there was a dragon slayer named Owen. He was the son of two great dragon slayers, the nephew of a third, and also the nephew of the greatest living smith. And even though he had only just turned seventeen, he already had some very complicated dragon battles under his belt, and more than a few slayings to his name."

Owen relaxed, just a bit, in the seat beside me. I took a breath and kept going.

"One day, Owen learned of a new hatching ground, north of where he lived and far from the control of the government. At first, no one believed him when he spoke about the danger, but soon everyone saw the truth and a great plan was made to keep everyone safe.

"The villagers and townspeople practiced diligently, until every one of them knew exactly what to do when the evacuation alarm sounded. Some went into their own shelters, and some went to their neighbors'. Dr. McQuaid went to the reinforced section of the hospital with her patients and waited in case any new injured people should be brought in by the brave paramedics.

"In Saltrock, Archie Carmichael led everyone into the mine, because Saltrock was going to be the most at risk, but in all the other towns, from Sauble Beach to Kettle Point, people made their preparations as well, so that everyone would be as safe and secure as possible."

That part was true. We'd seen the beginnings of it in Trondheim before we left, and I'd watched the drills in Saltrock enough times to know that they would go smoothly. And Owen was right: the other towns would be equally well prepared. Now came the hard part.

"The brave dragon slayers were ready too," I said, and somehow managed not to choke. "Aodhan and Catalina harried the dragon that had been sighted near the school board office, luring it in and then driving it off as they tried to buy time. Lottie Thorskard, the greatest dragon slayer since St. George himself, climbed to the top of the grain elevators, even though it pained her to do it on account of her leg, and settled in to wait. From her perch, she would be able to direct the other dragon slayers, and should a dragon make a run at her on her great height, she would still be able to pick it off as it dove for her.

"Hannah stood at the end of pier, waiting for the signal. When Aodhan gave it, it was Hannah's job to get to the ships moored offshore and evacuate the last of the skeleton crews to land so they could set off the explosions."

"I know all that," Owen said quietly, without opening his eyes. "What about us?"

"I'm getting to it," I said, dropping my storyteller persona a bit peevishly. I'd been on a roll. "There's a style to this sort of thing, you know. That's why you hired a professional."

"A thousand apologies, o bard," Owen said grandiosely. "Pray, continue."

I was still called "bard" infrequently enough that hearing him say it stirred something inside me. Even though he was making light, I knew he meant it. But this wasn't the time to stop and treasure moments. This was the time to plow on through them and hope for the best.

"But that was not the full extent of the plan," I continued the tale. "For Owen and his loyal bard were hastening north in the bard's intrepid Toyota Corolla—"

"Are you seriously referring to yourself in third person?" Owen interrupted, this time sitting forward and opening his eyes.

"*Style*, barbarian!" I said. This had clearly been a brilliant idea. Both of us were actually having fun and forgetting, for whatever short periods of time, what it was we were driving toward. "And stop interrupting."

"Okay," he said.

"For Owen and his loyal bard were hastening north in the bard's intrepid Toyota Corolla," I said again, backtracking to get back into the groove. "Their destination was Tobermory, and the small boat that would take them to Manitoulin Island, where the dragon eggs were waiting, unhatched and, if the lure in Saltrock had worked, unguarded."

I was so caught up in the story that I nearly blew through the red light where Country Road 10 turned into Highway 6 and intersected with 21. There wasn't anything around to hit, but it was the first traffic light we'd seen in an hour, and missing it would have been a shame. It would have been faster to take Highway 21, but that road hugged the lake and was, for obvious reasons, a bad idea tonight.

"After driving quite safely and legally all the way to Tobermory," I continued, having gotten the car back into fifth gear after its sudden stop, "Owen boarded the waiting tug and made his way to Manitoulin Island, where he found the waiting dragon eggs as unhatched and as unguarded as he had hoped.

"Using the flamethrower built by his multitalented Aunt Hannah, Owen ignited the eggs, causing flames from one end of the island to the other. They burned all day long, and when the sun set and the flames were extinguished, nothing remained of Manitoulin but the Precambrian Shield from which it came, and the dock where the boat was moored so that Owen could make his journey back to civilization."

"Convenient," Owen murmured. I ignored him.

"Thus did Owen, dragon slayer of Trondheim, return home to much glory and success. And birthday cake! As he had recently turned seventeen."

"I like that story," Owen said, after a few moments of silence had passed.

"So do I," I told him.

But that's not what happened.

THE ONCOMING ARPEGGIO

The boat was ready, just as promised, and rigged so that I could drive the car right onto the deck behind the wheelhouse. We were installed on the boat by just after three in the morning, having stopped for gas and a brief meal at the Mountie station. We weren't due to take the boat out until daylight, or until the dragons deserted the island, whichever came first. Even though I thought I was too tightly wound to sleep, I must have drifted off because the next thing I remember after putting the parking brake on was Owen gently shaking my shoulder to wake me up. There was a strange sound, unlike anything I had ever heard before. It was like the softest percussion imaginable played by hundreds of musicians; the slow, soft roll of brushes, multiplied a hundredfold.

Owen was leaning forward and looking up. I unfastened my seatbelt and mirrored his movement, squirming to avoid accidentally pressing the horn. What I saw very nearly stopped my heart.

There were dragons in the sky, hundreds of them, and some not very far above the car. The whisper I could hear was the sound of their wings cutting through the morning air as they flew. They were leaving Manitoulin, and they were heading for Saltrock.

I like to consider myself a fairly rational person. I knew that these dragons had already zoned in on a carbon source and were unlikely to turn away from it for any reason. I knew that the car hadn't been turned on in hours and that any carbon it had emitted had long since dissipated. I knew that the dragons were flying so quickly they probably didn't even see us. But that didn't stop the bubble of absolute panic that rose in my chest. I fought down a scream and sat back, my knuckles whitening around the steering wheel.

Owen pried my fingers loose, also careful to avoid the horn, and laced his fingers with mine. We sat there in complete silence, hardly daring to breathe, until the last of the dragons passed over our heads and out of our sight down the coastline. Then I pulled my hands back into my lap and took a deep breath.

"Next time," I said when I got my voice back, "you can feel free to let me sleep through that."

"Next time?" Owen said, but his voice cracked a bit, and that rather perversely made me feel better. He'd woken me up because he couldn't face the dragons on his own.

"You know what I mean," I said. I looked around again, making absolutely sure it was safe to get out of the car. I reached over to put the keys in the glove compartment and then opened my door. "Let's get this show on the road."

Dragons fly much faster than boats putter across nearly

open water, so by the time Owen and I made landfall on Manitoulin, Aodhan and Catalina had already engaged the main horde in Saltrock, with Hannah helping out where she could and Lottie monitoring them from above. The dragons had begun to fight amongst themselves over the burning ships almost immediately, but there were other sources of carbon in Saltrock, and a group of them had splintered off and headed for the downtown core instead of in the general direction of Michigan like we had hoped they would.

But I didn't know any of that as I maneuvered the tug up alongside the sturdiest-looking of the piers that still remained standing at South Baymouth.

"Tie us off as close as you can," I shouted to Owen. "We have to get the car on there."

"In hindsight, ATVs might have been a better idea," Owen said, but he did what I told him.

"Where would you carry your sword?" I asked.

"Good point," he replied, pulling as hard as he could. "That's as good as it's going to get."

I looked at the mooring, not entirely pleased with what I saw.

"Okay, this is what we'll do," I said. "Take everything out and put it on the deck. Then I'll get the car onto the pier and drive to land, and then we'll load back up again."

"You are not ending up in the lake!" Owen said.

"Not on purpose," I said. "But no one has put anything but illicit drugs on this pier in two and a half decades. I can swim to shore from here. Our stuff can't."

"Fine," Owen said, but I could tell he wasn't happy. "Roll down the windows."

Once everything was unloaded, I started the engine and tried not to think about the fact that I was probably the only source of carbon emissions between here and Sudbury. Hopefully all the dragons were gone. I carefully drove onto the dock, thankful for the hours my father had made me spend parallel parking, and then inched backward until I was on solid ground that I think had, at one time, actually been a road surface.

"Okay," I called back to where Owen stood watching. "We can reload now."

Owen took the opportunity to reorganize, unwrapping both his usual sword and mine so the latter lay across the backseat and the former was tip-down between his knees, his hands resting on the pommel. I repacked the trunk, removing some of the breakfast food that Hannah had packed, and passed Owen some beef jerky, which I knew he liked better. I checked the flamethrowers to make sure that nothing had shifted and made sure the gas cans were still closed properly. Then I closed the trunk and got back in the car.

"You ready?" I asked.

"I am," he said. I knew he meant it. "Just do me one favor."

"Today you can have anything," I said.

"When you tell people this story, don't mention any of the times I throw up," he said.

"As long as you don't do it in the car," I told him.

I put the car in gear and we pulled out of South Baymouth on what remained of the Highway 6 extension. It was eerie, driving through ghost town after ghost town. This island had once been a tourist destination, where people from the city came to escape the brutal Toronto humidex and spend their time swimming and boating. You could see the skeletons of old vacation memories, stretching thin fingers out of the scorched shells of restaurants and hotels and creeping along the edges of signs for fish bait, miniature golf, and small motor repair. It was like some kind of nightmarish theme park.

Evidence of draconic occupation was all around us. There were gutted animals everywhere, insides ripped out and hides left behind like some sort of half-finished taxidermy project. That meant corn dragons, which were picky eaters and didn't like fur. There were also smashed cement blocks and torn-up beach front, signs of *urbs* and *lakus*. And then there were the soot stains, long and dark against the grass, or mixing in with the sand. There were soot-streakers to be found here as well.

I found that I was cataloguing each observation, like Aodhan had taught us to do, and was a bit relieved to learn that under stress I still maintained some of my higher faculties. Owen was scanning the sky, while I did my best to avoid some of the more egregious potholes.

"Where are you?" he whispered. "Where are you?"

We continued on Highway 6, through The Slash and past the oddly named Squirrel Town. As tempted as I might have been to see what the town of Two O'Clock looked like, we stayed on the highway and made for Manitowaning.

By now, the only thing keeping Owen from rocking back and forth in his seat was the fact that he would put his sword through the floor of my car if he leaned on it any more heavily. He was driving me crazy, but I knew better than to try to stop him. I couldn't drive very fast, because of the road, and that was only making his anxiety worse. But even with the worsening roads, we were making good and careful progress. More important, we didn't see any dragons.

"Turn left," Owen said. "I can see a lake."

We'd overlooked Manitoulin as a good place for a hatching ground because Lake Huron was so big and lacked many concealed bays. In doing that, we'd forgotten that, as the largest freshwater island in the world, Manitoulin actually contained lakes inside it. The sign said we were coming up on Lake Manitou, and the vista we could see from the car looked like a page straight out of the Dragon Education and Defense Manual.

The town was called Vanzant's Landing, and when it had been a town, it hadn't been very big. There was a burned-out hotel, presumably called the Manitoulin Resort based on the unscorched letters, and not very much else. The lake was blue to match the sky, and dark where there were clouds above it, but neither Owen nor I was really looking at the lake.

All along the shoreline, in burned-out swathes or half-buried in the sand, were the eggs. The smallest were the size of my head, and the biggest were larger than the car. They were light brown and speckled with dark blues and greens and golds. They were almost beautiful. Or they would have been, had I not known what they contained.

And there were hundreds of them. Thousands, probably, but I couldn't see that far. I didn't know what we were going to do.

Owen didn't hesitate. He undid his seatbelt and leaned across me to pop the trunk. While I sat there, in more than a bit of shock, he got out and removed the flamethrowers from the back. Hannah had rigged the harness so that there was enough space for him to put his sword across his back as well, and she'd set a smaller harness for me and the sword that I carried. Owen pulled me out of the car and put the flamethrower on my back. By then, I had taken the sword in my hands, so I put that away myself. He reached in, awkwardly because of his burden, and turned off the car.

"Leave the keys in," I said. We might need them in a hurry.

"Okay," he said. He turned back to me. "You ready?"

"As I'll ever be," I told him.

"Siobhan?" He said it like a question.

"Yeah?" I replied.

"Would it be okay if I asked Sadie out, do you think?"

"Really?" I said. "Now?"

"I figured you'd be honest," he replied.

I hadn't said anything about Sadie yet because I knew she wanted to make her case herself. It never even crossed my mind that Owen would clue in before she worked up the courage to talk to him. Still, I was nothing if not honest, so I told him the truth.

"You know she's only interested in you because she wants to be a dragon slayer, right?"

"I think that might be why I like her," he admitted.

I was profoundly relieved that he wasn't harboring unspoken feelings for me. I really didn't know what I would have done with that, and we were about to face extreme danger together, which, as fiction has shown me, often brings out inconvenient feelings in even the most levelheaded of people.

"Well, I don't think it would be weird," I told him. In fact, I thought it would be a really, really good idea, but there was only so much honesty I could handle right now. My nerves were starting to get the best of me.

"Good," he said. He reached for my hands, which were shaking, and held them still. "And Siobhan?"

"Yes?"

"I'm glad we were late for English."

I smiled. The shaking stopped, and not just because he was holding me still. The path that had brought us here was bizarre and twisted, and I wasn't sure I bought into the whole epic destiny thing, but I couldn't deny that we were here, and we were probably here for a reason.

"Me too," I said.

And then—

And then, there was fire.

FIRE

It was like no dragon battle I had ever been a part of before. There was no defense from the air, no reason to draw swords and engage at close quarters. To be completely honest, it seemed a little one-sided, but I knew that there was no other way.

Starting on the shores of Lake Manitou, Owen and I burned our way across the island. As we went along, we got better at it, and we realized that whatever Hannah had put into the tanks was very efficient at lighting dragon eggs on fire. It took very little to ignite the eggs, and if we cracked them a little bit first, they went up in flames all the faster. Once an egg was lit, it would overheat in a matter of moments and explode, causing a chain reaction all along the beach. It was simply a case of getting any that got missed in the spray.

I watched the first egg burn the whole way, though. I don't know why. I guess I thought that if I saw the dragon, it would make me feel better. The thing that was left over after the egg burned looked like a dragon, but it was slimy and covered with membranes and goo. After that, I just followed Owen's lead and progressed as robotically as possible across the beach.

We left Vanzant's Landing just after lunch and headed back to Highway 6. There was smoke and fire and the sounds of explosions in the rearview mirror, and neither of us was very hungry. I made Owen eat more of the jerky, though, and choked down some as well. We also drank water. I felt a bit better after eating, but it helped to ignore the smoke.

Owen's phone beeped. We hadn't been sure if we would get cell coverage this far in the middle of nowhere, but apparently the towers in Tobermory and Spanish were pulling their weight, and a text got through.

"They're all okay." Owen said, and I could tell he was relieved. "The dragons attacked exactly as they hoped."

"Can you get a message out?" I asked. "Let them know we've started?"

"I can try," he said. "Hopefully it'll get through."

I let him type for a bit. I was dying to know how my parents were doing, even though both of them were in considerably less danger than Owen's family. Finally, I saw him press SEND.

"I told them to tell your parents you're okay if they can," he said. "I'm sure Hannah would have told me about them if she knew anything."

"I'm not worried," I lied. "Dad's in the mine and Mum's in the hospital, which is probably safer."

"That's true enough," he said. He looked thoughtful. "Why is it, you think, that you can lie so well to reporters and so badly to me?"

"It's not just you," I told him, glad for the levity and the part where he wasn't pressing the issue. "I am terrible at lying to all real people."

"Reporters aren't real?" he asked.

"For a certain value of real," I said. "You know what I mean."

"If you say so," he said. We drove in silence for a little bit. "Stop here," he said. "There's a small lake over there, and we're past the limit of our fires."

"There's going to be a clear path back to the tug, right?" I said. "I mean, I would like to be able to go home when we're done here."

"We're okay," he said. "The wind is blowing north again, so we can go anticlockwise around the island and not paint ourselves into a corner, as it were."

"If you say so," I said and killed the ignition.

This time the eggs were all small, *siligoinus* and the like, and they burned quickly. The lake was small enough, and the eggs densely packed enough, that we only needed to ignite a few of them and then watch the line of flames surround the whole thing.

"What about those islands?" I asked.

"Nothing's perfect," Owen said. "We might have to do some cleanup later. We're only supposed to get most of them."

"Right," I said. "I forgot."

"No worries," he said. "It's been a busy day."

"You are a very annoying person sometimes, you know that, right?"

"I do my best," he said and shrugged off his harness so we could get back in the car.

We continued on, turning off of Highway 6 when it headed north toward the causeway to the mainland and taking the smaller County Road 540 instead to go west and south. The smell of fire and chemicals clung to my skin and my clothes and my hair. There was also a weird miasma in the air that I didn't think could possibly be healthy, but we kept on. We had to refill the tanks twice as they emptied, and we stopped to wash our hands in nearly every body of water we passed.

It was getting dark by the time we reached Monument Corner, which was in the south-central portion of the island, and close to our finishing point. There was an orange glow beneath the horizon all around us, evidence of the fires that still burned. When the eggs were consumed, the fire jumped to whatever grass and trees it could reach and burned on. Sometimes it came to unoccupied lakeshore and stopped. Sometimes it destroyed the standing bones of whatever small town had once occupied that ground. Sometimes—most of the time—it encountered more eggs and burned them too.

Owen was sure that our exit was still accessible, and since the eastern sky was free of orange fire, I believed him. We were exhausted, running on adrenaline and beef jerky, plus the fumes of whatever we had been inhaling all day, and I hoped that the boat ride back to Tobermory would be peaceful, and that I could nap at the Mountie station before we went back to Trondheim. This was back in the days when I still planned ahead for the best-case scenario.

We were fixated on the shore of Mindemoya Lake, our eyes on the ground. We were entranced by the rhythm of burning fires and exploding eggs. We watched for the direction the fire took, but we didn't look up any higher than it took to check the wind. We were tired, and we forgot about the sky, with the dangers it could unleash.

I saw the dragon bearing down on us at the last possible moment.

"Owen!" I screamed at the top of my voice.

He reacted on instinct—what he'd been born with, descended through his bloodline, and what he'd honed with training and practice. He practically ejected himself from his flamethrower, correctly surmising that it was the source of carbon that the dragon was headed for. I threw mine off as well and scanned the sky to see if there were any more beasts incoming, but it seemed like the one headed for Owen was the only thing we had to worry about.

It was more than enough. Owen had rolled to get some kind of advantage by hiding behind the frame of what had once been a decent-sized rowboat, left abandoned all those years ago when the island was evacuated. It was only then that we realized the flaw in Hannah's design.

The packs were light, even when they were fully loaded with fuel, and the straps were positioned in such a way that we could both carry our swords strapped into the rig without hitting our heads on the pommels every time we turned. And therein, of course, lay the problem. Owen's sword was still attached to his backpack, and so was mine.

"Owen!" I shouted again, in case he was so focused on the imminent battle that he hadn't noticed yet. "Your sword!"

But it was too late. The dragon had landed between Owen and his pack, cutting him off from his weapon. It was small, but it was big enough, and Owen was unarmed. My pack had landed closer to the flames than I'd intended, and before I could pull it back toward me, the straps caught fire. I retreated, hoping Owen's hiding place was keeping him safe enough, and when my pack exploded in a ball of fire, the dragon turned toward me with a sharp keen of inhuman joy. I had what it wanted now, and it was coming to get it. My body froze, overwhelmed by the music that blared in my head.

"Siobhan!" Owen shouted. "Siobhan, run!"

That's what you do when it's a *siligoinus*. That's how the song goes. You run and you hide, because *siligoinii* are stupid and they will never find you. That's what people who aren't dragon slayers do. They run and they hide and they get out of the way so that the dragon slayers can get their job done. Owen was already scrambling around the dragon's tail to get to his sword. All I had to do was play my part and hide, and Owen would do the job he'd been born to do.

"Siobhan!" Owen was screaming now. My legs were missing their cue. "For the love of God, GET OUT OF THE WAY."

In desperation, he flailed against the dragon's tail with his bare hands, battering against the spines and scales. I thought that would probably be ineffective, but it was apparently annoying enough to divert the dragon's attention. Perhaps it thought it would have to share, and it wanted to take away any threat of a competitor to its feast. I saw the dragon start to turn, its tooth-filled mouth flaming, and I knew I wouldn't miss my cue again. It was a small dragon, but it still would have eaten him in one bite, unarmed as he was.

In the instant before the dragon turned, I saw the opening. Its twisted neck and bent back spine revealed the soft part of its chest. For a fleeting moment, I thought I could actually see its hearts beating there, two drums calling out for a blade.

Without thinking, I reached into the fire and grabbed my super-heated sword in both hands. I slid the blade between the dragon's ribs, severing both its hearts with one blow. It wasn't until I felt its blood stop pumping that I realized that I was burning too, and started to scream.

D.C. AL CODA

My name is Siobhan McQuaid, and I know things that no one else knows. Most of them, I will never tell, because they are not important to the story. But this is, and so I will tell it.

I know why Aodhan Thorskard is afraid of fire. It isn't because he's not brave. He is among the bravest of anyone I know, because he is afraid of fire and he walks toward it every day. And I know why Lottie Thorskard thinks fire is the enemy. She has seen it issue forth from the gaping maws of countless dragons, she has fought its rage with her every effort as it spewed up from oil-rich ground. And I know why Hannah MacRae thinks that fire can be controlled, used and shaped like the metal she turns into swords.

I love Hannah, but Hannah is wrong.

Once upon a time, I was a piano player and a weaver of notes onto staff paper. Mine was the trade of fingers and fingertips. Of scratching with a pencil across multi-lined paper. Of gliding up and down the keyboard, or running up and down the scales with the wind from my mouth blowing beneath the finger pads. Mine was a gift that few others had, the ability to tease out the notes I heard in the ether and commit them to paper for others to read, for others to play, and for myself to listen to when I sat on the piano bench. I saw music in the world, and I could play it back for everyone else to hear.

And all of that ended the day I set myself on fire to save Owen Thorskard.

It wasn't a tragic end. If anything it was a semi-heroic beginning. I didn't hate Owen for what I'd had to do, and I didn't lose my music completely. Everything just got harder, from doing up buttons and opening the pickle jar to tuning a horn by pulling on a slide or turning the handle on a door. It wasn't the end of me as his bard, either. I still traveled with him, but he drove now, and I scanned the skies and cradled his sword between my knees, while he watched the road. And it wasn't the end of the Story of Owen. That had years to go.

When I woke up in the hospital, I was very confused. It smelled too clean, so unlike the chemical hell of the island, and I didn't remember how I got there. I hoped I hadn't driven.

"Mum?" I said, because I knew she'd be close by. She couldn't have treated me, of course, but no force on earth could have kept her from my room.

"I'm here, sweetheart," she said, and I could feel her holding a straw to my mouth so that I could drink. My throat was irritated, and I wondered how much smoke I had inhaled and if any of it would kill me. I was only attached to a heart monitor, though. I could feel it around my finger. Surely if I was poisoned, they'd have me hooked up to more stuff.

I couldn't see clearly yet, which made me wonder how long

I had been out, but I could tell Mum was crying. I started to panic, wondering whom we had lost, and since I was clearly not about to be eaten by a dragon, I let it wash over me in waves this time. The monitor raced, and a hand closed on my shoulder.

"It's all right, Siobhan," said Lottie. "We all survived."

"Owen didn't drive here, did he?" I asked, my mind turning so fast that I said the first thing I thought of, even though it didn't make sense. "He doesn't have his license yet."

"They came for us with a helicopter, Siobhan," Owen said. My vision had cleared now, and I could see him standing at the foot of my bed. My dad was beside him, and Hannah was standing next to Lottie. I saw a tall shadow in the hall and knew that Aodhan was close by. The danger must be gone if they were all here.

"I wish I'd seen that," I said. I squinted at him and saw that his arms were bandaged, and there were new burns on his face. "What happened to you?"

"I had to put you out," he said. "You were on fire."

Memory flooded back: the packs, the swords, the fire. My hands. *My hands.*

They were under the blanket and I was tucked in so tightly that it took me a second get free. No one tried to help me, even when I got tangled in the monitor cord, and I was grateful for small mercies. It couldn't be that bad if they didn't have to help me. I got my hands free of the blanket and saw that they were both shapeless; wrapped in bulky white gauze, except for my left index, where the monitor was clamped. Whatever pain medication I was on prevented me from feeling my fingers, assuming I still had them.

296

"How bad?" I directed the question at my mother. She winced.

"Owen had to break your fingers to get them off the hilt," she said. "The heat had fused your skin to the metal, and you had pugilized before he got the flames out." She held up her own hand, pulled into a claw to demonstrate.

"I'm sorry," Owen said. "I didn't know what else to do. You were on fire."

"What—" I started to talk and choked. I cleared my throat and started again. "What will they heal into?"

"The doctors were able to prevent any infection, which is the worst fear in burns, but it meant they couldn't set the bones properly." She looked straight at me when she said it, and I understood why she had been crying when I woke up.

"I'll never play again," I said.

"You will," said Lottie. There were tears in her voice, and the trumpet blew bubbles. "You will play again if I have to keep breaking your hands until they set properly."

"It's not that easy, love," Hannah said softly. Lottie released my shoulder and looked away. Hannah pulled Lottie into her arms. Lottie looked so small, like my sword had.

"It's okay," I said. "I know what she meant."

"You'll lose a lot of your movement," Dad said. "Your dexterity, that sort of thing. But with physical therapy, you should regain some of it."

"So she will play again?" Owen asked.

"No," I said. Somehow, my voice stayed level. "I won't be able to manage the woodwinds anymore, or any of the valves for the brass. Certainly not the piano."

"What about writing?" Hannah asked.

"It'll never be easy again," Mum said. "But her typing should be okay. And she can compose on a computer. There are programs now where you can sing a line and the notes will come up on staff paper. Your throat's just irritated, not burned. Your voice and lung capacity won't diminish. It might take longer, but you can still write operas if you want."

I closed my eyes and breathed, listening to the heart monitor that paced out my new life in measured stanzas. I could already see the notes above and below the tone, shaping into the song of healing that would help us piece ourselves, and our towns, back together. When I opened my eyes again, all the grown-ups were looking at me like I might go into hysterics, but Owen had a small smile on his face.

"I read about someone who learned to play the trombone with his feet. Maybe I could do that," I said, and everyone relaxed. "What happened to Saltrock?" I asked.

"Most of the dragons went for the burning ships," Hannah said. "But a few of them went into the town. There was a lot of property damage, more than we expected. The Hub is nearly leveled and there were power shortages and gas leaks, but repairs are already underway."

"Death toll?" I asked, preparing for the worst.

"Fifteen," Dad said. "One of the tanker crews got turned into the lake and nine of them drowned. Four people died because they wouldn't leave their houses, and Mr. Knott's heart gave out when he was underground. And one of the foremen from the mine stayed up in the catwalk to make sure someone could warn those below if more of the dragons turned inland. The catwalk caught fire, and he couldn't get down. That's just Saltrock and Trondheim, though. We don't know about anywhere else yet."

Fire again.

"Okay, I'm not your doctor, but you really need to rest." I think my mother had some sort of undisclosed superpower, because she knew that I was about to break. "And since I *am* everyone else's doctor: go get some rest."

The adults grumbled good-naturedly and left. Lottie squeezed my shoulder again, and Hannah leaned over to kiss me and whisper "I'm sorry."

"It wasn't your fault," I said.

"It was a stupid mistake," she replied. "I should have seen the flaw in the design."

"We're the ones who were too stupid to watch the sky," I said. "If you're looking for someone to blame."

"It's easier to blame myself," she said.

"Well, I don't," I told her. She kissed me again and followed her wife out of my room.

Mum and Dad left too, giving me a moment with Owen before he was packed into the car and subjected to whatever terrible forms of over-parenting resulted from having four parents, none of whom were legally barred from giving him medical advice.

"Thank you," he said.

"For what?" I asked.

"For being late for English," he said, again. "And for slaying that dragon. It probably would have eaten me if you hadn't gotten it in the hearts."

"Yeah," I said. "You pretty much owe me forever."

"Hey, I did extinguish you," he protested. "You weren't exactly in the headspace to stop, drop, and roll."

"Okay, so we're even," I said.

"And still a team," he said, gently bumping his fist against my bandages.

"Really?" I said. I hadn't expected him to drop me entirely, not after everything, but I had suspected some kind of change in the roster.

"Of course," he said. "Don't think I'm replacing you just because it'll be harder for you to write songs now. Besides, you're pretty good with a sword in a pinch."

"I think that was a bit more than a pinch!" I protested. "And anyway, if you thought algebra was bad, you have no idea what you're in for with calculus next year. Mrs. Postma stops playing nice for that."

"Fine, I owe you forever," Owen said. "Or at least until we graduate."

"Speaking of, did the school survive okay?" I asked.

"Yeah, more or less," he said. "I mean, it was on fire when the helicopter landed, and a soot-streaker was attacking it. I managed to take it out, though. I had the helicopter drop me off right on the roof. I wish you'd seen it. It was very action hero."

I was almost positive he was making it up.

"You didn't even think about just letting it burn?" I asked.

"I gave it some thought," he admitted, and I could tell by his face that the part where the school had been on fire was true, though I still had my doubts about the part with the helicopter. He smiled at me. "But then where would we have the prom?"

And that was how it started.

THE STORY OF OWEN

Once upon a time, there was a dragon slayer named Owen. He was brave and strong, and he wasn't afraid of anything. He was very good at soccer and he was terrible at math. When his town was attacked, he defended it. When his friends were in danger, he saved them. And when he had to, he risked his own life to do it.

One day, Owen went on a perilous voyage to a faraway island to rid his home of dragons forever, or at least reduce the population to a manageable number. Though he was beset by bad weather and cold water, he neither quailed nor flinched away from his quest. And he got to that island, and he lit it on fire, and he burned away the dragon eggs before they could hatch into a ravening horde that would put his house and the houses of the people he loved in harm's way.

When he came home, there was a parade, and a street named after him, and a medal of honor from the Prime Minister himself. And when all the pomp was over, Owen got back into his car and went out to slay more dragons, because that was his job. He can be seen all over Huron County, defending farms and chickens or making sure that the high school formal doesn't get set on fire. He does his duty, working hard and working alone, as heroes always do. And because of that, the people of Trondheim are safe.

That is the Story of Owen, dragon slayer of Trondheim. And it is more or less true, but you can believe whatever you want.

ACKNOWLEDGMENTS

If it takes a village to train a dragon slayer, it also takes a village to write a book about one.

Thank you so much to Agent Josh, who almost always calls while I am driving, and to Editor Andrew, who said, "You've kind of written a Socialist Tract," and meant it as a compliment.

I thank my support group. Faith King, Laura Josephsen and Emma Higinbotham are the writing partners of my heart. Jo Graham and Natalie Parker stopped me from outright panic when it came time to send out query letters. RJ Anderson and Tessa Gratton believed in this book SO HARD, and spoke up about it on my behalf. Colleen Speed, Amy Hetherington, Emily Wilkinson, Rachel Mikitka, and Kathleen Dorsey are test-readers beyond compare.

To my family, who kept me and fed me, and did their level best to be understanding and patient: I love you all so

much! Special thanks to EJ and Jen, and to Auntie Jo, without whom I couldn't have done any of this. And to Eli, who sat very patiently on the swing while I was babysitting him, listened to the first two chapters, and said, as four-year-olds do, "Auntie Kater, is there really a dragon on the CN Tower?"

And I would be remiss if I failed to mention my f-list on livejournal, whose encouragement never fails. In particular, huge thanks to irony_rocks, lanna_kitty, oparu, mylittleredgirl, cincoflex, eolivet, amenirdis, penknife, dbalthasar, shadadukal, colej55, miera_c, and melyanna. You are not only the reason I write, you are the reason I am starting to get better at it.

The Story of Owen was born in Alberta, the subject of much discussion in Ohio, and written in the Erbsville Starbucks in Waterloo.

ABOUT THE AUTHOR

The cool things about Emily Kate Johnston are that she is a forensic archaeologist, she has lived on four continents, she decorates cupcakes in her spare time, she adores the Oxford comma, and she loves to make up stories.

The less cool things about Kate are that she's from a small town in southwestern Ontario, she spends a lot of time crying over books in random coffee shops, and she can't play as many musical instruments as she wishes she could. Visit her online at ekjohnston.ca.